HIS

Ruthless

BITE

BROOKLYN ANN

Published by Broken Angels, an imprint by Brooklyn Smith

http://brooklynann.blogspot.com
annarkie12@gmail.com

Dedicated to Karen Ann
(06-11-62 ~ 02-14-09)

One

London, 1824

The vellum note shook in Lenore's trembling fingers, blurring the letters.

Not that it mattered, as she'd read the missive twice. Rafael Villar, the interim Lord Vampire of London, requested her presence.

When his carriage arrived to fetch her, it took every vestige of her will to leave the comfortable townhouse Lord Villar had leased for her, and accept his driver's aid into the ornate conveyance.

Her shivering increased as the carriage rolled down the cobblestone street, despite the warmth of her fur-lined cloak. She tried to remind herself that Lord Villar had always been kind to her, even more so since she'd saved his reign— and likely his life— by reporting his former second in command's treachery to the Elders.

Yet the prospect of facing the stern, surly Spaniard whose authority held supreme power over her fate turned her blood to ice.

The shivers turned to full-fledged tremors when the carriage drew to a stop in front of the gargantuan Elizabethan manor.

"It will be all right," the driver said as he opened the door and beheld her pallor. "You've done His Lordship a great service. His summons can only mean he wishes to reward you further."

She ran a nervous tongue across her fangs and nodded as he helped her alight.

The last time she'd been to Burnrath House was when Lord Villar had held a party in her honor for aiding him. He'd presented her with a deed to a cozy townhouse so she no longer had to spend her days sleeping in the crypts.

She suspected this visit would be less festive. Villar was not a man given to social niceties or casual meetings. Since he'd already expressed his gratitude, he'd only call her to him to issue a command or a reprimand.

Her breath constricted in her lungs as her heart pounded. The tremble in her hands spread throughout her limbs. Another attack threatened. Lenore closed her eyes and focused on breathing slow and deep while she focused on things that made her happy. Hot tea… a warm fireplace… a kitten's purr. By the time the butler took her cloak, Lenore had a tenuous grasp of control.

The interim Lord Vampire of London awaited her in his study, his scarred face grave. His newly Changed wife leaned against the desk beside him, offering Lenore a reassuring smile.

"Thank you for answering my summons so promptly, Lenore." Lord Villar's voice was rife with forced gentleness. "How are you this evening?"

"Uneasy," she answered honestly.

His scars pulled taut as he smiled, though his amber eyes remained dark with… pity? "I understand." Reaching into his pocket, he withdrew his cigar case.

Lenore watched with rapt awe as he lit the cigar with a hand that had once been so crippled from burns that his entire left arm had been paralyzed. But then Cassandra, formerly his mortal prisoner and now his bride, had performed a miracle and repaired it. She was now the first vampire physician in London.

"I've received a letter from the Lord of Rochester." Rafael gave her an expectant look, as if she should know what this had to do with her.

Lenore's attention snapped from Rafael's hand, her eyes darting up to meet his face, though her mind conjured the image of another, more potent, visage.

Only last autumn, Rochester had found her stumbling within the boundaries of his territory, broken from multiple assaults, starved, and so weak she had collapsed before him. He'd revived her with his own blood and aided her in making the most important journey of her life.

She'd thanked Rochester profusely for his kindness.

He'd laughed coldly.

"Oh, I would not say I am helping you out of kindness. You will owe me a favor for this, Lenore, as will Lord Villar. And I always collect my debts."

Lenore's breath left her body as those past words slammed her back into the present.

"He has called in the debt I owe him," she whispered.

Rafael blinked in surprise. "Actually, he is asking for what *I* owe him for his aid in my battle against Clayton. I hadn't known that you owed him a price as well." Blowing out a cloud of blue smoke, he shrugged. "Though now the price he is asking of me makes more sense."

"What does he want?" Lenore asked through numb lips.

Villar's low answer was like a thunderclap. "You."

"Why?" Trepidation gave way to puzzlement. Her encounter with him had been so brief there was no possible way for her to have left much of an impression on him, other than for him to discern that she was among the weakest and most pitiful of Rafael's people.

Why on earth would he want her?

Rafael took a sheet of parchment from the desk. "According to his letter, he says he could use more vampires with your loyalty."

"He wants me to move to Rochester only for that?" She couldn't conceal her suspicion.

The vampire's lips thinned in a grim line. "I'm certain he has other motives. However, he has given me his solemn oath that he means you no harm."

"You would relinquish me to Ruthless Rochester?" Her fear returned as she spoke the moniker that Rochester's own people had dubbed him.

Lord Villar spread his arms in a helpless gesture. "With the terms of my bargain with him, I'm afraid I have no choice. I promised him anything short of my lands or my bride. Without his aid, I would have lost both." He reached out his left hand and patted her awkwardly on the shoulder. Lenore couldn't help but flinch. "I will keep in contact with you regularly, and if he does do anything less than honorable, I will do everything in my power to bring you back to London."

"Thank you, my lord," she replied, not in the least assured. "When shall I be leaving?"

"At the end of the week. Cassandra and I will personally escort you."

It took all of her effort to bow in obeisance and not flee from the room.

Lord Villar gave her another pitying look that set her teeth on edge. "Do you have any questions?"

"No." The word came out harsher than she intended. Softening her tone, she struggled to appear calm. "That is, I need a night to absorb… all of this. May we speak on the morrow? I would like to go home now."

Lord Villar inclined his head. "Of course."

Cassandra's gaze fell heavily on Lenore. "May I see you home?"

7

Lenore wanted to refuse, only wanting to flee and hide under her bedcovers. Instead she managed a reluctant nod.

The lord's wife remained silent until they were safely ensconced in the carriage. Then she placed her hand over Lenore's. "How are you, really? Have the, ah, bad dreams, melancholy, and the... anxious episodes abated at all?"

Lenore suppressed a bitter smile. She was speaking with the physician, not the Lady.

"They *were*, until your husband gave me his news." Lenore sighed and softened her tone. "I'm sorry. I don't mean to sound churlish. I know I can never repay you for all that you and Lord Villar did for me after..." She broke off before memories of shackles, starvation, and assaults drowned her.

Cassandra shook her head. "Nonsense. We are in *your* debt. Besides, I haven't done enough." Remorse and frustration laced her voice as her fists clenched in her skirts, wrinkling the expensive fabric. "I know nothing of healing wounds on the inside."

"Yes, but you and Dr. Wakley introduced me to Dr. Elliotson." Lenore insisted. "And *that* has helped me more than you can fathom."

After months of attempting to treat Lenore for the trauma she'd endured when held captive, Cassandra consulted her mortal colleague, who then recommended Lenore to Dr. John Elliotson, a physician who specialized in a new treatment technique called mesmerism.

Lenore was astonished to witness a human utilizing an ability she'd thought only vampires possessed. Just like a blood drinker, Elliotson put mortals into trances. Though rather than to feed from them, he coaxed people to pour out their heartache and willed them to feel at ease when they regained their senses.

Even with such unique talent for a mortal, Lenore was not surprised when Elliotson was unable to mesmerize her. And she was intrigued at the idea of using her own preternatural powers to heal people, rather than take from them. Lenore became Elliotson's student, assisting him in treating poor women from London's East End— the only place where he could find willing patients for his unconventional treatment.

Helping others had given her a purpose and a distraction from her own inner turmoil. Now that she was going to Rochester, her work would end. What purpose would she have now? How would she keep her nightmares— or were they day-mares— at bay?

"I need to see Elliotson." Lenore couldn't keep the urgency from her voice. "I need to say goodbye."

Cassandra glanced over her shoulder as if she feared Lord Villar was following the carriage. Finally, she nodded. "Very well. I *would* like to speak to him further about his stethoscopes."

Lenore called out to the driver, "To Whitechapel."

"Whitechapel?" Cassandra gasped. "But he lives near Marlborough!"

"Yes, but he usually comes by the factories on Wednesdays to check on his patients."

Cassandra abraded her lip with her fangs, a bad habit for a new vampire. "Well, it is a less than desirable destination for two women alone. However, given our... *attributes*, I believe we should be safe enough."

As the carriage slowed to a stop on Whitechapel Road, the driver sniffed in disgust at the sight of the ramshackle hovels and stark brick factories spitting out plumes of coal dust.

"Mind yerselves, ladies," he grumbled as he withdrew his pistol. "The master will have me hide if aught happens to ye."

Cassandra bared her fangs. "We're not frail human debutantes, James."

Lenore inclined her head in agreement as they alighted from the vehicle.

A group of women gathered in the square outside of an imposing factory. They stared raptly at a young man sitting on a large crate. Despite his finer clothes and imposing mutton chop whiskers, John Elliotson's casual demeanor and slight height put them at ease.

He had his hand on a woman's shoulder as he spoke to her in a melodic, soothing voice.

"When I snap my fingers, Prudence, you will awaken feeling as if a great weight has been lifted from your soul."

Prudence's shoulders straightened and her posture became alert.

Elliotson withdrew his hand. "How do you feel?"

"Much better." The woman breathed in awe. "It's a miracle!"

He gave her a smile before his gaze suddenly lit on Lenore. "Miss Graves and Dr. Villar! How wonderful it is to see you here!"

Cassandra beamed at the address, even though they both knew that in the mortal world women could not be physicians. Elliotson's audience gawped at the Lady Doctor a moment before showering Lenore with cheered greetings.

"Miss Graves." A frail woman with morosely dark circles beneath her eyes rushed forward and grasped her hand. "I'd prayed you'd come tonight. Begging Dr. Elliotson's pardon, I wanted you to help me. I stayed behind after my workday to wait for you."

Lenore looked into the woman's dark eyes, shadowed with pain, and forgot her own despair.

"What is your name?"

"Mary."

"All right, Mary. Look at me and focus only on my eyes and my voice." As she used her otherworldly power to mesmerize the woman, Lenore fought back the predatory urge to sink her fangs into Mary's throat, and instead spoke softly. "Now tell me what is hurting."

The woman poured out the tragic tale of her youngest son dying of consumption and her will to overcome her grief and gain the strength to continue to work to support her older boys.

Lenore blinked back tears for Mary's plight. She couldn't imagine the burden of such heartache. At least Lenore had been childless when her employer cast her into the streets after her lungs became afflicted with consumption. Still, she willed her patient to persevere and to gain comfort from her remaining children. As Mary's eyes filled with blissful relief, warmth suffused Lenore's heart.

After Mary thanked her and stepped aside, Elliotson patted her shoulder. "You have such a tender, effective way with them. How you do it, I'll never know."

Lenore closed her eyes to hide any revealing emotion. "Thank you."

"I plan on inviting some of the more severe cases to my home the following Thursday." Elliotson continued. "I do hope you would like to come assist me? I made certain to tell them to come in the evening."

"I'm afraid I cannot. I... I have to move to Rochester." A fresh wave of cold dread threatened to engulf her. What did Rochester want from her?

Elliotson frowned. "I am aggrieved to hear that. Are you going to continue your work there?"

Lenore began to shake her head —then froze as the question struck her full force. *Could* she continue her work in Rochester? Surely there were women in need there as well.

There were women in need all over the world.

"I hope to do so," she said finally. "But I don't know how I would begin." Or whether her new lord would tolerate such a thing.

"Perhaps I could pay you a visit. I have a cousin in Rochester, after all."

"That would be lovely." The words left her mouth before she thought.

Cassandra lifted her head from the stethoscope she held to a woman's back. Her eyes widened in alarm. "We must go now, Lenore, if we are to make our engagement on time."

Lenore needed no further urging. "It was a pleasure to see you, Dr. Elliotson."

"You as well, Miss Graves. Do send me a letter when you're settled in." He bowed. "Good night, Dr. Villar."

The moment they were away from earshot of the mortals, Cassandra gripped Lenore's arm tight enough to hurt. "What were you thinking? You know we're supposed to limit our association with mortals. Rochester will be livid if this man comes to his territory to consort with you."

"I know," Lenore replied glumly. But she couldn't bear to lose one of her only friends, much less her new reason for living.

She hadn't even arrived in her new lord's territory and already she had disobeyed him.

Two
Rochester, England

Gavin Drake, Baron of Darkwood, and Lord Vampire of Rochester, coolly surveyed the rogue vampire chained before him. Even though the creature was disheveled and trembling, a glimmer of insolence remained in the rogue's beady eyes. Or perhaps Gavin was imagining it.

He'd developed an extreme aversion to rogues of late.

When Gavin's second and third in command had captured this rogue, he had claimed to be from Bristol on legitimate business for his lord, though his accent was clearly from Dover.

Taking no chances Gavin had chained the vampire in the cellar and sent an inquiry to the Lord Vampire of Bristol.

As expected, Bristol denied any claim on the vampire. Shortly after, Gavin's spies reported that the Lord of Dover had cast out a vampire matching this one's description. There were only a handful of reasons for a Lord to banish one of his people: disobeying one's Lord Vampire, theft, and in some cases, rape, though the latter often warranted execution, as it did in Gavin's lands. Crimes such as killing another vampire, Changing a mortal without permission, killing humans, and revealing oneself to mortals merited death.

Further inquiries revealed that this one hadn't committed theft or disobeyed an order.

Banishment was seen as an act of mercy, for it gave the rogue a fighting chance. In truth, exile was more often like an extended death sentence.

If any Lord Vampire caught a rogue in their territory, he or she had full right to execute him, unless the lord decided to allow the vampire to become one of his subordinates.

It hadn't taken long for Gavin to decide which he would do.

"Harold?" he raised an inquiring brow at the rogue.

The vampire looked up at him with hopeful eyes. "Yes, m'lord?"

"I received a letter from the Lord of Dover. Your name is *Timothy* and you were exiled for rape." Gavin despised liars. And rapists.

Timothy cringed and struggled once more in his chains. "M'lord, I can explain. I—"

"I, Gavin Drake, Lord of Rochester sentence you to death." He turned to his second. "My sword, please."

The rogue's struggles increased, along with his piteous bleating, as Gavin lifted his ancient broadsword. "M'lord, please have mercy! I didn't know! The woman teased me, she—"

Gavin silenced him with a blade thrust through the heart. As Timothy's eyes glazed with death, Gavin's second and third in command unchained him so Gavin could behead the body. The remains would be placed in the rear courtyard to be destroyed by the sun before the human servants rose.

"Has Cecil returned from his errand yet?" he asked as he cleaned the blood from his blade.

Benson, his second, shook his head. "No, my lord."

"Send him to the Chattertons' manor when he does."

"You're going to that ball?"

Gavin raised his gaze heavenward. "If I do not, they'll come here and call on me, and I cannot have any interruptions for the next few nights."

Benson gave him a rueful smile. "Doubtless you're right."

After taking a bath, Gavin changed into black breeches, a black tailcoat, and a claret waistcoat embroidered with jet. By the time he tied his cravat, his carriage was readied.

When he arrived at the ball, Lady Chatterton did not greet him with censure for his tardiness as he'd hoped. Instead, she eyed him with avarice and prattled on about her daughter.

Gavin gnashed his fangs in impatience as yet another blushing young girl was thrust in front of him.

"My Lauren sings like a bird," her mother crowed proudly. "You must attend our musicale this Wednesday and hear for yourself."

The tips of Lauren's ears turned red as she curtsied. Gavin inclined his head and resisted the urge to glare at the mother. This girl looked to be still in the schoolroom. If she was anywhere near the age of majority, he'd eat his cravat.

"It dismays me to say that I have another engagement." Bowing, he turned away from the avaricious matchmaker only to walk headlong into another's clutches.

Lady Summerly gushed. "It is so good to see you, Darkwood. Have you heard that Jenny had her come-out this Season? We were so dismayed not to see you in London."

He bit back a sigh and stepped out into the gardens the moment he was able to extricate himself. It was happening again. Throughout his every incarnation as the Baron of Darkwood, his mortal peers inevitably took a vexing interest in his marital status— or lack thereof.

Though he avoided the London Season like the plague, the summer country parties were impossible to escape without causing undue gossip. Unfortunately, he'd discovered over the last century that remaining a bachelor also prodded tongues to wag. After he'd had to fight a duel back in the 1735 for allegedly ruining some whey-faced debutante, Gavin knew that something had to be done.

Gavin's thoughts broke off as his preternatural senses detected the approach of one of his vampires. Moments later, Cecil appeared in the garden.

"Lord Villar is delivering the vampire you requested tonight," he said with a bow. "They should arrive in little more than two hours."

"Splendid. Now I have an excuse to make an early departure. Tell Jane and Benjamin to keep an eye on their progress and notify me if anything befalls the carriage, and then you are free to enjoy the rest of the night as you please."

The first time Lenore had come to Rochester, she'd been so weak she could barely walk, and rogues had been pursuing her.

This time she'd arrive here safe, and in much better condition.

"Yes, my lord." Cecil bowed again and departed as unobtrusively as he had appeared.

After Cecil departed, Gavin lingered in the garden. He wondered how Lenore had reacted to his calling in her debt, and how she would respond to his reason for it.

Although he'd known exactly what he wanted from her the night he'd joined his forces with the Lord of London's to do battle with a usurper, he'd waited.

She'd been through an unfathomable nightmare, and he wanted to give her time to recover. His spies kept him informed, and he was pleased to hear that Villar had displayed proper gratitude for Lenore's service to him and leased a townhouse for her. Apparently before that, she slept in a crypt with London's poorest vampires.

Villar's physician wife also saw her regularly, though his informants were unable to see or hear what transpired during those visits.

But it wasn't nearly enough. Gavin clenched his fists. After everything Lenore endured and accomplished in service of her Lord Vampire, she deserved far better recompense. And far more effort to ensure that her inner wounds healed.

He would easily accomplish the former.

Unfortunately, he was less confident in regards to the latter.

***

Lenore peered out the window at the full moon nestled in a ring of silver clouds. The tranquil sight was at odds with the hammering of her heart and the jolts of the carriage on the rutted country road. In mere minutes, she would see the Lord of Rochester again... and be relinquished to him. He'd handily trapped her in this arrangement, knowing she would have no choice but to obey Lord Villar. And she mustn't forget that she owed Rochester a debt as well. Would her moving to his lands pay her debt as well as Villar's? Or did he want something further from her?

In mere minutes she might learn why they called him ruthless.

Thankfully, Lord Villar and his wife remained silent throughout the journey, as if they sensed that even mild conversation would take a toll on her jangled nerves.

But when the carriage trundled down the driveway of a vast estate, Cassandra reached forward and patted her hand. "Breathe, Lenore."

Swallowing, she nodded, knotting her fists in her skirts as the conveyance rolled to a halt. Rafael exited first, helping his bride with one hand while gripping his jeweled walking stick with the other. The cane concealed a narrow, but deadly blade.

Courage bolstered by their determination to protect her, Lenore accepted the footman's assistance out of the carriage.

Instead of being greeted at the door by the butler, Rochester himself met them in the drive. Somehow he looked even larger than he had when they'd first met. His eyes, black as sin, roved over her, searing her body with awareness of his danger. Quickly, she curtsied.

His lips curved in a smile that looked oddly triumphant before he addressed them all. "Miss Graves, Lord Villar, Lady Villar. I am happy you arrived. I trust you had a pleasant journey?"

Rafael's eyes widened at Rochester's greeting Lenore before a fellow Lord. Lenore met his stunned gaze and shook her head in confusion as Cassandra answered curtly, "Indeed, my lord."

Rochester ignored Cassandra's suspicious tone and kept his smiling gaze on Lenore. "Splendid. Now if you'll follow me inside, I have refreshments waiting."

Lenore started forward, but Rafael gripped her shoulder, stopping her in her tracks.

"First I want your oath that no harm will come to her under your care." A thread of steel underlined Villar's soft voice.

For a moment Rochester's eyes narrowed dangerously as he stared down the Lord of London, then he inclined his head. "Very well, I swear upon my honor as Lord Vampire of Rochester, that no harm will come to Lenore under my care..." His countenance darkened once more. "...unless she does something to merit punishment."

"Of course," Rafael spoke through clenched teeth.

Rochester turned to Lenore and smiled. "But I know I won't have to worry about that from you, will I?"

Lenore shook her head. "No, my lord." What else could she say?

His grin broadened until she glimpsed the tips of his fangs. He extended his arm. "Shall we?"

Her belly quivered as she placed her fingertips on the sleeve of his greatcoat, feeling his muscles flex in answer to her touch. Unbidden, the memory of being in his arms washed over her in a potent wave… his wrist pressed to her mouth as his powerful blood rejuvenated her starved and weakened body. The rough timbre of his voice as he'd coaxed her to drink… the softness of his bed, the feel of her mouth on his flesh.

She licked her lips in remembrance of his taste.

He'd saved her life that night, so she truly believed he didn't mean her any harm, but what *did* he intend?

Her thoughts buzzed like a swarm of bees as Rafael and Cassandra followed them in.

Lenore's eyes widened at the vast and elaborate estate, which was even larger than Burnrath House. Rather than one sweeping staircase leading into the foyer, there were two. Ancient tapestries from centuries past adorned the walls, interspersed with gilded sconces in fanciful shapes.

Her feet sank into the plush Aubusson carpet as they entered a receiving room that was more imposing than cozy. Instead of inviting maple wood chairs with flowery embroidered cushions, Rochester's chairs were large and elaborately carved of wood so dark it looked black. Fitting for the Baron of Darkwood. Lenore's lips twisted in an ironic smile.

Rochester caught her gaze. "Please, take a seat. The chair won't bite."

But you will. Lenore thought silently as she did as bid, sitting next to Cassandra.

The countess ran a finger along the arm of her chair, admiring the carvings of leaves and a coat of arms. "The craftsmanship is exquisite," she said somewhat grudgingly.

Rochester inclined his head, ignoring her tone. "Thank you. They were part of the manor when it was first built. This home has been in my family since the Fourteenth century. My father was a one of King Edward's most loyal vassals."

Lenore's chest tightened at the daunting weight of his age and sense of history. *My father was a chimney sweep.* Her shoulders slumped before she caught herself. *I do not belong here.*

Rafael lit his cigar and narrowed his amber eyes on Rochester. "Enough prevaricating. Just what, precisely, are your intentions toward Miss Graves?"

Rochester chuckled. "I am glad someone finally asked. You were so concerned about what I what I *won't* do with the lovely Miss Graves that I never thought I'd have the opportunity to discuss what I *do* intend. And I can assure you that my intentions are honorable." A glint of humor lit his eyes as if he were savoring some private jest.

Before anyone could prod him to elaborate, the Lord Vampire of Rochester rose from his seat and approached Lenore. He took her hand, his grip strong, yet reverent, and sank to one knee. Lenore was so distracted with his touch that she nearly missed his words.

"Lenore Graves, would you do me the honor of becoming my wife for the next five decades?"

Three

Gavin watched Lenore's already large brown eyes widen in astonishment. He did so enjoy her surprise. Poor, frail younglings likely never received proposals from Lord Vampires.

"What?" she whispered softly.

"I would like you to be my baroness."

Her lush pink lips parted and her lashes fluttered like captive butterflies. "Why?"

"As I'd told your lord," Gavin paused to grin at Rafael, who continued to gape at him. "I admire your loyalty and could find it very useful."

Lenore shrank back in her seat, looking at Gavin like he was a monster about to devour her. To his surprise, her blatant terror at his proposal stung, despite the fact that he'd expected some measure of trepidation.

Before Lenore could reply, Cassandra rose from her seat and strode over to Rochester, fangs bared, green eyes blazing with unholy fury. "No! As her physician, I object to Lenore being subjected to marital duties. You know what she has been through. How could you ask that of her?"

Gavin had to fight to maintain his composure at the dismal reminder. Yes, he remembered how pale and battered Lenore had been when she'd stumbled onto his territory and fainted in his arms. *Fainted.* He'd never seen a vampire so weak that they fainted. And when Gavin discovered that she had been raped, his very bones burned with an unsettling combination of protectiveness and rage.

How he'd wished that he could have torn the bloody curs limb from limb. But he'd only been able to kill one of the rogues during Lord Villar's battle with a would-be usurper. Gavin's satisfaction of driving his blade through the bastard's groin before disemboweling him was short-lived, for the Lord of Cornwall had slain one and chained up the others and delivered them to the Elders. Damn Vincent and his law-abiding honor.

Though the rogues had been executed, Gavin had wanted to slaughter them himself. Make them suffer as they'd made Lenore suffer. All four of them. His stomach quailed at the number. He despised rapists, and the idea that they'd done such things to a vampire so fragile and brave as Lenore amplified his outrage.

Yet despite all the unspeakable horror that she'd endured, Lenore had not only managed a clever escape from her captors, she had also mustered unfathomable strength to flee to his territory and then embark on a journey to face the Elders and inform them of Clayton's treason. She'd also lied to protect her Lord Vampire. Rafael had been unable to Change his captive, Cassandra, because he'd illegally Changed another human recently. Rochester had long guessed that illicit truth from Rafael's pleas to other vampires to solve his dilemma, and became certain the moment Lenore stood, unflinching before the Elders and told the lie that saved both Villar and his lover.

Though she now trembled before him, Gavin knew that Lenore possessed an iron will and phenomenal inner strength. Strength that drew him to her with a mysterious pull.

Lenore took a tentative step forward. "May we speak in private, m'lord?"

He took in the sight of her blushing cheeks and heard the slight trace of Cockney accent that she was usually able to hide.

Embarrassment and fear emanated from her in tangible waves that made his chest constrict.

"Of course, Miss Graves. After all, this is an intimate subject and inappropriate to discuss in front of others." He cast Lord and Lady Villar a censorious look for broaching a topic that rightfully should have remained between him and Lenore.

As he took her arm, Rafael fixed him with a glare. "If you need me, Lenore, do not hesitate to call out."

Bristling with Villar's constant intrusion, Rochester ground his teeth as he escorted Lenore up the stairs and to the library. He willed himself to maintain civility. After all, soon Rafael and his wife would depart for London, leaving Lenore with him, and they would no longer interfere with his affairs.

He closed the door and spoke as softly as possible, though with their preternatural hearing, Lord and Lady Villar would still hear snatches of their conversation.

"There is no need to worry about consummating the marriage." His gaze held Lenore's large brown eyes. "Our union will be in name only, unless you desire otherwise."

Lenore's taut shoulders visibly relaxed at his words. "Do you mean that truly, m'lord?"

Gavin nodded. "I may be strict when it comes to ruling my lands, but I am not such a beast as to force my attentions when they are not wanted."

"I, ah," she looked down and fiddled with her skirts. "I need time to think."

This time Gavin brought forth his ruthlessness. "There is no time to think, Miss Graves. This is the price I shall have for aiding you." He strode forward and seized her arms with a firm, albeit gentle grip. Yet still she cringed. He nearly released her and apologized, but instead he held firm, trying to prove that he would not hurt her. Though he softened his tone. "Now think about this. All of London's vampires know the lurid details of your captivity. I imagine you've endured some discomfiting scrutiny."

Biting her lower lip, she tentatively nodded. "Yes, but—"

"But," he cut her off, "here in Rochester, your past is unknown to my people. You could begin your life anew here."

For a moment, hope flashed across her delicate features like a ray of sunlight. Then her trembling resumed. "But I am not suitable to be a baroness. I was a match girl, and after that, a mere laborer in a factory. I wouldn't know the first thing about the duties of a Lady."

"Not to worry. One of my people shall help instruct you in all you need to know. Elena was a viscountess in her mortal years and poses as one to this day."

Lenore's full lips curved in a frown. "Then why don't you marry *her*?"

Gavin laughed. Ah, there was that thread of iron. "I did, last century. Alas, she finds widowhood more agreeable."

Her hands crept up to push him away, then they halted and rested against his chest. A frisson of pleasure jolted through him at the contact.

Those large brown eyes remained wide with bafflement. "Why do you want to marry *me*?"

He sighed. "The mortals in my lands pester me incessantly when I remain a bachelor too long. I could become a recluse, as so many other vampires in my situation have done, but being a shut-in is far too dull. I enjoy attending balls and the theater. Therefore, there is only one thing I can do to fend off the matchmaking mothers. I find a female vampire to pose as my wife for a few decades."

Anne was usually amenable to playing the part, but unfortunately she'd recently fallen in love with the Lord of Salisbury and moved there. And Elena had no desire to repeat the role of mistress to his estate.

Now Gavin needed a bride, one who would fulfill the role as his baroness quietly and demurely, never causing any scandal. One who would bore the peerage to death, leaving them to turn their attention to another unfortunate bachelor. But most of all, one he could trust.

Running his fingers lightly along Lenore's upper arms, Gavin's lips curved in a satisfied smile. "Your loyalty and cleverness are the very qualities I seek in a wife."

"I see." A tiny frown line appeared between her dark brows as if she were unaccustomed to such praise. "And you swear that our m-marriage will be in name only?"

"Yes," he said once again. "Unless you change your mind." And God help his blackened soul, part of him prayed she would. Even when he'd seen first seen her, bruised and bedraggled, there had been something about her that drew him.

Her cheeks turned crimson. "When?" she asked.

"I'd say two months. There will be a small scandal at such haste, but that shall quickly abate when my neighbors see that you do not increase." Gavin outlined his plan. "Tonight you will go to Elena's. You shall be her cousin, come to visit, and catch the most eligible bachelor in the village."

Lenore shook her head slowly. "Your neighbors will find it hard to believe someone like me would be capable of such a thing."

"When they see me lose my heart and woo you, they'll believe it." The words came out impatiently. For some reason he disliked her lack of self-regard. "Now, do we have a bargain?"

Her eyes narrowed. "You never gave me a choice."

"That is true. As I said before, marriage is the price I ask for helping you last autumn," he said with a shameless grin. "But things will proceed much easier if you agree to say 'I will'." A strange weight settled in his stomach. What if she refused? Shaking off the unsettling sensation, he continued on. "Which would you prefer? Living in discomfiting notoriety in London, or being a grand Lady here and forging her own future?"

Lenore froze, her body vibrating with tension. Gavin's own muscles tightened as he studied her face, watching a multitude of expressions flit across her delicate features. Her eyes looked through him, past him, to some other far off world that he could never see.

"Very well," she said so softly he almost didn't hear.

Gavin released a breath he hadn't realized he was holding. He held out his hand for her to shake, and fought back a tendril of desire as her warm palm clasped his. "I will treat you well, I promise. I may be strict, but you will see that I am also capable of generosity." He released her hand slowly, part of him crying out in reluctance. "Now that we have an agreement, let us rejoin your former lord and assure him that I haven't devoured you."

A bright blush infused her pale cheeks and Gavin suddenly wanted to do just that. With great effort, he tamped down his desire. No, after all she'd been through, Lenore needed time. He'd just vowed to treat her well.

"Yes, my lord." Her cockney accent vanished, though her voice still held a tremor. Gavin wondered who'd taught her to speak like a Lady in the first place. Elena would be able to help her polish up her graces.

"Please, call me Gavin." He bowed and extended his arm.

Pink tinged her pale cheeks like a wallflower at a ball. "Yes... Gavin," she said in a breathy whisper that made a shiver run all the way down to his toes.

He took her arm to escort her back to the receiving room and she flinched again. Damn those rogues. Still Gavin did not release her, though he stroked her sleeve in gentle, soothing circles. She needed to learn to trust him.

Lord Villar and his wife rose from their seats the moment Gavin and Lenore returned, gazes roving over their former charge like protective mother hens. Gavin resisted the urge to growl at them and carry Lenore off away from their accusing eyes.

"Well, Lenore," Rafe said, though his blazing amber gaze remained fixed on Gavin. "What have you decided?"

Lenore met her former lord's gaze, face now crimson. "I have agreed to marry Rochester... ah, Lord Darkwood— in *name* only." She stressed the last.

"And he did not coerce you?" the Lord of London asked sharply.

Lenore shook her head vigorously. "No. He needs a bride to avoid undue gossip from the villagers. And I will have the opportunity to start a new life where no one knows about..." She looked down at her feet. "My past."

Rafael scowled, but Cassandra nodded in comprehension. She flicked a glance at Gavin and her emerald gaze softened. "May I look in on her from time to time? She is my patient, after all."

"You may attend the wedding, but other than that, no."

Cassandra frowned. "Why not?"

"I cannot have another Lord Vampire or his consort traipsing onto my territory with such frequency." Besides, something about the hot-tempered Spaniard irritated Gavin, no matter the fact that he held a grudging respect for him.

Rafael nodded in reluctant understanding. If a Lord Vampire was making constant visits to another's territory, others would speculate that the two were planning some sort of illegal coup... or worse, that a vampire was too weak to hold his territory and needed the assistance of another. Gavin would die before he allowed that misconception to flower.

Lady Villar gave Gavin a pointed look. "But if we leave Lenore here alone under your roof, surely that will cause the very gossip you are trying to avoid."

"She will not reside here until we are wed. I will take her to stay with another of my vampires who will pose as Miss Graves's cousin and educate her in her duties as my Baroness before I arrange for us to meet and begin our courtship." Gavin waved an impatient hand. "All preparations have been made."

Rafael inclined his head in a curt nod. "Very well, we shall take our leave then." Lady Villar took his arm and together, they strode over to Lenore.

Gavin stepped back and allowed them to say their farewells, fighting back his irritation as he overheard them reassure her that if she was unhappy, they would do their utmost to bring her back to London. Treating their bargain as if it were a frivolous thing.

Gavin ground his teeth. Lenore was *his* now. She would not be going back, not until she'd served the half century he asked of her.

And they were all going to have to become accustomed to that.

Four

Five rogues stood downwind as they watched the interim Lord Vampire of London and his wife drive away in their carriage.

Rolfe, a rogue who'd been banished from Dartford for stealing money from his lord's third in command, looked at their leader. "They left the youngling behind. I wonder why?"

Justus shook his head. "Perhaps the Spaniard has installed a spy in Rochester's household."

Will, the third rogue, frowned in confusion. "But Rochester aided the Lord of London in battle only months ago. Why would he want to spy on him?"

"I cannot fathom, though I know Rochester and Villar have long shared a misliking for each other." Justus's eyes narrowed against the dust of the departing carriage before turning back to glare at the manor. "If Villar is planning something against Rochester, he bloody well better wait." He bared his fangs. "Damn it all, it is *our* turn for vengeance."

It had been eight years since Rochester exiled him. Justus had been Gavin's second in command, hell, his best friend. And now, thanks to Gavin's heartlessness, he was nothing but a rogue, living on the fringes of towns and villages, always on the run and subject to scorn and violence from any vampire who encountered him.

Justus quickly learned that the only way to survive was to join up with other rogues. Before he knew it, he found himself the leader of a small band. At first their only focus was finding safe places to hunt and spend their day rest, but once the burning haze of pain and betrayal eased, anger at Gavin's exiling him— and making the woman he loved vanish— gnawed like a cankerous sore.

Before long, Justus found himself resuming one of his old duties as Rochester's second in command. Though now instead of spying *for* him, he spied *on* him.

One night soon he would find the key to ruin Rochester.

One night soon, Rochester would learn what it was like to be cast out, to be humiliated and to lose all he held dear. To suffer as Justus had suffered.

***

After Lord and Lady Villar departed, Lenore's flesh tingled with awareness that she was alone with the Lord of Rochester. That soon he would be her husband. Even if the marriage was a farce, playing the part would surely result in more intimacy than she'd ever experienced.

He'd promised that the marriage would be in name only. Unbidden, his words whispered in her thoughts. *"Unless, you change your mind..."*

As always, memories of her captors' brutal assault battered her in a sickening deluge. But then, the flashback suddenly faded to a vision of lying in Rochester's bed, the chains and stone walls that had imprisoned her now replaced with a downy mattress, fluffy pillows, and silken sheets. Instead of reliving painful, pinching fingers and slobbering mouths, she found herself imagining Gavin's gentle hands on her upper arms when he'd held her earlier, the softness in his voice when he assured her he wouldn't hurt her.

Then the rogues invaded her mind again. Those endless hours of torment and pain.

Her stomach roiled, her flesh went cold as if doused in ice water. Willing off another attack, Lenore forced her mind to other prospects of her impending nuptials. First she would be attending fancy country parties like the elegant debutante she'd daydreamed about being when she was a young girl. And just like those old fantasies, she'd be courted by a dark and dashing gentleman.

And then she would be a baroness, presiding over this opulent estate. Lenore closed her eyes and remembered playing with the dolls her mother had made out of discarded scraps of fabric, placing them around a broken barrel in the alley behind their flat, and presiding over them for tea. All she'd had for "tea" was one cracked cup that her father had found for her in a rubbish pile, but she'd treasured it all the same.

Oh, how Lenore had longed to be one of those grand ladies that she'd sold matches to in Covent Garden. She'd long admired their sweet smells, their vibrant gowns and elegant hats, their soft, dulcet voices that sounded like angels.

At first her mother had been perplexed when Lenore had tried to imitate the upper classes, but when she noticed that her young daughter had an aptitude for it, she pressed upon her husband, who had been the youngest son of a vicar, to teach Lenore to read.

Sometimes, her great aunt, a governess, would come visit and expand her lessons. Sometimes she'd even brought her a book.

It wasn't until Lenore turned twelve that she learned she'd never be able to become a lady. Her mother had encouraged her because she'd thought Lenore could seek employment as a Lady's maid. When she'd recovered from her dismay, Lenore had accepted that even that would be a vast improvement to her circumstances. And she would still get to live in a great house, dress hair, and handle fine silks and muslins. With a new, albeit more practical motivation, Lenore increased her efforts in improving her speech and mannerisms.

By the time she was sixteen, she could hide her cockney accent and had ramrod straight posture and perfected a curtsy fit for a drawing room. Alas, she could not style hair, for she was unable to secure pins, brushes, and irons. And she did not know how to dress a lady, for she did not know any to allow her to practice.

Alas, her efforts came to naught. All of the households she applied to wouldn't even let her past the doors of the servant's entrance, for she didn't have any references.

Impotent frustration had welled in her being. How could she secure a reference if no one would give her an opportunity? The scorn of the housekeepers who'd impatiently listened to her application before turning her away had burned like acid. It was as if they could smell her inferiority.

Dejected, Lenore had leapt with muted joy when one finally offered her a situation as a scullery maid. Her parents had been so proud. Unfortunately, her employment did not last long and she then ended up in the same textile mill that ultimately claimed her mother's life.

Lenore swallowed the lump in her throat and chased away the painful memories.

If someone had told that young dejected girl that she would become a baroness, she would have spit on the ground in derision at having her leg pulled.

And only God knew how she would have responded if she'd been told she'd become an immortal blood drinker.

A small noise that was part chuckle and part indelicate snort escaped her.

"May I be privy to the jest, Miss Graves?" Gavin's deep voice rumbled behind her.

Heat infused her face. "'Tis nothing, m' lord." She bit her lip as her studies came back to her. *My lord, not m'lord.* How many times had she slipped up on that crucial detail this night?

His brows drew together and he frowned a moment before his features smoothed. "Well, let me see you off to Elena's."

She took his proffered arm, relieved that she didn't instinctively recoil this time. Already she'd grown to loathe the look of pity in his gaze whenever she drew back from his touch. Just as much as she detested herself for her unreasonable response to such meager contact.

If Lenore was to gain anything from wedding Rochester, the very least she hoped for was an end to pitying glances.

Gavin donned a surprisingly shabby coat from a rack in the foyer and then led her out of the servants' entrance to a plain carriage. When they passed the other carriage, lacquered and sporting the Darkwood crest, Lenore glanced down at Rochester's rough spun coat in comprehension.

To protect her reputation, his carriage could not be seen driving her anywhere before they began their courtship. So he was disguising himself as a hackney driver. She'd pretended to be a Lady and now he was pretending to be a commoner. The juxtaposition brought forth another irrepressible chuckle.

Rochester halted and glanced down at her with overwhelming intensity. "Please let me in on the jest."

Lenore managed a tremulous smile. "I don't yet have the words, my lord, but I vow I will confide in you when I find them."

A potent, inscrutable look filled his black eyes as he looked down at her. "I know this must be overwhelming for you, but I promise, everything will be better once we endure this bothersome courtship. And please, call me Gavin."

For some reason the fact that he assumed her amusement came from nerves made her bite back full blown laughter. The irrational mirth sobered her. Perhaps he was right.

"You'll find that things are not too different than they were for you in London. All the rules are the same. Do you remember the rules?"

Lenore recited them with a nod. "No Marking or Changing a mortal without permission. No Changing children ever. No leaving your lord's territory without a writ of passage. No killing mortals, or exposing them to our secrets. No feeding on other vampires without consent. No theft. And," her eyes narrowed in fury. "No rape... mortals *or* vampires." She nearly spat the last.

His dark gaze softened and his knuckles brushed her cheek. "Very good, Lenore."

As Rochester assisted her into the carriage, Lenore saw that someone had already loaded her trunk and valise onto the conveyance. The sight proved that not only had he planned out this endeavor with meticulous detail, he also would have never allowed her to refuse his proposal.

She suppressed a shiver.

Rochester climbed up on the driver's perch and flicked the reins. A weight settled in Lenore's chest as she grasped the carriage strap, alone in its dark confines. Surely she wasn't disappointed that His Lordship was not in here with her?

In what felt like mere minutes later, the carriage rolled to a halt in front of a cottage that was more like a small manor. Rochester— *Gavin*, she corrected herself— took her hand and helped her alight. His grip was strong and warm through the thin fabric of her gloves.

He then effortlessly hefted her trunk and valise from the boot.

A female vampire with reddish-gold curls and glittering green eyes greeted them at the door. Though her gaze lit with recognition when she saw Rochester, she lifted her chin and looked imperiously down her nose at him. "You may carry the trunk upstairs to the second chamber on the right."

Lenore stared as, rather than berating the vampire for her insolence, Gavin shifted the luggage to one shoulder and doffed his cap. "Yes m'lady."

After he went upstairs, the vampire turned her cool gaze on Lenore. "So you are to be the new Baroness of Darkwood."

Lenore curtsied. "Yes, my lady."

"Do that again," Elena commanded. "But straighten your back, hold your skirt with two fingers instead of three, and do sweep your left foot behind you."

Lenore curtsied again and the vampire tsked. "No, like this." She demonstrated.

After her third attempt, Elena gave her a brisk nod which hopefully signified approval. "I cannot fathom why he chose such a mouse for his bride, but we shall have to make do."

Gavin returned downstairs and Lenore felt a wash of relief to no longer be alone with this viper... until he said, "I bid you good night for now. I shall see you again as soon as is proper."

He bowed and lowered his head to kiss her knuckles just as Lenore had daydreamed about in her mortal days.

"Not until you are formally introduced!" Elena hissed.

Gavin withdrew and scowled. "Blast it, Elena. Must you be such a dragon?"

"It will take a dragon to carry off this madcap scheme. Though this little mouse may speak well, anyone with a pair of eyes and ears will know she's of common stock. I have my work cut out for me, and you must behave with utmost care if you want to avoid the wagging tongues." She bared her fangs, eyes glowing with unholy light. "In the old days, we simply could have torn out their tongues and not had to bother with such silly farces." Lenore must have made some reaction, for Elena turned to her. "Show me your teeth."

Reluctantly, Lenore opened her mouth.

Elena smirked. "So you *do* have fangs. I had begun to doubt it."

Gavin sighed. "Elena…"

She waved a dismissive hand. "I needed to make certain you hadn't gone as mad as the Duke of Burnrath and are trying to wed a mortal. Now shoo. I need to start on her lessons at once if we expect her to be ready for the Haversham's party."

Gavin gave Lenore an unreadable look before turning on his heel and leaving the cottage… leaving her alone with the dragon.

Elena's narrowed gaze looked her up and down with discomfiting scrutiny. "Come, sit in the parlor with me."

Lenore's gaze surveyed the immaculately clean cottage that somehow managed to be elegant and cozy at the same time. The rose colored damask wallpaper with gold gilt cabbage roses complemented the cherry wood table and chairs. Small sculptures, candelabra, and vases filled with fresh cut flowers stood upon lace doilies on every available surface. Lenore eyed the blooms and wondered if Elena had a hothouse.

…Or if Gavin had brought them to her.

Once they were settled in high-backed chairs, Elena arranged her skirts. Lenore did her best to imitate her, though her gown was not as voluminous.

"Were you a merchant's daughter?" Elena asked.

Lenore shook her head. "My father was a chimney sweep."

The vampire's brows rose to her hairline. "Oh my. I suppose I may have underestimated you. Your speech may hold a touch of the lower classes, but I never would have fathomed *that* low. Can you read?"

"Yes," Lenore said, bristling with irritation. She may be weak and born of common stock, but she wasn't a half-wit.

The vampire ignored her irritation. "Can you dance?" Her voice seemed to hold a taunting edge.

Dismayed, she shook her head. "The vampire who made me taught me a few reels and a country dance or two, but I cannot waltz."

"And what of ladylike pursuits?" Elena continued her interrogation. "Do you paint, sing, or play the pianoforte?"

Lenore's shoulders slumped. "No. I never had the means." She didn't even know how to ride a horse.

"Well, I knew we'd have much work to do. Lord Darkwood would not have sought my aid otherwise." Elena's gaze softened. "Do not look like the end times have come. If you were quick-witted enough to learn how to read and speak properly as a mortal, learning a few mortal frivolities shouldn't be over-difficult." She rose from her seat. "Come, I will help you unpack your things and show you where we shall take our day rest. And then we shall waltz."

As Lenore followed Elena upstairs, she glared daggers at the vampire's back. She didn't want to spend any measure of time with this vampire, much less dance with her.

To her surprise, she found that she missed Rochester.

Gavin, she once more corrected herself.

Five

Gavin sat by the fire in his study, sipping a snifter of brandy and gazing into the flames.

He'd heard her laugh tonight.

Despite the countless other, far more important matters demanding Gavin's attention, he could not stop hearing Lenore's laughter in his mind, and picturing the way her lips had curved with genuine humor. Although he knew that people under extreme duress were prone to outbursts of mirth, tonight had proved that Lenore was at least still capable of laughter.

Irrational relief permeated his conscience. She was so solemn and timid every time he'd seen her. Perhaps there was hope that she would find some measure of joy.

Gavin frowned at how much he cared about her feelings. It shouldn't matter whether Lenore was happy or not. All he needed was for her to fulfill her requisite role. Yet he found himself hoping that she would enjoy playing her part.

He wondered how Lenore was getting on with Elena. Hopefully Lenore was not too overwhelmed with the vampire's intensity. He'd seen her shrink back from Elena's scrutiny, and he doubted she'd also seen the glimmer of compassion in Elena's piercing gaze.

Though Elena possessed a brusque exterior, she concealed a kind heart and a zest for mischief and adventure, the latter of which Lenore was painfully lacking.

And yet, she'd laughed tonight. That laughter continued to haunt his memory. Like the chiming of silver bells, the sound seemed to light up the night.

He would do all he could to make her do it again.

Taking a final sip of the fine vintage, he savored the fiery heat that burned down his throat. However, another thirst needed slaked, and Gavin rose from his chair, donned his greatcoat, and went out in the night to feed.

At first Gavin considered going by the King's Arms for a drunken harlot, but then he realized that Elena would likely be taking Lenore to hunt soon.

Perhaps he should discreetly look in on them and make certain they were getting on well.

As he neared Elena's hunting grounds, Benson, his second in command intercepted him.

"Yes, Benson?" he struggled to conceal his impatience.

The vampire spoke quickly, eyes wide with urgency. "Another rogue has been spotted, near the quarry. Alec and Cecil have already given chase."

Gavin cursed. "Bloody hell, there seem to be more of them popping up every night."

"Should I send a message to the Lord of Maidstone?" Benson asked with a nervous blink.

Gavin thought for a moment. On one hand, it would be the courteous thing to do to make Maidstone aware. On the other… "No, he vexed me last spring when he allowed some of his people to invade my lands for the May Day festival without my leave. Let him contend with intruders this time." He turned on his heel and said over his shoulder, "I am off to have a bite. We shall speak tomorrow night."

Benson bowed. "Yes, my lord."

After his second departed, Gavin rushed off toward Elena's preferred hunting grounds in a burst of preternatural speed. He took a circuitous route to Knight Street, remaining downwind so the females wouldn't detect him.

Moments later, he caught their scents. Elena's always struck him as a bit tart, like Bordeaux wine. Lenore's was subtle, yet evocative, like a calla lily. Only meager power radiated from her. If the vampire who'd Changed her was older than a century, he'd eat his boots.

Gavin paused. Who *had* Changed her anyway? Why hadn't that vampire been looking out for Lenore? Had he— or she— abandoned her? Or were they dead? He resolved to ask her at the earliest opportunity.

Hushed voices, too low for a mortal to hear, reached his ears.

"Just wait, and some sotted bucks will be shambling along from the pub." Elena's voice carried in a hungry whisper. "The ones around here are usually quite brawny from working on the cathedral."

Lenore's response was so soft he couldn't make it out, or maybe it was the flare of irritation at the thought of her fangs in some young muscled male's neck that blotted out his hearing.

Gavin shook his head. Why in the name of heaven should it matter who she fed on? She was a vampire, it was what they all did.

"Are they well fed?" Lenore's voice reached his ears.

Elena sounded perplexed. "The ones I've bitten appear to be so. Why do you ask?"

"I won't feed off of those who are malnourished." That quiet, yet implacable will once more imbued Lenore's tone.

Elena chuckled. "A vampire with principles, how quaint. Not to worry, there are very few underfed in the country. Unlike that squalid city you came from."

Gavin bit back a laugh. He'd forgotten how much Elena had loathed London. She'd held a pomander to her nose the entire time. In that aspect, at least, Lenore had more fortitude.

Now that he'd assured himself that Elena had things well in hand, he ought to depart and seek his own meal, but something held him in place. He wanted to see Lenore feed.

Unbidden, the memory of the bite of her fangs on his wrist, the feel of her mouth on his flesh, and the golden glow of her eyes as she'd fed from him with kitten-like ferocity teased him.

Gavin shivered in delight. The sound of drunken laughter and a human's voice raised in garbled song brought him closer, despite his better judgment. When Lenore and Elena came into view, he couldn't help comparing the two.

With Elena's vibrant hair, confident poise, and sleek movements, she radiated predatory grace. Lenore, on the other hand, appeared meek and unassuming as a wallflower at a ball. Even her cloak and dress, while new, were drab. However, such an unimposing impression would indeed make her the superior hunter, if she knew how to utilize her persona.

Leaning back against a wide oak tree, he watched to see if she did.

Two human males staggered into sight, arm in arm in the type of brotherly love that only copious amounts of spirits could invoke. When they spied Lenore and Elena, they stopped so abruptly that they nearly fell on their faces.

The first one doffed his cap and steadied his friend with a hand on his shoulder. "What are pretty gels like ye doin' about at this hour?"

Elena gave them a winsome smile and hooked her arm through Lenore's. "It is a secret, I'm afraid."

"Waiting for a moonlight tryst?" The other man hiccupped. "Well, 'tis awful late, so perhaps they've lost their way." He staggered forward. "But if ye both are still feeling randy, we will gladly accommodate ye."

"Aye." The first one reached for Lenore. "And who is this shy little flower?"

Lenore stepped back. Elena frowned and bent down to whisper in her ear, too low for the mortals to hear, but easy for Gavin to catch. "What are you doing? *We* are the predators here. *They* are the prey."

Even in the dark, Rochester could see her face flush. Once more he cursed the rogues for reducing her to this state. How had she been able to feed after what she'd been through?

Lenore nodded and forced a smile as she approached the man who leered at her.

Gavin clenched his fists, ready to destroy the human if he tried to harm her.

"I'm sorry, sir, I am shy." She took another dainty step toward him. "That is a very nice scarf you are wearing. May I look at it closer?"

"Of course, m'lady." The man bent down and Lenore captured him with her gaze. Elena did the same with the other man, beckoning him with fluttering lashes before she bent his will to hers.

Lenore lowered the human's scarf, wrinkling her nose as she exposed his neck. Then, touching him as little as possible, she lunged, sinking her fangs in his throat with surprising fierceness. Gavin saw her eyes light with a flash of fury, and he wondered if she imagined retaliation for those who had wronged her.

The wrathful expression vanished as quickly as it appeared, and Lenore closed her eyes, a small, content sound rumbling in her throat as she fed.

Gavin felt a surprising twinge of envy, along with a sudden urge to feel her mouth on *his* neck instead.

He paused and shook his head. He'd never been all that interested in doing such an activity with any of the female vampires he'd been with before. Though he'd been happy to oblige them, if that was what they desired. Feeding from another vampire during lovemaking could be pleasurable, after all.

Lenore clearly never wanted to touch a male ever again. Which made his inclinations towards her all the more ludicrous.

Satisfied that Elena and Lenore had things well in hand, he departed to seek his own meal.

***

Justus watched Rochester leave from spying upon the new youngling and Elena. For a moment, he'd thought that Gavin had sensed him when he'd nearly stumbled upon him in the forest, but Rochester had passed by, oblivious to his presence.

And that was bloody unnerving. Although Justus was relieved to have not been caught, he was also perplexed as to why that little whey-faced youngling held Rochester's attention so thoroughly.

He hadn't kept her in his home, so she wasn't intended to be a servant or a bedmate. Her being with a vampire as old and powerful as Elena implied that the youngling was an orphan in need of a mentor, but the fact that she had been delivered by the Lord of London himself convinced Justus that there was more to the situation— Especially with Rochester keeping such a close eye on her.

And he was damned if he knew what.

Six
One Week Later

Lenore's hands trembled as Elena buttoned the back of her gown. Tonight they were going to the Haversham ball, where she would "meet" the Baron of Darkwood and their courtship would begin.

"Stop shaking, little mouse," Elena scolded, albeit not unkindly. "You've learned the dances expected of you, we've practiced polite conversation until we both drooped in boredom, and we have the start of your wardrobe. By the by, where did you learn such fine stitching for those alterations?"

Lenore laughed and ran a hand down her sleeve of her white satin ball gown that used to be Elena's. "Aside from the benefit of my improved eyesight, compared to the clothing I made when I was young, this was much easier." She turned around and faced the other vampire. "Having a sharp needle helped immensely as well."

"Yes," Elena stroked her chin, eyeing her with what looked like admiration rather than scorn. "You *would* have made your own clothing…" Her words broke off as she cocked her head to the side. "This must be quite a change for you."

"Indeed," Lenore drawled in her best impression of an aristocrat, warming to the understanding in the older vampire's voice. "Even more of a change than becoming a vampire, to be truthful."

They both laughed as Elena wrapped Lenore in a cashmere shawl that warmed her almost as much as the vampire's kindness.

To Lenore's everlasting relief, Elena did not turn out to be the merciless dragon she had first perceived her to be. Throughout their lessons, the vampire was exceedingly patient and tempered her sharp tongued criticisms with witty jests. She seemed to take untold delight and amusement in turning a factory worker from the London East End into a grand lady.

Lenore, on the other hand, had begun to wonder why she had wanted to be a lady in the first place. There were so many rules with countless caveats, and she was supposed to behave like an insipid twit until she was wed.

Her chest grew tight beneath her stays. "You have only been teaching me for a week. What if I give myself away?"

Elena shrugged. "As you are posing as my poor relation, a slip or two will be forgivable. And between the two of us, we can wipe their memories of any significant gaffes." She adjusted Lenore's coiffure threaded with a strand of seed pearls. "Though I must say that you will be thoroughly loathed by the end of the evening, no matter how much we've polished you."

Lenore frowned at her reflection in the mirror. "Why?"

"Because you're about to catch the most coveted bachelor in this borough." Elena placed her hand over her breasts with melodramatic flourish. "That, and since the Season began, all who remain here are baronets, knights, squires, and untitled gentry who cannot afford to leave for the London Season just yet, or at all. That seems to make them all snobbish and mean-spirited to newcomers who are lower-ranking than themselves." Elena smirked, showing a glimpse of her fangs. "Just remember, if anyone treats you too shabbily, you can always bite them."

Lenore's lips curved in a smile. When she'd been Changed into a vampire, all she'd cared about was that she was no longer dying from consumption, that she had escaped the factory, and would no longer starve. She'd seen feeding as a necessary evil, one that filled her with remorse. Yet she could not deny that Elena's perspective of preying upon mortals who wouldn't hesitate to prey on them... and even the concept of a spot of revenge for those who slighted her had its appeal.

All her maker had cared about was survival. And look where that had gotten her.

Lenore shivered. She hadn't thought of Blanche in months. And all of London had already forgotten her shortly after Blanche had vanished during the Duke of Burthrath's reign.

The sound of horse hooves reverberated outside, interrupting her reverie.

"Time to begin our act." Elena fastened Lenore's ivory velvet cloak with a pearl-encrusted clasp. "You look lovely, little mouse. A delectable debutante sure to have Lord Darkwood smitten." She winked at her jest.

"And you look like Queen Titania stepped out from the pages of *A Midsummer's Night Dream*," Lenore murmured. *And a much more suitable bride for Lord Darkwood*, she added silently as she studied Elena's elaborately curled sunset tresses, glittering peridot eyes, and elegant gown of sea green brocade embroidered with silver thread.

Elena gave her a warm smile. "With such endearing charm, I would not be surprised if you won the cold heart of the Lord of Rochester in truth."

The thought made Lenore's belly turn over. She didn't know if Elena was jesting again or not, so she remained silent as Elena led her out to the waiting barouche. The coachman tipped his hat and assisted them into the plush vehicle, which was nearly as fancy as the Lord of London's.

Elena now posed as a widowed viscountess, taking impish delight in being higher-ranked than Gavin in the human world. In truth, she had been a French courtesan in her mortal years. Lenore had blushed to hear Elena's confession… and her cheeks heated further on all the questions dancing in her mind that she didn't dare ask.

Haversham House resembled a Grecian palace more than a country manor, with its wide columns that may have been real marble, and the wide pitched roof. As Elena and Lenore joined the receiving line, she saw that the inside was just as opulent, with plush carpets, ornate statues, and crystal chandeliers illuminated with hundreds of candles.

"Lady Broussant and Miss Graves," the butler boomed, tapping his cane on the polished floor.

As they removed their carriage boots and donned their dancing slippers, Lenore sucked in a breath as all eyes swiveled to land upon her and Elena. Fans flicked open and Lenore's preternatural hearing caught their whispers.

"She's the daughter of a banker, I'd heard."

"Well, she'd better stay away from my Andrew. Nothing less than a Squire's daughter shall do for him."

"She is rather plain… though I suppose she has nice eyes and good posture."

A woman chuckled. "I wager ten quid that she'll be a wallflower for the duration of her stay."

"I'll take that wager," another man whispered to his companion. "Lady Broussant is a merry dame. Surely her cousin will succumb to her gaiety."

"Just as half the men here already have?" A woman replied archly. "Did you hear that she…"

The conversation drifted away from Lenore, their curiosity ebbed in favor of a more delicious source of speculation.

Elena's lips curved in an amused smile as she introduced Lenore to Lord and Lady Haversham. It wasn't difficult to play the shy, demure maiden as the hostess's gaze dissected her like one of Lady Villar's surgical implements.

Lenore curtsied as she was taught. "It is an honor to make your acquaintance, My Lady."

"I'm certain I'm delighted," Lady Haversham said absently and moved on to the next group of guests.

Indifference was certainly preferable to disapproval, Lenore thought as Elena introduced her to those who had already greeted the hostess. Elena had warned her that introductions were made as quickly as possible so that the dancing could commence. In fact, they proceeded so quickly that the names and faces swirled in her mind in a chaotic soup.

And then she saw him. Her breath froze. Gavin Drake, Baron of Darkwood, Lord Vampire of Rochester... her soon to be husband. No matter how many times Lenore pondered the latter, she still could not fathom it.

Unbidden, her lips parted as she took in his powerful frame, emphasized by his black tailcoat, burgundy waistcoat, and charcoal knee-breeches. His long, dark curly hair was tied back, emphasizing the sharp angles of his cheekbones. His harsh black eyes surveyed the assembly with a look of practiced boredom. When Lord Darkwood's gaze flicked across hers, a jolt of lightning seemed to pierce her heart.

Elena touched her elbow. "Don't stare."

Quickly, Lenore directed her gaze elsewhere, though it was hardly necessary as all eyes were on Darkwood. Aside from his wealth and rank, surely they had to sense the aura of raw power that emanated from him. Perhaps even some primal instinct recognized that he was like a wolf among a herd of deer.

Her neck strained with the effort to not turn in his direction. She fanned her heated cheeks as her ears picked up the deep timbre of his voice when he greeted the hostess. Even his words dripped with authority.

And then he was before them. "Lady Broussant," he said with a bow, "It is a delight to see you once more. I heard your cousin is visiting." His gaze once more roved over Lenore as he let his words hang in expectation.

Elena curtsied. "Miss Lenore Graves, allow me to present to you, Lord Gavin Drake, Baron of Darkwood. Lord Darkwood, allow me to introduce you to my dear cousin, Miss Lenore Graves."

Gavin bowed deeply. "Miss Graves, I am pleased to make your acquaintance. How are you enjoying your stay in Rochester so far?"

"It is very lovely, Lord Darkwood." As Lenore curtsied, she realized she meant every word. Rochester was a beautiful borough, with its grassy hills, quaint cottages, and tall trees. The land seemed painted with green, so abundant were the flowers and foliage. Countless birds and animals she'd never before laid eyes on surprised her every time she ventured outdoors. The air smelled clean and fresh and best of all, it was quiet. At first the silence had alarmed her after the constant noise and bustle of London, but now the peace of the land settled over her like a downy blanket.

As his dark eyes met hers and his lips curved in a smile of approval and amusement at their farce, Lenore couldn't help but wish they had truly met under these circumstances. Did he fancy her gown and painstaking styled hair? Or did he still see her bruised and battered, collapsed in the mud at his feet?

His words that night rang in her mind. *"Get up. I will decide whether or not you should fall to your knees in supplication…"*

She shivered and forced a polite smile.

How savage and cruel he had been at first. Although he had gentled when he discovered the reason for her presence in his lands, Lenore couldn't help but fear that she'd see that harshness once more.

Lord Darkwood inclined his head once more before asking Elena to partner him for the first set. He wouldn't ask Lenore until the set before the supper, that way he could sit next to her while they dined. And then he wouldn't dance with her until the end, when they played the waltz. When he escorted her and Elena to their carriage, he would ask permission to call on her tomorrow. Lenore hid a disbelieving smile behind her fan at how meticulously their feigned courtship had been planned.

Which meant she would be dancing with mortals at first. To her surprise, Lord Haversham partnered her in the first Cotillion. Straightening her spine, Lenore focused on executing the steps as Elena had taught her. Not too slow, not too fast… and only utilizing her vampiric speed to correct a wrong motion.

Thankfully, she did not make a cake of herself on the floor. And even more importantly, to her relief, her lessons had rewarded her. With her confidence in her appearance and concentration on all that she'd been taught, the proximity and light touch of the men dancing with her did not bring back her attacks of panic. She said a silent prayer of thanks to Elena for reminding her of her strength.

I could bite them all if they gave me offense. Tear open their throats and drain them dry. Lenore smiled as she turned to meet her next partner in the line. Perhaps that was why Elena had not taken her to hunt before the ball.

She bit back a surprised gasp as Lord Darkwood took her hands and spun her in the reeling dance. "You seem to be adapting well, youngling," he said too low for the other dancers to hear.

Lenore tried to ignore the heat creeping into her cheeks at his touch. "Elena says I am a quick learner."

His lips twitched again. Was that pride in his eyes?

She didn't have time to discern his expression as she was handed off to the next man, who was slightly clumsy, though she pretended not to notice. The floor rumbled with the rapid steps of the dancers, the strains of the orchestra competed with the animated chatter of the guests. The air was redolent with the scent of beeswax, perfume, sweat... and blood. The sound of countless heartbeats roared through her ears, amplifying the sudden onslaught of hunger.

Lenore swallowed as saliva filled her mouth and her stomach rumbled. Elena hadn't warned her that her hunger would be spurred. Of course, Lenore had never told them just how much of a youngling she truly was. She'd only been a vampire little more than three years. And Blanche had kept her far away from mortals much of the time, so she'd had little opportunity to practice control.

I can do this, she said silently, willing herself not to look at the pulsing veins in the women's exposed throats. Thank heavens the males' necks were covered with their stiff cravats, else she may have fed on one of her dance partners by now.

When at last the music ceased, she quit the floor and went to the dressing room as soon as was acceptable. She paused at the door as she heard two women laughing.

"Did you see how she held her fan?" one woman said with an audible sneer. "Breeding does tell. Even her surname is common. Graves."

"She does have a nice curtsy and danced well," the other said. "Really, Harriet, you shouldn't be so nasty. Just because she's a poor relation doesn't mean she doesn't have prospects."

Lenore licked her fangs before entering the room, features composed in a carefully placid countenance to conceal her raging blood thirst. One girl blushed at the sight of her and fled the room with a quick curtsy while the other glanced at her with a smirk. The malice in the girl's green eyes vanished, however, as Lenore captured her gaze and fed.

After drinking a pint, Lenore bit her finger and healed the girl's wound with her blood, leaving the dressing room sated and satisfied with the spot of vengeance.

When she returned to the ballroom, Lord Darkwood regarded her with a raised brow and a glimmer of amusement as if he knew exactly what she had done. She wondered if he'd fed from someone at the ball as well. Her belly turned over at his smile as he bowed.

"May I have the pleasure of dancing the next set with you, Miss Graves?"

Even a human could hear the gasps from the other guests at Lord Darkwood's request. Even though this whole endeavor was a ruse, Lenore couldn't hold back a thrill of triumph to dance with the county's most coveted bachelor. She hid a grin beneath her fan at the jealous glares the other young women cast her way. Wallflower indeed.

The Master of Ceremonies called for a Quadrille and Lenore and Gavin lined up with the other couples. The intensity of his gaze as he bowed nearly made her falter in her curtsy when the musicians struck up a jaunty tune.

His hand grasped hers, the solid heat of his grasp palpable through the fabric of their gloves. His other hand lightly touched her shoulder and Lenore felt a tremor of something other than the usual fear. Not ready to ponder her strange response, she focused dutifully on her steps and turns.

"You dance very well, Miss Graves," he said low, so the mortals couldn't hear. "Elena taught you well."

The compliment eased her tension. "I never imagined the steps were this energetic. They're not too different from the reels in the East End."

"Truly?" he laughed before his gaze roved over her with an entrancing smile. "Though I'm sure the manner of dress is quite different. I confess, you look even lovelier in a ball gown than I'd anticipated."

"Th-thank you, my lord," she stammered as his words sent her heart pounding.

When she was passed to a new partner, she found herself missing Lord Darkwood. The human was polite enough, but he didn't smell right. He also had an unnerving habit of peering down her bodice.

Her next partner was much more courteous, yet she still craved Gavin's presence. Was it because he was familiar? Or also a vampire? Or was there another reason?

All thoughts fled as she was once more reunited with him. They moved in perfect tandem, the steps suddenly wrought with magic. Lenore gazed at him in wonder as they moved to the beautiful music. This was exactly what she had imagined when she was a young girl.

Her tongue slid along her fangs as mirth bubbled within her being. Well, maybe not exactly.

"What are you thinking about to bring such an enchanting smile to your lips?" Gavin asked.

"Just how different everything is." Lenore's cheeks heated with his mention of her lips. "And truly, you do not have to flirt with me when our arrangement is a forgone conclusion."

"But I am enjoying it." He grinned. "This courtship is the most diverting of any I've orchestrated."

But why? she wanted to ask.

Seven

Gavin tried to hide his wonder as he escorted Lenore to the dining room. She played the part of an innocent debutante to utter perfection. He marveled at her rapid learning and adaptability. And when he'd danced with Elena, she'd told him that Lenore was an accomplished seamstress, so much that the ball gown she'd worn tonight was one of Elena's old dresses that she'd altered herself.

That could prove useful for the duration of their marriage. It was dreadfully difficult to bribe a tailor into seeing him after dark. Their weak mortal eyes required so much light.

Once more he glanced down at her, trying not to be caught staring. Her transformation was beyond astounding. Gone was the plain, waifish female he'd first encountered. In her place, a radiant angel walked beside him. No, an angel was too pure for the primal visions that Lenore incited, Gavin thought as he eyed the small, yet delectable curves of her breasts rising up from her gown and the smooth, delicate column of her neck that begged him to take a nip.

Her crowning glory, however, was her hair. A rich mahogany, it shone like polished bronze and his fingers itched to run his fingers through the curled tendrils to see if it was as soft as he remembered. As Elena made a delicate sound behind him, he realized he'd been staring more than was appropriate. Damn these societal strictures. He wanted to drink his fill of the sight of her beauty. But he couldn't risk damaging Lenore's reputation. His bride must be untarnished to avoid unwanted attention after this scrutinized courtship concluded. The rushed wedding, though necessary, would draw enough talk.

As they neared the long table, loaded with so many dishes that it practically groaned, he felt Lenore's arm stiffen as she froze beside him. Looking at her wide eyes, he wondered what was amiss. Elena had assured him that she'd taught her proper table etiquette and use of silverware, but perhaps she hadn't mastered such complexities in so short a time?

He lightly stroked her upper arm in effort to soothe her. It didn't matter if she made mistakes. Once their engagement was announced, her status would be beyond reproach. As he pulled out her seat, he saw her staring at the array of food as if beholding one of the wonders of the world. Comprehension dawned and he smiled. Since she'd come from the lower classes, she'd likely never seen such a vast repast. Pity she was unable to enjoy it as a human could.

"I do hope there is not something amiss with the table," one young woman said, eyeing Lenore with amusement.

"Not in the slightest," Lenore protested. "I was only admiring the beautiful arrangement."

"Did you not have suppers like these where you come from?" The chit's lips curved in a mocking smile. She glanced back at her friends and they tittered behind their fans.

Lenore shook her head, not catching the implied insult.

Gavin ground his teeth. He hoped that viper had been the one Lenore had fed on in the dressing room earlier.

He watched with fascination as she took a delicate sip of the leek soup and closed her eyes in pure bliss. Vampires couldn't digest food very well, but they could at least enjoy small tastes.

He himself took a sip of the Madeira and hid a wince at the vinegary aftertaste. His own stores were far better. He would be sure to serve it at his ball after the wedding.

The fish course was brought out next and Lenore took a small bite of buttered turbot and actually moaned softly. Arousal shivered down his spine. If only he could make her moan like that. But he never could. Not when their marriage would be in name only. Gritting his teeth, he willed his lust to abate and focused on making polite conversation. The bane of all social gatherings.

He couldn't wait to be alone with Lenore so they could speak of things that actually mattered. To the devil with the weather.

To her credit, Lenore managed to make the boring topics bearable with her shy smiles and becoming soft voice. The partridge and pheasant were delivered and she sampled that as well. And then a piece of fruit.

Too late, he realized just how much she had eaten. "Lenore," he whispered, hiding his lips behind his glass, "You must stop eating, or you will become ill."

Her two front teeth worried her lower lip, almost revealing her fangs and she nodded quickly before lowering her fork to toy with the venison a footman had set before her.

But when the berry custard was offered to her, he caught her slipping a spoonful of the creamy confection into her mouth. Her moan of pleasure was audible to some of the other diners and they glanced at her with veiled expressions of disapproval.

Gavin hid a sigh. Foolish youngling. What was she thinking?

"Is the custard to your liking, Miss Graves?" Lady Haversham asked.

Lenore nodded. "Oh yes. Everything is wonderful. I have never before enjoyed such a fine meal."

Gavin's eyes widened as comprehension dawned. Of course, not only would she not have seen so much food before, but as one who had grown up starving, she would have difficulty resisting temptation to eat what was set before her. Especially such delicious delicacies.

His chest tightened in pity for the difficult life she must have led. But he couldn't have her casting up her accounts all over the dining room table.

"Lenore…" he said sharply, though still too low for the humans to hear.

She flinched and dropped her spoon.

Though he was pleased with her obedience, he did wish she did not react to his reasonable requests like a startled hare.

After the dishes were carried away, he breathed a sigh of relief that temptation had been removed. He and the other men who wanted to dance escorted the ladies to the dressing room while the others remained behind for port and cigars.

While he waited for Lenore to powder her nose and adjust her coiffure, he realized that he was looking forward to the waltz. It was likely the only time he'd be able to hold her in his arms. They'd danced together so well, despite their disparity in height. This next dance promised to be exquisite. He tapped his foot in impatience, eyeing the door. What was taking her so long?

When she emerged, the reason for her delay was apparent in her ashen complexion, which almost had a greenish cast.

Lenore shakily curtsied. "My lord, I'm afraid I am feeling a trifle out of sorts. May we postpone our dance?"

"Of course." Gavin inclined his head in assent. "But please permit me to take you outside for a bit of fresh air once we locate your cousin to chaperone us."

As if summoned by his words, Elena materialized behind him. "I would be delighted to take a turn around the gardens with you. I want to see if anything is budding yet." Her eyes roved over

Lenore's face with growing concern. "Let us change back into our walking boots."

Gavin frowned as he once more found himself waiting by the door. He hadn't sensed Elena's approach. His worry for Lenore had taken over his awareness. That was dangerous.

When they made their explanations to their hostess, Lady Haversham nodded agreeably, though her eyes glinted with curiosity with Gavin's unprecedented interest in Miss Graves. Truly, taking a walk with her gave an even greater impression of his impending courtship, though he still would have preferred a waltz.

As he'd expected, a few matrons suddenly decided that they wanted to take in some of the night air on the terrace, where they could conveniently observe most of the gardens.

Gavin caught Elena's gaze and tilted his head in the direction of the peeping mortals. "We have spectators."

Her arm hooked with Lenore's, she gave an almost imperceptible nod before pointing at the rose bush, pretending to be extolling its virtues while she looked down at her charge. "What were you thinking, little mouse? Vampires cannot handle an overabundance of solid victuals."

"I'd been told," Lenore replied miserably. "But I didn't know how little I could abide. It's just that I'd been hungry all my life and the food… It tasted like heaven." She looked up at Gavin with pleading eyes. "I'm sorry I ruined your plans, my lord."

"It is quite all right." His words came out sharper than he meant.

The thought of her being so hungry that she couldn't restrain herself at a meal infuriated him for some reason. And Clayton, the vampire who'd captured her last year had starved her as well. Why did the world have to be so cruel to some people?

"And I told you to call me Gavin," he chided, a little softer.

"I cannot use your Christian name when we've just been acquainted," she protested. "It would be—" she broke off with an alarming choking sound as her face paled further.

Elena quickly led her behind a hedge, pretending to need to adjust her bonnet laces.

The sound of retching reached his ears and he hoped the nosy hens on the terrace didn't hear. Gavin turned his back and looked up at the moon, feigning polite boredom while inside he seethed. This evening had become a travesty.

No, he corrected himself, this unfortunate incident truly wasn't a significant inconvenience. There would be other dances, other suppers and musicales for them to act out their courtship. Then why was he so vexed? Perhaps it was merely the fact that things had not gone exactly as planned. Yes, that must be it.

Lenore emerged with Elena, dabbing her mouth with a handkerchief. Her cheeks were ashen and she looked ready to topple over with a slight breeze. Gavin's fists clenched with furious impotence that he couldn't do anything to abate her suffering. He'd never seen a vampire become ill before.

Her eyes met his and a bright flush crept up her cheeks, visible in the moonlight. Though her embarrassment was unfortunate, Gavin was pleased to see some color in her face. "Do you think you shall feel well enough for me to call upon you tomorrow?"

She nodded, appearing to be too exhausted to speak.

He offered his arm. "Then let us make your excuses so you may depart and rest. I had hoped to present you to my people this evening, but that shall have to wait until tomorrow."

Even though she tried to hide it, he did not miss the flash of fear in her eyes at the prospect of meeting his other vampires.

Once back in the manor, he hung back as Elena spoke with the hostess. Lady Haversham eyed Lenore's pale complexion and clucked like a mother hen. Gavin wished he could follow them in their carriage, but such would be unseemly. Instead, he contented himself with assisting Lenore and Elena in fastening their cloaks and asked permission to look in on them tomorrow evening.

He kept his gaze firmly on Lenore as he spoke, leaving no doubt to the spectators as to his true intentions.

Since he no longer had the diversion of waltzing with her, he retired to the card room for the remainder of the evening. He played a simple game of Hazard, and was surprised to be losing. And losing to humans at that. Tonight's events had driven him to distraction.

Once more he pictured Lenore eating the human food with blissful abandon. The truth was now clear. Whoever had Changed her clearly could not have been around long enough to educate her on even the basics of her new position in life. He resolved to teach her how to be a proper vampire as soon as possible. He never wanted to see her ill or in pain again.

Setting down his brandy, he wondered why he cared so much.

Eight

Lenore lay on Elena's aptly named fainting couch as the other vampire dabbed her forehead with a cool cloth.

"You'll need to feed again. I do hope you recover before dawn," Elena said.

Though Lenore's nausea had abated, her stomach continued to churn with agony like she had swallowed broken glass. If she was making such foolish mistakes now, what did that impart for her future as a baroness? Her stomach lurched again.

Even that pain didn't hurt nearly as badly as the anger in Rochester's eyes at her gaffe. What if he changed his mind on marrying her? What if he sent her back to London? That was what she wanted... *wasn't* it?

Her stomach gave another lurch.

"I do not think I am well-suited to being a vampire," she groaned aloud.

Elena chuckled. "Well, that is not something you can go back and change, I'm afraid." She gently dabbed Lenore's eyelids with the cloth. "How long ago *were* you Changed?"

"A little over three years."

"Had your maker never told you that we cannot digest solid food well?" Her tone turned curious. "Where is the one who made you?"

"She's dead. Or at least, I'm fairly certain she is. Only a few months after Blanche Changed me, she disappeared after we lay down for the day sleep. And after that, I heard talk that a vampire

Hunter had been in Town, and the Lord Vampire's wife had killed him." Lenore shuddered as the painful memories flitted through her mind like captive birds. If the Hunter had checked the other part of the crypt, he'd have found and slain her too. "Blanche had no reason to leave London, much less abandon me. She saved me from death because she had a kind heart and she was lonely." She sighed, not wanting to talk of Blanche anymore. "Yes, she *did* tell me that we should not eat food. But since we never had any, I never before experienced the temptation to do so. Tonight, everything tasted so good, I just could not stop. You must think me such a fool." And the heavens only knew what Lord Darkwood thought.

Elena moved the cloth back up to her forehead and Lenore opened her eyes to see the vampire shake her head. "No, I think you are a bit of a green-girl, but not a fool. Only one who has been deprived of so many things."

"Do you think Lord Darkwood will change his mind about wedding me?" To her surprise, the prospect did not fill her with as much relief as she'd anticipated.

"I doubt it. He seems to genuinely like you. And Gavin does not like many people." Elena smiled.

"Why didn't you want to marry him this time?" she blurted the question without thinking. "I'm certain you make a far better baroness."

Elena tapped her lower lip with her finger. "Aside from the fact that a widow has much more freedom than a wife, the deception grew heavy upon me after awhile. If I were to wed again, I would want it to be for real. For love."

Lenore frowned. "He didn't love you?" Who wouldn't love such a vivacious, beautiful woman?

The vampire laughed. "Now you sound like a fool."

"What was it like, being married to him?" She held her breath, unbearably curious.

"Not too different than any other marriage in the nobility. I ran his household and hosted his parties. He provided me with an exquisite wardrobe and gave me a free hand in decorating. Many of my furnishings are quite out of date, so you will want to give the place a fresh look when you take up residence." She dipped the cloth into a bowl of water and smiled. "The only real differences were that I naturally couldn't receive callers during the day and I had no obligation or ability to provide an heir."

Lenore lifted her chin to peer up at Elena, eager to glean as much information about her impending fate as possible. "He didn't require you to do your wifely duty?"

"Require?" Elena laughed. "Of course not. Though we've shared a tumble a time or two, when we were between lovers. I do hope you're not envious. It was a long time ago and we never suited in that way."

Lenore shook her head, though admittedly she felt a twinge of... something. "Not at all. I asked Lord Rochester, I mean, Lord Darkwood, for our marriage to be in name only."

"That is probably wise, as such intimacy can muddle up such an arrangement." Elena stroked her lower lip with a pensive look. "But I must ask, do you not find him attractive?"

"I do," she answered quickly. "That is, he is very handsome. Just the sort I used to dream about when I was a girl." Her cheeks heated saying it aloud. "But, I'm afraid I can't... can't..." she trailed off as even the word of such an act filled her with terror.

"Because someone misused you?" Elena said softly.

Hot and cold chills wracked her body along with a roiling fury. "He told me my reputation would not follow me here! He said that he wouldn't tell anyone and that I could start anew."

"Be calm, little mouse. Gavin didn't tell me anything of your past. I only discerned that you had been assaulted from the bad dreams you've had, and just now when it was written all over your face." She ran a soothing hand through Lenore's hair. "Would you care to talk about what happened?"

"*No.*" She nearly spat the word.

Elena drew back slightly. "Alright then, I will not pry. And I will not reveal your secret to anyone."

Lenore softened her tone. "Thank you. I did not mean to sound so waspish."

"It is quite all right." The vampire patted her shoulder. "I would be much more vicious in such a situation, I am certain."

Just as Elena adjusted the pillow under Lenore's head, there was a knock at the door. Elena smirked as if she knew who it was. Perhaps one of the lovers she'd spoken of had come to call? Lenore wanted to get up and follow her, but her stomach gave another stab of pain when she tried to move.

"Stay there, little mouse," Elena scolded and crossed the room to open the door.

Rochester's frame passed through the doorway. "How are you feeling, Lenore?"

For a moment, Lenore couldn't speak, she was too overcome with shock that he'd taken himself from his countless duties as a Lord Vampire to look in on her. Especially since only hours ago he'd said he wouldn't call on her until tomorrow. Finally, she managed, "Much better, my lord. Once more, I apologize for my foolishness."

He held up a hand, dismissing her apologies. "Do not apologize for not knowing what your maker failed to teach you."

She bristled at his callous censure of Blanche. "That wasn't her fault. We never had food to avoid in the first place."

He held up his hands in mock surrender. "Alright, I apologize for my assumption." His polished black boots echoed lightly on the smooth wooden floor as he crossed the room to approach her. "I trust you've learned to listen to me from now on?"

Although she was slightly irritated at his autocratic tone, Lenore nodded. "Yes, my lord. But I'd thought you'd said you were going to call on me tomorrow."

"And so I shall." He chuckled and perched on the arm of the fainting couch, mere inches from where she reclined. "But it is my duty as Lord Vampire of this borough to look after the welfare of my people."

Behind him, Elena made a small sound that might have been a laugh. Rochester darted her a sharp look and she grinned. "Of course it is."

Lenore looked up at him, suddenly having trouble breathing from his nearness and spicy scent of power and masculinity. "That is very noble of you. My stomach ache is nearly gone."

Her words only quavered slightly as her mind roiled. Although Lord and Lady Villar had often checked on her, the real Lord Vampire of London, Ian Ashton, Duke of Burnrath, had barely spared her a thought after Blanche had disappeared. He hadn't even spoken to her directly, merely sent one of his other vampires to question her on her maker's possible whereabouts.

Yet Ruthless Rochester was here simply because she had an upset stomach... which she'd brought about with her own stupidity. She didn't know what to make of such solicitousness.

All thoughts ceased as he took a lock of her hair and gently twirled it between his fingers. His touch electrified every inch of her flesh, but it wasn't the cold, queasy sensation she usually experienced at a male's touch. This was something different, alarming because she wasn't sure this feeling was unpleasant. Except for the perplexing flutter in her belly. Was her response from his touch, or a new reaction to the food she'd eaten?

Rochester's rumbling voice silenced her inner prattling as his knuckles grazed her forehead. "Your color seems to have improved, though you appear as if you need to feed."

Since she'd vomited up the blood she'd drank along with the food, he was likely correct. Humiliation welled within at the reminder that she'd been sick in his presence.

Elena nodded. "We shall hunt before dawn if she's feeling well enough. If not, Lord have mercy on the sod she feasts on at dusk." She chuckled.

"Elena," His glare was sharp with warning. "You remember the law."

Full blown laughter trickled from her lips. "Come now, I was only jesting. Your little mouse is too small to drain a man dry."

"I came close once," Lenore retorted, reminding them both that she was perfectly capable of speaking for herself. "The night you and I first met."

"Are you saying you nearly killed a human on my land?" Darkwood raised a brow.

She sat up quickly, fear coursing through her veins. "No, my lord, it was in Dartford, and I'm certain the man lived." Dizziness washed over her, making the room spin.

A gentle hand grasped her shoulder. "Lenore, please do not be overwrought. I am well aware of what you'd been through before I found you that night."

"Oh." Her words came out in a shaky whisper.

"Please, lay back down and rest. I shall see you on the morrow." Gone was his harsh air of authority. In its place, was a soothing rumble, almost a purr.

Lenore did as bid and froze as he bent down and lightly pressed his lips to her forehead. The brief kiss spread warmth through her limbs, even as it set her heart to beating like a moth's wings.

Her lips quavered to form a response as he bowed and strode out the door.

Elena clasped her hands together. "Well, this is certainly a diverting courtship."

Diverting wasn't the word Lenore would have chosen, however, she couldn't come up with one that suited this situation. If Darkwood made her mind turn upside down with such brief interactions, how would he affect her when she was under his roof?

Nine

Gavin sighed with impatience as his second and third in command intercepted him on his way to Elena's the following night. He wanted to show Lenore some of Rochester's most famous landmarks and hoped to do so before her presentation to his people.

"My lord, we've received some information from the Maidstone's second in command that you should hear," Benson said.

The urgency on his second's face could not be ignored. Still, Gavin couldn't suppress a weary sigh. "What is it?"

"He said a band of rogues has been observed roaming about all of Kent. And that they appear oddly organized for rogues. Thus far, they haven't made any sort of move to invade or harm any occupied lands, but all who have seen them wish to discern their motives," Benson said, eyes grave with concern.

Rogues in a group? That was all he needed. Rogues were much more difficult to capture when there was more than one. Thankfully rogue bands rarely lasted long, because though there was strength in numbers, grouping together also made them easier to find and their hunting more difficult.

"Do you have descriptions for any of them?" Gavin demanded.

Cecil nodded. "Three were seen by Maidstone's second only a sennight past. One was said to be portly, with mud brown hair, another has yellow hair. And the one presumed to be the leader, was said to be lean, with a mane of dark red locks, so that will make him easiest to spot.

Gavin paused at the last. That wasn't the most common shade of hair, however it wasn't all that rare either with vampires. Red hair darkened when denied sunlight, after all. The darker the shade, the older the vampire. He wondered…

Benson voiced his thought. "Do you think that could be Justus?"

Gavin thought for a moment, then shook his head. "No. Aside from the fact that he knows I'd have to kill him if he entered these lands again, he made it very clear that he never wished to lay eyes on me again, after what happened with that girl."

Justus. Gavin's gut tightened at the name. The vampire was once his second in command and closest friend. All of that vanished in an instant when the he'd disobeyed a direct order and then done the unthinkable.

Benson nodded, though his frown remained dubious. "If you say so, my lord."

"Keep your eyes and ears open at any rate," he instructed them before continuing on it way.

As he continued his walk to Elena's, thoughts of his former friend haunted his memory. If only there was something else he could have done. Alas, Justus's hazardous actions merited a death sentence. Exiling his former second had already caused Gavin to lose face as it was. Some now thought him weak, though most understood that he could not bear to slay his closest friend.

When he reached the door of Elena's cottage, the hurt in Justus's eyes flashed in his mind, like a recurring nightmare.

"Have we done something to cause offense, my lord?" Elena's voice pierced his consciousness.

"Not at all," he said quickly. "I merely had some old business on my mind. How is Lenore?"

The vampire gave him an arch look. "Completely recovered, albeit somewhat nervous. She's never been courted before. Poor thing hasn't had much of any life's pleasures."

"Well, I shall have to do what I can to rectify that." He followed Elena into the sitting room and, blissfully, the memories and guilt fled as soon as he beheld Lenore.

The youngling rose at the sight of him. "My lord," she said so quickly that he was unable to discern whether she was happy or wary at his presence.

Dressed in a gown of pale blue velvet with navy trim, Lenore looked too delicious for words. All signs of last night's illness had vanished as she curtsied for him. Her complexion was creamy with a slight blush that either meant she'd fed, or that she was somewhat pleased to see him. He hoped it was the latter.

He took her hand and brushed her gloved knuckles with his lips. Bare skin would have been more preferable, but her deepened blush was more than worthwhile. "You look very becoming, Miss Graves."

"Thank you." She sat back down on the settee. "What exactly does one do when a gentleman calls?"

"If we were human and proper, I suppose we'd sit and talk while our chaperone watches us like a falcon." He grinned at Elena's snort of laughter. "However, since we are not, we shall do something even more diverting." He held out his hand. "Come, I'd like to show you something. You may want to fetch a cloak and better boots."

Elena darted him a curious glance as Lenore rose to comply.

"I'd like her to see some of her new land," he said without elaborating further.

The vampire pouted, though her green eyes glittered with merriment. "You never gave me a tour."

"I didn't need to." Gavin laughed. "You undertook your own exploring before I had the opportunity to offer."

Elena's laughter echoed his own. "That is true."

Lenore emerged, wearing smart black walking boots and a dove gray woolen cloak. Thicker cream kid leather gloves covered her hands to ward off the still-chilly night air. He offered his arm and was gratified when she took it with no hesitation. However, he still felt a slight tremble in her grip. Would he ever be able to dispel her fear of him... or any man?

Leading her to the rear door, he turned back to Elena. "Meet us at the gathering place in two hours." If only they had more time.

The moment he and Lenore stepped outside, he asked her, "Do you know how to *run*?"

She looked up at him, lips curving slightly with confusion. "Run?"

"As a vampire runs, with inhuman speed," he clarified as they walked the path of the rear garden.

"Once, and only for my life." She looked down and shivered.

When she'd escaped the rogues who'd assaulted her. Rochester cursed himself for bringing shadows of pain to her eyes. But he was resolved to do everything in his power to help her banish that poison darkness and not let it rule every aspect of her life.

"You've never attempted to do so for enjoyment?" He studied her, unable to comprehend what it was like to not indulge in that simple pleasure.

She shook her head. "For one, it feels a little odd to run like that. For another, there was little room to do so in my part of London. I did not want to risk a mortal seeing me."

Gavin accepted that logic and crossed his arms. "Well, there is no time better than the present."

She looked doubtfully at the high stone wall.

He chuckled. "You can leap that easily." To demonstrate, he vaulted to the top. His shoulders shook with mirth as she fiddled with her skirts. "Come on now. At least reach the top. And if you make it all the way over, I shall catch you."

Eyes wide with trepidation, Lenore took several steps back and ran towards the wall— faster than a human— but still slower than she was capable of— and leaped. Just as he'd anticipated, she cleared the wall by several feet.

Gavin jumped down quickly, admiring the sight of fluttering petticoats and teasing glimpses of her bare legs beneath her skirts before holding out his arms and catching her. Lenore was light as goose down in his arms, yet warmer and more potent than he could have imagined.

For a moment, he simply held her, feeling her chest rise and fall against his and the heat of her rapid breaths against his neck. She fit against him perfectly, he realized, like a missing stone in an arch.

Suddenly, she stiffened, breaking the spell. He gently set her back on her feet, gratified by the sparkle of triumph in her large dark eyes. "I did it!"

"Yes, you did." He couldn't hide his pleasure in her joy. "Now we run."

She looked up at him, less afraid this time. "Where?"

He grinned down at her, eager to make her smile again. "Take my hand." As her small, warm fingers entwined with his, a pang of tenderness tugged at his chest. "Since I am far older and more powerful than you, I am faster than you. Therefore, you must keep hold of me so I may match your pace. Are you ready?"

She took a deep breath and squared her shoulders. "Yes."

"See that tree with the split top?" At her nod, he continued. "We will stop there." He squeezed her hand tightly before saying, "Now!"

At first, it took utmost effort not to fly to the tree in a blink of an eye, but as her tiny fingers gripped his, he found himself not only guiding her pace, but molding to hers, as if they were one force cutting through the night like a single blade. The wind whipped across their faces and their feet barely touched the ground. Gavin glanced over at Lenore to see her hair pulling free from its pins to brush across her cheeks and fly behind her like a banner. He'd never seen anything so enchanting.

Together, their hands struck the bark of the tree so hard that pine needles rained down around them. Bright flags of color stained Lenore's rounded cheeks, visible even in the meager moonlight. Rochester closed his eyes in ecstasy as the most unrestrained, joyous laugh he'd ever heard trickled from Lenore's lush lips.

"That was... incredible, my lord," she breathed, eyes still shining with unabashed joy.

"Gavin, please." It took every vestige of his will not to bend down and claim her lips in a devouring kiss. "I am glad you think so. I'll teach you to be a proper vampire yet."

"Such running does not feel so very proper," she replied, an awestruck smile still playing across her lips.

Staring down at her mesmerizing mouth, he admitted, "Very little of what I will teach you is."

***

Lenore's heart thudded in her ears from their run. She'd never before experienced something so invigorating. It felt like flying! Blanche had told her they could move more swiftly than humans, but she'd never imagined this level of preternatural swiftness. True, she'd used this ability to flee from her imprisonment last year, but she'd been too terrified to enjoy it... or even recall the experience. Now she wished she could run this way everywhere.

Rochester continued to smile down at her. Something in his enigmatic black eyes made her belly turn over. Fighting the unsettling sensation, she turned away. "What did you want to show me, my lord... ah, Gavin?"

"One of our most ancient landmarks... the other you shall see later." He pointed and the clouds parted as if on command. A shaft of moonlight shone down on a massive and ancient cathedral.

Lenore peered up in awe at the massive stone structure wrought with medieval turrets, rounded arches, and crenellated parapets.

"It's beautiful," she breathed. She'd only been in a cathedral once, one of the few places the poor were allowed to venture. This one may be smaller, yet it was all the more noble, nestled in a lush valley and surrounded by nature instead of jammed between numerous other structures like the ones in London.

"It's a ruin... again." His lips curled in a mocking smile. "Half the roof is rotted away." He seized her hand, and just in time, Lenore caught herself from flinching. "Would you like to see inside?"

"Oh, yes." There was something tantalizing, almost sinful about entering such an ancient, holy place. She'd once read a book that stated that vampires could not enter a house of God, but after she'd accepted the fact that Blanche was dead, she'd tested the myth by walking into a small church by the wharf, and only received a scolding from a sleepy parson.

As they passed through the west door, beneath a tympanum of what looked more like a scene from Greek mythology than anything Christian, Rochester said, "We can only explore a few areas, lest we risk startling the few remaining clergy who make their home here."

Once inside, Lenore felt as if she truly were a little mouse as she looked up at the high pillars supporting impossibly high stone vaulted ceilings. "I thought you said the roof was rotted."

"It is, in the quire and south transept. In fact, the wall leans as well. They tried to repair it a century ago, but they seem to only have worsened the problem." He frowned with blatant disapproval.

He led her through the nave and the east transept, pointing out which sections had been rebuilt over the centuries, as well as the countless carvings and stain glass windows, and when each had been gifted or commissioned.

"You seem very familiar with this place," Lenore said.

"Yes, I was raised here. As a third son, I was to be trained to be a bishop."

He said the words so matter-of-factly that it took a moment to absorb their meaning. Lenore looked up at him sharply. "*You* were to be a man of the cloth?" She couldn't fathom such a thing.

His rich laughter echoed through the north transept. "Yes. Shocking, is it not? But I assure you, I was much more devout back then."

She giggled a moment, unable to picture this man, who was as handsome as the devil himself, being a humble and chaste servant of the Lord. *Humble, chaste, servant of God...* these words were the antithesis of the man who stood before her. He was arrogant, commanding, and from what she'd heard about him, *not* chaste. And oh, so wicked. Once more, a shiver coursed up her spine.

"You don't believe me?" He placed his hand over his chest, feigning a wounded look. "Well, perhaps I have a scrap of faith lingering in my black heart." He looked around the cathedral and smiled. "How would you like to have our wedding here?"

"If it please you, my lord," she breathed, overwhelmed at the thought of being married in this grand place with such a rich history.

"Although it is right that you should want to please me, I do like to please you as well. What say you, truly?" He looked down at her with such sincere concern that her breath fled her lungs.

The Lords and Ladies in London preferred Saint George's Church to plight their troth. Lenore had often spied many joyous wedding parties exiting the church, tossing bouquets of flowers and riding off in elegant phaetons. Rochester Cathedral dwarfed Saint George's and appeared to be ever so much more fine, even if it was missing half the roof.

His talk of wanting to please her struck a chord of unfathomed longing within her. "Yes, I would like that very much."

"Good." He smiled with genuine pleasure. "A church wedding should restore some propriety to our hasty marriage. Perhaps we may even have the banns read, though I still must procure a special license for us to be permitted to wed in the evening."

"I appreciate your consideration. A morning wedding would be most uncomfortable," she replied with a smile, trying to hold back the depth of incomprehensible emotion he'd invoked.

Lord Darkwood covered his mouth to muffle his laughter. "I do not believe I've ever heard you jest before. I hope to hear you do it more."

They laughed together until suddenly he fell silent, staring at her as if he'd never seen her before. Those sin black eyes held hers as he slowly lowered his head and brushed his lips over hers, soft as a whisper. Heat spiraled in her belly even as her thighs seemed to melt to liquid. Lenore reached for him, whether to hold on or to pull away, she did not know, for he withdrew before she could deduce her own intentions.

"I apologize," Gavin said softly, his voice cracking, as if he had difficulty speaking. "I'm afraid I was too swept up in our courtship. I didn't frighten you, did I?"

"No," she whispered, praying he couldn't see her legs wobbling beneath her skirts. His kiss hadn't scared her, but it had done *something* to her.

For a moment he looked like he wanted to press her further, but then he nodded. "Well, shall we proceed to the Gathering?"

The Gathering, where she would be presented to all of the vampires of Rochester as the bride to be of their Lord. Now *that* filled her with undeniable terror.

Ten

Justus led his band of rogues through the trees by the river in a circuitous route, hoping they didn't come near another Rochester vampire. He'd seen several during tonight's roaming, all headed to the ruins of the castle. There was to be a Gathering, it seemed. At first he'd been tempted to send his comrades away and see if he could spy upon it, but for one thing he wasn't quite ready to risk being sensed by Gavin or any of his people. For another, from the snatches of conversation he'd heard from the last vampires they'd passed, the Gathering was only so Gavin could present the new youngling to the others.

He frowned. Why in the blazes hadn't Rochester done that when the chit had first arrived? He knew that the Lord Vampire could be forgetful about some of his responsibilities, but for one thing, he hardly ever took in new vampires. For another, he seemed to take unseemly interest in this one, heaven only knew why. After several nights of watching the youngling, Justus had deduced nothing interesting about her, aside from the fact that she appeared to be laughably ignorant on how to use her new abilities... like she'd only been Changed yesterday. How the usually abrasive Elena remained so patient with that pathetic creature, Justus would never know.

Perhaps Gavin had delayed her presentation to educate her more so she wouldn't embarrass him with her ignorance. But that only brought back his original question. Why take in such a useless vampire in the first place? Did he owe the Lord of London a favor?

One would think, with Gavin's aiding him in battle last November, that Villar would owe Gavin.

Justus shook his head. Perhaps his old friend's mind was slipping. That happened to the old ones from time to time. He shook off a reflexive pang of sympathy. No, if Rochester was declining, it would be all the easier to cast him down.

He turned to the others. "Presentations usually last at least three hours, though they may be even longer if Rochester decides to hold court."

"What exactly happens at a presentation?" Charlie asked, eyes shining with curiosity beneath his shaggy blond bangs.

He'd forgotten that Charlie was a bastard of sorts, a vampire made by a rogue. He'd never had a city to call home, or a vampire to call lord. Justus was determined to change that.

Patiently, he explained. "The new vampire is introduced to the others and has a chance to become acquainted and begin to forge their place in the hierarchy. That waif we saw will be at the bottom rank for a very long time." He shrugged and resumed walking. "Either way, let us feed quickly while we have the land to ourselves."

As they roamed through the territory openly, Justus smiled as he observed their relaxed shoulders and the absence of watchful tension in their features. Some night soon they would be able to hunt freely like this all the time.

Once they returned to their lair beneath the crypt of the old cathedral, better fed than they'd been in weeks, Justus's cheer vanished like last month's snow melt.

Other vampires had been here. Their faint scent lingered in the air. One he couldn't identify, but the other had clearly been Rochester. The rogues halted behind him, growling and sniffing the air.

"Justus?" Will whispered tentatively. He was the youngest, only twenty years Changed, and had a frail, almost elfish form.

Justus held up a hand for silence. "Remain here. I will investigate. If I call out, I want you all to scatter and find somewhere safe to hide."

"But what if you're attacked?" Rolfe asked, glancing around for enemies lurking in the shadows. Built like a bull, he was capable of a good charge.

Justus shook his head, trying to focus on the trail of the scent. He brushed his red hair from his eyes. "If it is who I think it is, your assistance will do more harm than good. Now do as I say and be quiet."

It didn't seem as if Rochester had been inside this part of the cathedral directly. His essence was too faint. Still, Justus remained cautious as he slowly climbed through the carefully concealed trap door and into the crypt itself.

The scent was also faint here, carried lightly on a draft down the staircase. Holding his breath, Justus made his way up the steps to the main floor. Here the smell of Gavin and the other vampire was the strongest. He followed it in a clearly apparent line through the nave, the clerestory, and across the transepts. After following the trail, Justus confirmed that his enemy had not ventured into the crypt, much less below it... which was a godsend, since if he'd gone that far, he certainly would have smelled Justus's band. And he'd bet his soul that Rochester had avoided the cloisters.

But what had he been doing in the cathedral in the first place? Had someone seen Justus or one of his people near it? Was he searching for their lair? Or had he only been here to reminisce on his past? After all, Gavin had grown up here, had a history and dark past... which was why he typically avoided the place.

Justus shook his head. The reason for Gavin's visit didn't matter. Justus couldn't risk his people.

Returning to the hidden chamber, he breathed a sigh of satisfaction that his fellow rogues had obeyed him. Hidden in the shadows, they stood still near the entrance to the hidden tunnel, waiting for his orders.

"We have to move," he told them. "Tonight."

***

Lenore's next run with Gavin was not as thrilling as the first. Every muscle of her body quaked with trepidation at the prospect of being displayed before the Rochester vampires like a horse at auction. If it weren't for Gavin's grip on her hand, she would have lagged behind. As it was, she had to will every ounce of her concentration to maintain her speed and not trip, or career into anything.

Despite her efforts, by the time they halted in front of the ruins of an ancient castle, Lenore was covered in scratches from various tree branches and brambles.

Gavin surveyed her with a frown. "You are quite disheveled. We shall definitely have to practice your running." He punctured his index finger with a fang and gently trailed the bleeding wound along the scratches on her cheeks, instantly healing them. He did the same with her arms.

Every place his fingers grazed her skin tingled with warmth, whether from his healing or his mere touch, she could not say. The scent of his blood awoke a gnawing hunger that she struggled to suppress. Gavin then helped her straighten her gown and adjusted her cloak before moving on to her hair. Between either the first run or the second, her pins had flown from her sensible bun and now her hair tumbled down her back in shameful disarray.

As his fingers combed through her tresses, plucking out leaves and smoothing the strands, frissons of sensation cascaded through her body, similar to the feeling he evoked when he kissed her, yet with a different sort of intensity.

He stepped back and surveyed her with a smile. "There. You look like quite the picture... except for one thing."

"I know," she agreed sullenly. "My hair is down. I lost all my pins."

He shook his head. "Your hair is lovely. Many vampires wear their hair thus. Look, my own hair is free." He ran a hand through his own shoulder length locks, the curls the color of decadent chocolate. "The problem is that you look like a prisoner being led to the gallows, rather than a worthy vampire ready to meet her new kin and wed the lord of this land. Straighten your shoulders and look me in the eye." After she did as bade, he tilted her chin up with his thumb and nodded. "Yes, like that. If you show any fear, I will be sorely disappointed."

His foreboding tone made her belly quake. Walking at Rochester's side, Lenore held her spine rigid and tried to carry herself more like Elena. What she would give to have more of her tutor's courage.

Gavin guided her though a hidden door that opened to a tunnel that was dark even with her preternatural vision. The scent and essence of other vampires made the hair on the back of her neck stand on end.

I should not be afraid, she scolded herself. *I am one of them.*

But *was* she? All other vampires she'd met were so much stronger than her. Even the other younglings, who'd been Changed by older, stronger vampires than Blanche.

It didn't matter. Lenore closed her eyes and took a deep breath. She would not disappoint Gavin or embarrass Elena. She'd had her fill of embarrassment.

The tunnel gave way to a spiral staircase so narrow that she had to walk behind Gavin. Though he had a slender frame, she couldn't help but notice that his shoulders were very broad. And from their dance last night, she knew it wasn't padding.

Light glowed from below as soft mutters and whispers reached her ears. All fell silent when Gavin emerged into a large concave chamber deep in the castle bowels. Lenore took his proffered arm and nearly froze at the sight of so many eyes upon her.

Though Gavin had only a fraction the amount of vampires as there were in London, being the subject of such scrutiny made her shiver. But when Lenore's eyes met Elena's reassuring gaze, some of her tension eased.

Gavin surveyed them all. "Vampires of Rochester, with the greatest of apologies for the delay, I would like to present the newest member of our humble borough." He placed his hand on the small of Lenore's back and gently guided her forward. "This is Miss Lenore Graves, formerly from London. She has come to Rochester to be my wife for the next fifty years."

The vampires' eyes roved over her with surprise and disbelief. A few even darted glances at Elena, as if they couldn't believe that she was no longer fulfilling the role. Lenore could hardly blame them. She knew she didn't look the part of a baroness, much less a bride of a Lord Vampire.

One female vampire elbowed her neighbor before saying loudly, "Greetings and welcome, Lenore."

"Greetings and welcome, Lenore," the others echoed, looking slightly shamefaced for the delay.

"Greetings in return and thank you," Lenore curtsied, only half paying attention. Gavin's words still swirled in her mind.

Fifty years. Though Lenore knew that five decades was a trifle to most of the old ones, it was still a long time for her. If she'd still been mortal, she'd be an old woman by then! Could she and Rochester truly remain congenial for so long? She knew that many married couples remained happy together until the day they died, but they'd loved each other and wanted to marry. This was a sham, a business arrangement. Where was the chance of happiness there?

And yet the memory of the soft brush of his lips on hers teased her memory, along with his smile and gentle touch.

Rochester's voice broke through her frantic musings. "Lenore is currently residing with Elena, but she will take up residence in my home in about two months. I expect you all to treat her with as much respect and courtesy as you do with me and other high ranking vampires here." His black eyes surveyed them with a sudden harsh glare. "I will not have a repeat of last time."

Last time for what? Lenore made note to ask Elena.

"And now for other business," Rochester continued. "Myrtle, come forward, please."

A blonde female vampire sharply inhaled and darted nervous glances at the others as she lifted her skirts and approached her lord.

"You've been seen visiting Aylesford without permission on three occasions," Rochester said in a dangerous, silky voice. "Do you deny it?"

Myrtle opened her mouth and for a moment it looked like she would lie, but then she sighed and nodded. "No, my lord," she said sullenly. "I am guilty."

He nodded curtly before turning to his second and third in command. "Seize her and take her to my dungeon to be questioned further."

The other vampires gasped and muttered as the vampire was hauled off. "Please, my lord, have mercy! I can explain!"

Lenore suppressed a shudder as the captive vampire's pleas faded away.

Gone was the kind, laughing vampire she'd been running with. Gone was the handsome suitor who'd called her beautiful and kissed her. In his place was Ruthless Rochester and she now saw where he'd acquired that moniker.

Rochester turned back to the gathering of vampires. "There is one more matter to address before this meeting is adjourned." A foreboding expression shrouded his already stern countenance. "I've heard word of an organized band of rogues in the area. "Has anyone seen or heard anything of them?"

As the vampires shook their heads, Lenore's heart thudded in her throat. *Rogues!* She clenched her jaw tight to keep her teeth from chattering and to hold back a scream. Once more the memories of the rogues seizing her crashed through her mind. Their cruel hands upon her body, being chained, beaten, starved, and raped. *Oh God, what if it happens to me again? Or what if another vampire is captured? What if—*

Rochester's thumb stroked her arm in a soothing rhythm as he continued to address his people. "I want you all to keep a close eye out and report any suspicious sightings to me straightaway. I also advise you to try to hunt in pairs until further notice. Rogues can be very dangerous when they form a pack. If you encounter even one, do not attempt to engage them in combat. Run straight to me, Benson or Cecil and inform us."

His people nodded and Rochester's features softened slightly. "Good. Enough with the unpleasantness, I will now adjourn the official meeting. Wine and tea will be served in the old great hall while you have an opportunity to become better acquainted with our new vampire. If any of you have any concerns, you may voice them now, or approach me privately."

Everyone bowed and Rochester led her up another set of stairs to a vast stone chamber with trestle tables and rotting tapestries. Two tables were covered with snowy cloths and held glasses and decanters of wine as well as a tray of small biscuits.

Lenore accepted a glass that Rochester's second in command brought her, but declined any biscuits. She'd learned her lesson.

A few vampires approached her with genuine warmth, while others, mostly older females, gave her forced greetings and sauntered off to whisper amongst themselves, doubtless nothing friendly. Lenore couldn't think badly of them. It was understandable for them to be angry that a weak youngling held a higher status than them, and an outsider at that.

However, they were her people now, so she would have to learn to get on with them. Besides, she was pleasantly surprised and grateful that so many did accept her.

A voluptuous female vampire with a cap of yellow curls eyed her over the rim of her wineglass. "Well, you've certainly arrived during interesting times. An arrest and rogues all in one night. *Rogues.* Can you imagine? They hardly ever group together, and most know better than to venture anywhere near here. Ruthless Rochester despises their sort."

Lenore nodded and gave the only proper response. "I am sure our lord will deal with them accordingly." And she was. Gavin's hatred for rogues was apparent from the night they first met. Perhaps his ruthlessness would be a good thing in this case.

As long as he did not turn it on her.

Eleven

Gavin frowned as he escorted Lenore and Elena home. His bride to be had been silent throughout the entire walk. He hadn't missed the fear in her large brown eyes when he'd arrested Myrtle. A semblance of guilt niggled at him, but he shook it off. No, he had to maintain his strict rule. He couldn't be allowed to show weakness just to appease her delicate sensibilities, and she would have to grow accustomed to that fact.

Besides, it wasn't as if Myrtle would be executed, or anything so severe. Unless she was committing a serious crime. And he highly doubted that was the case. Usually when vampires crossed over into another territory, it was either because they'd developed a fondness for another vampire, or because there was a market or entertaining party they wanted to attend. He'd turned a blind eye to Myrtle's wanderings the first two times, but the third time, he had to punish her, lest all of his vampires decide that they could go wandering without consequences. He couldn't afford to have one of his people taken for a rogue because they had no writ of passage, or worse, for another Lord to accuse him of sending spies... which of course he did from time to time, but not in such a clumsy manner.

Too soon, they arrived at Elena's door. Gavin wished he could spend more time with Lenore, maybe accompany her hunting, but he had duties to fulfill before dawn.

"I must leave you now." He bowed. "Will I see you at Lady Stoat's musicale tomorrow evening?"

"Yes," Lenore replied softly as she curtsied.

He took her hand. "I shall count the hours." Bending down, he kissed her knuckles, gratified to see her cheeks flush a delicate pink.

He wished he could kiss more of her.

The severity of the wish startled him. He turned away before she saw the raw desire in his eyes. No need to frighten her further.

Gavin sighed. He needed a woman. It had been months since he'd enjoyed a good tumble. Unfortunately he had little time for such a triviality. Even if he did, he hadn't encountered one who appealed to him in some time, and he was not the type to visit a whore.

No, he enjoyed the chase. Unfortunately, the one he most wanted to chase had no interest in becoming caught.

And yet, Lenore allowed him to kiss her earlier.

Memories of the warmth of her mouth against his flickered through his mind like a candle flame that refused to dim, the feel of the soft curves and arches of her lips, her subtle, yet heady taste.

Could there be hope that she'd overcome her fear of a male's touch? Her fear of *his* touch? Could she one day allow him to hold her in his arms and show her how pleasurable intimacy could be?

Hot lust coursed through his veins at the thought before shame quenched the flame. He'd promised her that he wouldn't touch her. Was he such a monster as to ponder going back on his word?

Gavin quickened his pace. Hopefully a run would cool his mad musings. Making his way to the nearest inn, he fed on the first drunkard he stumbled across. The blood eased hunger in his belly but did nothing for his other craving.

By the time he made his way back to his manor, his mood had turned sour like wine turned to vinegar. Making his way down the hidden staircase to the dungeon where he held recalcitrant vampires, Gavin surveyed Myrtle's stricken face. Benson and Cecil had chained her securely, though they gave her enough slack so she could walk the length of her cell. A glass of wine sat on the table untouched.

"I'm so sorry, my lord, please," she whimpered, looking up at him with pleading eyes. "Don't kill me."

Gavin sat in a high-backed chair outside the cell which was used when a guard was necessary. "That depends on what you have to say for yourself, Myrtle. What were you doing in Aylesford? That's part of the Lord of Maidstone's territory, you know that."

Her blue eyes brimmed with tears. "I know, my lord. But I met a man and—"

"Human or vampire?" he asked sharply.

"Vampire," she answered quickly.

Gavin's shoulders relaxed with a measure of relief. The last thing he needed was to contend with one of his people falling in love with a mortal... again.

"And why didn't you ask me for a writ of passage?" he pressed.

"The first time I hadn't meant to go there. I was hunting and lost track of how far he walked." Myrtle twisted her fingers together, wincing at the clank of her chains. "And that is where I met Jack. We finished the hunt together and talked until it was nearly dawn." Her eyes turned distant and wistful. "He asked me to meet with him the following night, and I know I should have asked you for permission then, but I didn't want to trouble you or explain too much when I wasn't certain I would like Jack enough to want to keep visiting him. And from all the stories he'd heard about you... well, begging your pardon, my lord, but he was too afraid to come here."

Gavin stroked his chin. "I see... but what about the third night?"

Myrtle fidgeted in her seat. "I did try to seek you out for a writ of passage then, but you were away at a ball and..." She hung her head, shamed and chastened. "I didn't want to wait."

"Your impatience has a price, I'm afraid. I will have to punish you." As tears filled Myrtle's eyes, he continued. "If Maidstone had caught you gallivanting on his lands without permission, I would have been held liable. We already dislike each other, and you could have compounded the problem."

Gavin allowed her to sob a moment, utterly implacable. Tears did not move him, and they never would.

"I'm sorry, my lord I—"

He held up a hand. "You will spend a month imprisoned. Benson will bring you one meal a night. After you're released, I'll give you a writ of passage, and someday I may even ask Maidstone if you may move to his lands, if you prove yourself repentant."

Her eyes widened in disbelief. "Thank you, my lord! You are a true noble to have such mercy, you—"

"I wasn't finished." Gavin snapped. "If you ever disobey me again, you'll be exiled, or worse. Do I make myself clear?"

Myrtle hunched over and nodded. "Yes, my lord."

He left her and headed up to his study, pouring himself a draught of brandy from the Lord of Cornwall's stores. He should report the incident to Maidstone. It was only right to inform him that he'd had a trespasser and should keep closer watch on his borders. However, he really didn't care for the pompous, up-jumped squire of a vampire.

Besides, there were other trespassers to be concerned with. Taking a sip of the liquor, he sighed and took up his quill.

After composing four identical letters, as well as a longer one to the Lord of London, Gavin informed all of his neighboring Lords about the band of rogues and promised to send word if they were seen near any of their lands, though he hoped to capture and eradicate them himself. To Lord Villar, he also added a brief report about Lenore.

Miss Graves and I shall be wed in two months. For now she remains under the care of Elena, one of my most respected vampires and quickly on her way to becoming a grand lady. She smiles more every night.

Gavin paused, nearly dripping ink on the parchment. Now why did he write that?

He smirked and leaned back in his chair. To teach that arrogant son of a bitch that his accusations were ludicrous. What other reason would there be?

***

Rochester's courtship of Lenore flew by like a dervish. After the musicale, he began escorting her to every ball and supper until whispers roared from the rafters everywhere they went. The message was imminently clear that the Baron of Darkwood had an interest in Miss Graves.

Some of the gossip Lenore's sensitive ears picked up consisted of bitter ruminations that a plain-faced tradesman's daughter was an inferior choice for His Lordship. And that their noble daughters were far more deserving.

Other talk was far more malicious, inferring that Darkwood had less than noble intentions towards Lenore and that she would be ruined within the fortnight. At first their vicious words stung, until she heard Elena's unbridled laughter.

"Their envy amuses me to no end. As if Rochester would waste his time on any of them." She continued to chuckle beneath her fan. "But I cannot believe they have the gall to call you plain. Do they not possess mirrors?"

Lenore laughed lightly behind her own fan, warmed by the vampire's support. "You are too kind, Elena." Truly she was plain, her mother had assured her of that fact quite frequently.

"Tell me," Elena's eyes sparkled with mischief, "which one do you want to sink your fangs into tonight? I'm inclined to feast on Lady Chattertton, but it is only fair that you have the first choice as it is your character being maligned."

"You may have the lady," Lenore whispered with a smirk. "I want to bite her viper of a daughter. She tried to trip me on the dance floor earlier. If only she knew what I was sparing her from."

Elena raised a brow. "What do you mean?"

"Well, being a vampire can be a trial. I imagine she'd miss her morning rides. And to abandon her romantic dreams to play a role." Some dull ache throbbed in her chest at the words, though she couldn't discern why.

Elena sniffed. "Mortal wives have to play a role as well. There's no difference." She smiled over the lace edge of her fan. "Though you do have a point. Yes, Miss Chatterton *would* make a horrid vampire. And His Lordship would not be able to tolerate her, I would imagine. He will be much kinder to you. Ah, and here he comes to claim another dance."

"Miss Graves," Gavin bowed. "You look enchanting this evening. Would you do the honor of partnering me in the waltz?"

She curtsied and took his hand, still fighting off the sense that she was dreaming. Gavin had played the role of a smitten suitor so convincingly that Lenore constantly had to remind herself that his romantic words and gestures were a ruse. And even then the only thing that kept her from falling under his spell was the image of poor Myrtle being hauled off to a dungeon, pleading for mercy beneath her lord's cold eyes.

Lenore wanted to ask him what had become of the blonde vampire, but couldn't muster the courage. Elena had assured her that Myrtle hadn't been killed, but other than that, there was no information. The thought of the poor vampire being locked away made Lenore shudder, even if Gavin was only adhering to the law.

And yet she couldn't stop her pulse from rising at his mischievous smiles or heat spreading through her limbs when his lips touched hers in chaste kisses that surpassed her most fervent imaginings.

Now, as they turned on the dance floor in front of what felt like a hundred eyes, Lenore's belly fluttered with exhilaration at the admiration in his dark gaze, the warmth of his hand on her waist, and the way they moved seamlessly together in the most romantic dance of the century.

The music stopped, breaking the enchantment. As Gavin escorted her back to Elena, he accepted two glasses of champagne from a passing footman and handed her one. "Would you care to take a turn through the garden with me? There is something I wish to discuss with you."

Her heart skipped a beat. Was it time already? Feeling suddenly faint, she nodded. "Yes, my lord. That is if my dear cousin agrees to accompany us."

"Of course, darling coz." Elena rose and smoothed her skirts. "A bit of fresh air sounds like just the thing."

Hundreds of eyes bored into Lenore's back as they exited the French doors and walked to the garden. Naturally no less than ten other guests decided to take in the night air as well.

Perhaps she should be relieved that since their courtship was coming to the end, so would this incessant scrutiny. Yet though that would be a blessed relief, she couldn't help but wish she could enjoy Gavin's smiles, compliments, and gentle touches for a little longer. Some part of her even wished this was real. That he wanted her to be his wife because he loved her.

Don't be foolish, she scolded herself. *You cannot be a proper wife anyway. Not after what happened.*

Rage, fiery and black, welled through her in a sudden flood. If Clayton's rogues hadn't raped her, perhaps she could have had a chance at marital relations. Perhaps she might have even taken pleasure in it. Some women did. Elena definitely did. She'd told Lenore some tales that made her blush. Could Lenore have enjoyed sharing a man's bed?

Closing her eyes, she tried to picture sharing a bed with Gavin, but her mind wouldn't allow it. Instead she remembered him kissing her at the cathedral. The firm, yet soft feel of his lips against hers, the way he held her in his arms, much closer than when they'd danced.

And she'd liked it. If she enjoyed his kisses, then perhaps there was hope for more.

The thought excited and alarmed her all at once.

"Are you well, Lenore?" Gavin asked softly.

Her chest tightened at the warm note of concern in his voice. But was that false as well?

"Yes," she lied. "A goose walked over my grave, that's all."

His dark eyes narrowed with skepticism before he shrugged and spoke in a much louder tone, a gift to those eavesdropping. "I will be leaving for London tonight. I would like to pay a call on your father, if you do not think me too presumptuous."

Her father had been dead for years. Still, the image of the elegant, urbane Baron of Darkwood in the same room with the haggard chimney sweep made Lenore dizzy. Would Papa have approved? Doubtless he would be overjoyed that not only would there be one less mouth to feed, but perhaps better financial and social connections. He had been pragmatic, not one to care about something so frivolous as love.

Behind them, gasps and whispers erupted from the veranda. "He is going to propose!" Lady Haversham whispered loudly.

Rochester's lips twitched in amusement as he pretended not to hear.

Lenore was so captivated with his smile that she nearly forgot his question. "Yes, my lord. And if you could deliver him a note, I would be forever grateful." *Must keep up the pretense. Make everything look proper.*

He bowed and kissed her hand so tenderly that she felt the heat of his lips through the satin of her gloves. "I would be honored. And upon my return, I would like to invite you to Darkwood Manor."

She didn't have to feign a blush as she fanned her cheeks despite the cool night air. Though she'd already been to the manor twice, there was something about this particular invitation that warmed her belly. It reminded her of a romantic novel.

"You honor me, my lord." Her voice came out more breathless than expected.

His fingers continued to graze her knuckles, a forbidden caress. "Now that I've made my intentions clear, would you indulge me in a third dance?"

The fabled third dance. The one that was tantamount to announcing an engagement. Or ruin a maiden's reputation. "Shouldn't that wait until after…" she trailed off. "I mean, would it be proper?"

Those sin-black eyes danced with wickedness. "We could do with some impropriety."

Her belly fluttered. This sort of impropriety she would welcome.

And when they danced that third dance, she didn't even mind the flurry of gossip around her. All that mattered was the dreamy strains of the music and the feel of being in his arms. Every time she had to move to another partner, her soul protested. To her surprise, Lenore found herself anticipating the ride home in his carriage. Gavin had taken to holding her hand for the entire journey. Later, when certain no mortals were watching, he would return to Elena's to show her more of the countryside and run and hunt. And before he brought her back to her mentor, he'd kiss her, whisper soft, yet oh so warm. There were no witnesses for those stolen kisses, so Lenore dared hope that he did it out of genuine affection for her.

Would he kiss her when she was his wife? Part of her hoped he would. She did so enjoy his kisses. However, she wasn't naïve enough to believe that a man, especially one as old and urbane as the Lord Vampire of Rochester would be content with only that.

It would only be a matter of time before he came to expect more.

But was Lenore capable of giving him more?

Twelve

Justus laughed as his eyes scanned the *Medway Chronicle*. "So that explains Rochester's overabundant attentions to the little waif. He danced three dances with her at the Chatterton ball."

"So?" Charlie asked.

"So that means he intends to wed the chit," he explained impatiently. "She's his candidate for his half century of leg-shackling. I wonder why Elena was not his choice this time. Though she can be a bit shrewish, she is far more comely."

His shoes clattered on the stone floor of the castle ruins as he paced the underground chamber and pondered the riddle. To be honest, the youngling was a very odd selection indeed. And why wed a youngling to begin with? Why import one from London? Rochester barely tolerated the true Lord of London and liked the interim one even less. Justus had met the scarred Spaniard when he'd served as the Duke of Burnrath's second in command and had nearly had his head torn off when he'd speculated that perhaps the reason for Gavin's dislike of Villar was because they shared a similar temperament.

What was so special about this Lenore?

As if reading his mind, Rolfe spoke. "She would be an odd choice for a mortal baron, if the talk I've heard is to be believed. To them, she's Elena's poor relation. The daughter of a mere clerk. Some of the more malicious ones claim to detect a trace of Cockney in her accent. They say it's a love match." He rolled his eyes.

Love? The word filled Justus's eyes in a haze of red. Rochester was the last man alive to deserve love. Not after what he'd done.

Bethany... he almost whispered, but the name caught in his throat, receding to the aching pit where his heart used to be.

Justs still didn't know the manner in which he would orchestrate Rochester's downfall, but he did know one thing.

Somehow Rochester's bride would be the key.

***

Cornwall

Gavin looked out at the ocean waves crashing along the cliffs of the Cornish coast. "What a fantastic place you have here." *And what a nuisance that you insisted I come all the way here before giving me a straight yes or no as to my request.*

Vincent Tremayne, Earl of Deveril and Lord Vampire of Cornwall, stood beside him and nodded. "It will always be my home." He swiped his windblown silvery gold hair from his eyes. "However, managing such a large territory can be a trial, with my people being so spread out."

Gavin chuckled. "Not to mention your penchant for taking in misfits and miscreants." For a vampire so tall and so quick with a sword, Vincent was certainly soft at times.

The vampire shrugged. "Someone has to."

"Or we could just do away with the lot," Gavin suggested. Truly, Vincent's mercifulness could cause his own downfall one day.

Vincent frowned. "I'm beginning to understand why the moniker, 'Ruthless Rochester' was hung upon you." His eyes narrowed with derision. "Is it true that you've executed over two dozen vampires in your lifetime?"

"Actually, only twenty three, and most of those were rogues," Gavin answered, ignoring a twinge of distaste at the number of lives he'd taken... and anger at the judgment in Vincent's voice. "But I've also been merciful and exiled ten."

"Which only creates more rogues." Vincent replied in an indecipherable tone. "Didn't you exile your own second in command recently?"

Gavin bit back a growl as the old sadness and impotent frustration returned. "He told a *human* our secrets. By law I should have killed him, but due to his long years of loyalty, I spared his life." Desperate to change the subject, he fixed the Lord of Cornwall with a piercing stare. "You escaped a potential death sentence for Changing a mortal without sanction. I hear you were only fined. So I'd think you'd have some appreciation for my judgment."

"Lydia would have died if I hadn't Changed her," Vincent's features twisted with clear remembrance and pain. "And I was not disapproving of your act of mercy, I was only commenting on the fact that you've created rogues of your own." He sighed. "I wish there was some solution to the problem. We banish them, and they only run to cause trouble for someone else... until they're chased off or killed."

"I hear you *only* chase them off," Gavin countered, "Which keeps them alive to cause more mischief." He wondered if he should tell Vincent about the band of rogues now sniffing along his lands, but held back. Cornwall was too far away for him to be of any aid.

Vincent turned back to gaze at the sea. The moonlit rolling waves reflected in his blue-gray eyes. "Sometimes, if I do not take them in and make them legitimate citizens and thus keep them from causing further trouble."

Those words made Gavin pause. "You haven't taken in a red-haired rogue within the last eight years, have you?" If Justus was here, not only would he be safe, that would also mean he was not part of the band of rogues wandering his lands.

Vincent shook his head. "I would inform you immediately if I had."

"And what would you do with him?" Gavin dared to ask.

"I would hear his side of the story. According to the crimes you'd reported, I would most likely take him in." The Lord of Cornwall's eyes narrowed with censure.

After fighting a pang of guilt, Gavin concealed his relief that there was hope for his old friend to find redemption. "One would think filling your kingdom with disreputable miscreants would be unwise."

"Careful, Rochester," Vincent said. "Have you forgotten that you've come for aid from two of my 'miscreants'?"

"Not at all," Gavin answered with a wry smile, warming to the reminder of his mission here. "I did not say that I wouldn't benefit from your foolish penchant for softness."

But the Lord of Cornwall wasn't finished. "And have you forgotten that you've taken an orphan vampire yourself?" His lips twisted in a condescending frown. "I must say, I do not at all approve."

Gavin bristled. Why did so many of the other Lord Vampires think it was their place to judge him? "Not that your opinion on how I rule my own lands matters in the slightest, I am curious as to your objection. I have been nothing but kind to Miss Graves. I am elevating her position to one of a great lady. Hell, I am here to order her a passel of the finest gowns and fripperies."

"You're going to wed her," Vincent crossed his arms and gave him and accusing stare. "Knowing very well what happened to her. I do not know what possessed Lord Villar to agree to such a thing. If Ian had been there—"

"Ian never took notice of Lenore." Gavin retorted, irritation welling up within him. "To him, she was nothing but a nameless lowly orphan vampire, regaled to sleep in the crypts. She was also beneath Lord Villar's eyes until she saved him from the wrath of the Elders. And though he has rewarded her for her valiant deed, I do not think it was enough, which is part of why I requested her as my price for my aid in stopping Clayton's rebellion. Which Villar could not refuse, first on the account that he gave his word that I could ask for anything aside from his lands or his bride, secondly, he would not want to risk a war with me."

Vincent snorted. "Villar's vampires outnumber yours three to one. London would slaughter you."

Gavin's grin broadened. "True, but after having a battle break out in his own lands, how would the Elders perceive another battle in so short a time?"

Vincent's eyes widened in horrified comprehension. "You really are Machiavellian."

"At last, an accusation I can admit to." Gavin forced a laugh at the other vampire's righteous disapproval, though irritation gnawed at him that Vincent would think he'd orchestrated this plan to hurt Lenore. Not when his plan to wed her was the exact opposite.

The Lord of Cornwall turned his head and gave him a pointed look. "And which accusation do you deny?"

"That I have less than honorable intentions towards Miss Graves." He bit back a sigh. He was growing weary of having to clarify that. "She asked that the marriage be in name only and I will abide by her request." Unbidden, his lip curled back to reveal his fangs. "All of London and half of Cornwall know about what Clayton's rogues did to her during her captivity. Is it so hard to believe that I wish to give her a fresh start, without the pall of shame and scrutiny hanging over her head?"

Vincent sighed. "Yes, because you never do anything without some benefit to yourself."

Gavin spread his arms in the universal gesture of innocence. "Why, I shall have a wife to fend off the matchmaking mothers for the next fifty years. You should know all about how bothersome that can be from your time in London two years ago."

Vincent whipped around and gave him wide stare. "How did you hear about that?"

Gavin couldn't hold back a bark of laughter. "Come now, the notoriously reclusive Lord of Cornwall taking on a mortal ward and bringing her out for a London Season? Word about that spread across the entire United Kingdom, and probably to the Continent." Gavin stroked his chin and smirked. "It is amusing that you are accusing me of lechery when you couldn't keep your hands or your fangs to yourself."

"Careful, Rochester," Vincent growled, baring his own fangs.

Gavin dismissed the threat with an indolent wave. "But never mind that. I see that you and the new Lady Deveril are the happiest of couples and I am genuinely glad for you. Back to my point, As Lenore has proven her capacity for loyalty, she is a suitable candidate for the role as my baroness. I have no need for romance, only a wife."

To Gavin's vexation, the Lord of Cornwall continued to give him a skeptical look. Then Vincent sighed. "Very well. I suppose I have no choice but to take your word. Not that there is much I could do if you were lying."

"All this sudden care for a youngling that was invisible until four months ago," Gavin drawled, sick of the hypocrisy. "How odd our kind has become of late."

"And all of this sudden chivalry from you," Vincent countered. "Well, shall we look in on the Sidwell sisters and put in your order?" He turned on his heel and started walking off in ground devouring strides. "It is fortunate you came in before the Season. They would have been too burdened with orders to be able to accomplish what you want."

"Sidwell?" Gavin laughed once more. "You are still trying to maintain *that* deception? Even I've heard the true fate of the infamous daughters of Sarah Siddons."

"Then you know why I could not allow them to come to Rochester," Vincent said curtly, seemingly undaunted by Gavin's pointing out the truth.

"Are they as mad as they say?" Gavin couldn't hold back his curiosity. Allowing rogues to roam free was bad enough, allowing mad vampires to live? Now that was a dangerous endeavor.

Vincent shoved his hands in his pockets and ducked under a tree limb. "They're much better than they used to be, but that does not mean I will take the slightest risk of them taking off anywhere... especially not London."

Gavin raised a brow, unable to conceal his confusion. "Wouldn't Lord Villar arrest them and simply send them back to you?"

Vincent shrugged and walked faster so Gavin had to quicken his pace to keep up.

"My God," Gavin said as comprehension dawned. "You don't fully trust Villar. What happened between you two when you were last in London? The last time I saw, you two were the thickest of allies."

"Oh, we still are, and there was no incident when I was there to aid him," Vincent said amiably. "Rafe even aided me when the Siddons sisters nearly caused the Elders to have their heads, along with my own, when they tried to murder Thomas Lawrence."

What Gavin would have given to witness that debacle. "So what is your quarrel with him then?"

"If you must know, Rafe foolishly told the Siddons sisters that he would allow them to kill the bastard if he tries to pursue their cousin." Vincent's eyes blazed with unholy light. "Damn it, I cannot wait until that bloody sod dies of old age, or is run down by a carriage. They say our lives are so long that the years of a mortal pass in the blink of an eye, but this man seems to have lingered forever."

Gavin laughed as he tried to keep pace. "Blimey, Deveril, so you do have a ruthless side of your own after all."

Vincent sighed. "If I did, I would have disposed of the man myself. All I'm saying is that the sooner Sir Thomas sloughs off his mortal coil, the sooner Sally and Maria will forget him and truly begin to heal."

"They must be very talented seamstresses for you to keep them around," Gavin said, resisting the urge to jibe at the vampire's sentimentality.

"The very best," Vincent agreed firmly as they arrived at an elegantly constructed stone cottage. "Why else would you be here?"

That was true, Gavin admitted to himself. Elena's wardrobe mostly consisted of gowns made by the 'Mad Sisters of Cornwall,' as she called them. And for some reason, nothing but the best would do for Lenore. Again he wondered why he cared.

Although visiting a London seamstress was out of the question, given the tension between him and Lord Villar, there were dozens of reputed dressmakers closer to Rochester. But instead, he had written to the Lord of Cornwall to request the coveted gowns sewn by the Siddons sisters.

Because she is to be the Baroness of Darkwood, he reminded himself. *How well she is garbed reflects on me.* Of course that was why.

Wasn't it?

Thirteen

Justus paced through the underground chamber beneath the castle ruins, working out the first step in his plan to discredit Gavin. Every cell of his being quivered with impatience to begin now, however, wisdom dictated that this strategy would be more effective once Lord Darkwood was wed and tied to that London youngling for the next half century... not that she'd live that long if things progressed to their full potential.

And he couldn't do much of anything while Rochester was absent. Not even spy upon Elena and the youngling. Gavin had doubled the guards he'd assigned over them before he departed. Justus frowned. Where had he gone? With the new alliances Gavin had forged last year, who knew what plans he could be hatching?

As if reading Justus's mind, Charlie looked up from his dice game with Will. "With the lord absent, why can't we venture out more? I'm starving."

"Because Rochester tightens his vigilance tenfold when he has to leave here," Justus explained. "There are thrice as many patrols, and thus three times the likelihood that we will be caught."

Will nodded, eyes wide and fearful. "Rolfe has been gone awhile. You don't suppose they got him, do you?"

Justus went cold. Rolfe had been with him for far less time than the others. And though he possessed more courage and strength than Charlie and Will, Justus had the disquieting feeling that if interrogated, he would be the one most likely to confess everything.

For what felt like an eternity, they waited in silence, watching the tunnel for the slightest hint of light or movement.

At last, they heard Rolfe's familiar gait shambling through the passage, and detected his scent. Justus's nostrils flared as another ominous odor reached him. *Vampire blood.*

Rolfe burst into the chamber, panting with exhaustion, eyes still glowing with vampiric fury. Fading bruises covered his face and he bled from a wound in his arm.

"What happened?" Justus demanded.

"Got into a tangle with one Rochester's main vampires." Rolfe rubbed his jaw with a dark scowl. "I would 'ave 'ad him if the other one hadn't interfered."

"Which one?" Justus asked sharply. "Benson has dark hair, while Cecil has yellow hair like Will."

"Yellow hair," Rolfe answered. "Dressed like a dandy... fought like one too." He spat on the dusty stone floor. "If I get that blighter alone, I'll—"

"You'll do no such thing," Justus growled. Good God, Rolfe had fought with Cecil? That could have been bad. No, not *could have*, it *was* a travesty. Now Gavin's third likely had Rolfe's scent memorized.

"Why not?" Rolfe protested. "Why are we cowering down here when Rochester is gone? I say we go up there, slaughter his strongest vampires and take this land for ourselves."

"If we did that, the Elders would slaughter *us*." Justus rubbed his eyes, suddenly weary. "You will listen to me and follow my plan, or you will leave and find some other place to hide."

For a moment it looked as if Rolfe would argue, but then he gave Justus a sullen nod and sat down to join the dice game.

Not for the first time did Justus regret taking the hot-headed rogue under his wing. If Rolfe ruined his plans for vengeance, Justus would kill him.

***

Lenore paced back and forth in the drawing room, nearly spilling her tea on the Persian carpet.

Elena's voice chided behind her, "A lady never walks with a cup of tea."

"But we can carry flutes of champagne and punch at a ball," she argued, growing weary of her training in ladylike decorum.

Elena's hands gently took the cup from hers. "I never said the rules were consistent. Now sit down before you wear a path in my rug. Honestly, I don't see why you are so nervous about a night with a forgone conclusion."

Because I did not know until last night's invitation to visit Darkwood Manor was delivered that Gavin had returned, she wanted to say. *Because Gavin sent a messenger to deliver the invitation instead of coming here in person. Because I'm not certain if I'm brave enough to ask him for something.*

But all of that sounded foolish, as if she'd been deluded into thinking that this was a real courtship, rather than the farcical business arrangement that it was. Lenore smoothed her violet skirts as she joined Elena on the settee. "I suppose I am in need of a diversion after our hours of lessons. The intricacies of seating arrangements made me veritably dizzy."

"Yes, they rather are," Elena chuckled. Both froze at the sound of horse hoofs and carriage wheels coming down the drive. "Here is your diversion now."

Lenore's stomach fluttered like a captive bird as Elena opened the door to admit Gavin. Was it possible that he had grown even more handsome in the five nights that he'd been absent? And where had he gone to take so long for his pretense to call upon her father? Did he have a mistress tucked away somewhere?

The flutter in her belly gave way to queasiness. She tamped down the feeling. A man had to fulfill his needs somewhere and since she would not... Besides, she had a more important matter to be concerned with.

Her thoughts broke off as he bowed and took her hand. "Miss Graves, you have grown even more enchanting in my absence. I do hope your glow is not due to another suitor usurping me while I was away?"

"Of course not, my lord," she said quickly. "I would never be so fickle." Why must he tease her?

"No," he said, his eyes suddenly solemn. "You would not." His thumb grazed her knuckles, sending shivers down her spine. "Well, shall we be off? I confess that I very much look forward to showing you my home... even though you've already seen some of it."

During the carriage ride, he held her hand just as he did when he first started courting her. Lenore fought the compelling urge to fall back under the spell of his fairytale courtship. He could reveal his other side soon.

"Did your journey go well?" she asked tentatively.

"Oh yes, it was most diverting. I paid a call on the Lord of Cornwall," he said with a conspiratorial smile. "And I brought you back a surprise, well, several surprises, though those will have to wait."

The Lord of Cornwall. A measure of tension melted away. She remembered the tall lean vampire who'd allied with Lord Villar. She'd even heard that he'd slain one of Clayton's rogues, split the cur in two with a sword that was as long as a normal man's height. And of course, she'd never forget Cornwall's wife, a vampire even younger than Lenore who wielded a pistol like a marksman and exuded the confidence of a much older blood drinker. Lydia, her name had been. She'd spoken to Lenore after the battle, but Lenore had been in too much of a daze to recall the conversation.

Another thought intruded. Gavin hadn't been with another woman! *Hush,* she scolded herself. *He has every right to be. Besides, he could have met with one on the way.*

"Ah, we're here already," Gavin broke off her racing thoughts.

From the moment she entered the foyer, Lenore saw Rochester Manor with new eyes, now that she was to be its mistress. Unlike Haversham House's attempt to resemble an ancient Greek structure, this house was truly ancient, with worn stone walls covered with tapestries for color and warmth, and wood-walled rooms further inside.

Some rooms looked more modern, with porcelain vases instead of pewter, and floral patterned wall paper.

He'd told her that she was to redecorate the place. Lenore could scarcely fathom it. In the tiny flat she'd shared with her family, the most she'd been able to do was trim the curtains with a piece of ribbon and fill a gin bottle with wildflowers scavenged from the edges of Hyde Park. Now she could do whatever she liked with countless rooms, gardens, and fields.

Her first priority would be the room full of nothing but the mounted heads of animals... or so she thought until she encountered a parlor done in nauseating pastel blues and pinks, over-gilt with gold and overflowing with horrid cherubs.

Had one of his previous wives furnished this room? The place was ghastly. Lenore vowed to pack away every last cherub at the soonest opportunity.

After they made their way back to the main floor, Gavin turned to Elena. "Lady Broussant, I would like to speak to Lenore alone, if I may be so bold."

"Certainly, my lord," Elena's eyes sparkled with amusement at his formality. "Though do not tarry too long."

Lenore's heart hammered against her ribs as Gavin led her out into a rose garden. Tiny green leaves and dark red buds peeked out from a forest of thorns.

To her astonishment, the Lord Vampire of Rochester sank to one knee before her. She reached down to stop him.

"That really isn't necessary, my lord. You've already proposed on bended knee."

"That time did not count, as I was only announcing my intentions." He grinned and placed his hand over his heart, like a suitor overcome with ardor. "Now that we've enjoyed a sufficient courtship, I must insist on completing all of the formalities."

She bit back a giggle at his foppishness. "But there is no one here to witness that."

"That doesn't make it less enjoyable… in fact, it heightens the fun." With a wicked gleam in his eye, he once more knelt and took her hand. "Lenore, I am awed at your beauty and enchanted with your charm and wit. Would you make me the happiest of men and do me the honor of becoming my wife?"

She looked down at him, mesmerized at his smile and beautiful words. *If he can take pleasure in the pretense, why can't I?*

For a moment she allowed herself to imagine that he desperately loved her, that their life together would be full of magic and warmth.

Her lips curved in a wistful smile. "Yes, I will marry you."

He rose and pulled her into his arms. "I will do everything in my power to make you happy, I promise."

As Lenore rested her head against his chest and listened to the steady beat of his heart, a soothing sense of warmth filled her at his words. He sounded like he actually meant them.

When he withdrew, part of her cried out in helpless longing. But all thoughts ceased as he bent down and claimed her lips in an intoxicating kiss.

Warm shivers wracked her body, as she clung to his broad shoulders. His tongue delved between her lips like the flicker of a flame, lightly caressing hers, making her limbs turn to liquid and her stomach flutter in the most alarming matter.

A low growl rumbled from Gavin's throat, and his grip tightened around her, restraining her. Lenore stiffened, fighting back shadowy memories.

He released her so suddenly she stumbled.

"I'm sorry," his voice was thick and husky. "I forgot myself. It shan't happen again."

Lenore lifted her finger to her tingling lips. She wasn't so certain she wanted him to never kiss her like that, but the words froze in her throat. How could she say anything when she didn't know what exactly it was that she wanted? Or if it was even proper to want at all?

Shaking of the muddled thoughts, she took a deep breath a faced Gavin with a direct stare. "If you truly wish to make me happy, my lord, I do have one boon to request."

"A boon?" Gavin arched a brow. "How formal. Well, I did say anything, as long as it is within my power."

Lenore lifted her chin and didn't break her stare. "That vampire you have imprisoned. Would you free her?"

His expression darkened like a thundercloud. "How very clever you are," he laughed, but the sound was tinged with some deep-rooted emotion that was not amusement. "Most would use an opportunity like this to plead for jewels or a fur. But not you. No, all of your thoughts are for others, as always." He spread his arms wide as if in mocking surrender. "Well, you've trapped me, so come along and let us fetch your prize."

Elena's eyes widened as they filed past her and down to Rochester's dungeons.

To Lenore's surprise, the stone chambers were warm, dry, and well lit. No dank and chilly cells in sight. And when she spotted the prisoner who'd kept her awake in the daylight hours, rife with worry, Lenore froze so suddenly that Elena bumped into her.

Myrtle's cell held a cot covered with warm blankets, a table with paper and quills, and a glowing lantern. A small bookshelf stood in the corner, full of countless selections. Myrtle herself sat on a pillow by her cell door, playing a card game with the guard through the bars.

A far cry from the pitiful, abused creature Lenore had imagined. Guilt flooded her for assuming the worst of Gavin.

Myrtle quickly stood, scattering her cards. "My lord! I hadn't expected to see you for another month."

"My bride to be has requested your freedom as an early wedding gift." When the vampire's face broke into a wide grin, Gavin shook his finger. "You are still forbidden from going to Aylesford until I receive a response from the Lord of Maidstone. However, you may write a letter to your lover and explain your absence."

Myrtle turned her shining gaze to Lenore. "Thank you, my lady. You possess the mercy of an angel."

Lenore inclined her head, still speechless at the prisoner's lavish accommodations. She wasn't even chained anymore.

"Do not expect such generosity a second time." He turned to the vampire guarding Myrtle. "Escort her home and inform Brian and

George to keep an eye on her. One of you may deliver Myrtle's letter to Aylesford. Decide amongst yourselves and I'll sign a writ of passage."

After the vampires departed, Gavin led Lenore and Elena back upstairs. "Did my gift of mercy please you, Miss Graves?"

"Very much, my lord... ah, Gavin," she breathed.

As warmth unfurled in her heart at his kindness in granting her request, her stomach also knotted with fresh shame for misjudging him. Shame, followed by a fresh tremor of fear.

If Gavin wasn't the cruel and merciless vampire that he was reputed to be, and if his kindness and generosity toward her was genuine, how could she stop herself from falling in love with him?

Fourteen

Seemingly moments after Lenore finished dressing for the evening, there was a knock at the door. Was Gavin calling on her so soon? She couldn't hold back a smile. Perhaps he did have genuine affection for her.

Their engagement ball last night had been magical. For the first time ever, they had been able to dance every dance without censure. And there wasn't a moment that Gavin did not smile at her and look at her like she was the only woman in the room. They'd even hunted together, feeding on the Earl and Countess of Bromley in the conservatory after Lord Bromley had protested Gavin's exuberant attentions to Lenore and Lady Bromley had implied that Lenore was less than modest.

Now, even though it had been mere hours since she'd last been in his arms, Lenore's pulse fluttered in anticipation to see Gavin again.

But when Elena opened the door, it wasn't Gavin. Whoever had come to visit, he or she was too short.

"And who might you be?" Elena asked, voice laced with suspicion.

"Dr. John Elliotson, my lady," a familiar voice said politely. "I was hoping to look in on Miss Graves."

"She is not ill, to my knowledge." Elena said sharply. "Who summoned you?"

Lenore strode to the door and nudged Elena away before she bit the poor man. "Dr. Elliotson is my dear friend from London." She took Elliotson's hands in her own. "How are you?"

"Quite well, though still a trifle weary from my journey." The short doctor's kind eyes smiled up at her. "I see you are still a night owl. I called earlier in the day, but the housekeeper said you would be abed until dark."

Elena's narrowed gaze darted between Lenore and Dr. Elliotson, her lips thinned in disapproval. Lenore looked down at her hands, avoiding her gaze. In the midst of her occupation with Elena's lessons, the whirl of balls and musicales, and the enchantment of Gavin's courtship, she'd forgotten all about Dr. Elliotson's intentions to come to Rochester. Still, it was a joy to see the familiar face of an old friend.

After a discourteous pause, Elena's shoulders relaxed with an inaudible sigh. "Of course a friend of Miss Graves is welcome. Please, do come in and I will ring for tea."

"I would be most delighted," Elliotson said as he removed his hat and hung up his coat.

Lenore led him to the parlor, rampant with curiosity about how his treatments had progressed without her.

"How are the women?" she asked the moment Elena left to find Mrs. Branson.

"Mary seems to be completely recovered, while Louise is still having a rough time of it. They all miss you dearly and were even more devastated when I left. If only I could open a clinic and fill it with capable staff." He leaned forward, eyeing her intently. "Have you continued your work here?"

Shame sank in Lenore's gut like a stone as she shook her head. "I'm afraid that my cousin has had me too occupied with showing me the countryside and socializing... and then," she looked down at her lap, "the Baron of Darkwood began courting me. And now we're to be married." How frivolous that sounded, though she couldn't explain that her marriage to Gavin was the price of an alliance between two Lord Vampires.

Instead of frowning in disapproval, Elliotson's face broke out in a wide grin. "Why, that's wonderful! As a Baroness, you'll have so much more influence—"

"Influence for what?" Elena asked sharply as she entered the room with Mrs. Branson trailing behind with the tea tray.

"To do great works," Elliotson answered with a broad grin. "In London, Miss Graves was my student in mesmerism, and later my assistant."

Elena raised a brow as she poured their tea. "And what, pray tell, is mesmerism?"

The doctor's eyes shone with excitement as he explained his obsession. "Mesmerism is a process in which I place a patient into a trancelike state where, through powers of suggestion and harnessing the imagination, spiritual and sometimes even physical healing can be achieved. The human mind is a powerful thing and my techniques are utilizing those powers."

"And how do you place your patients in such a state?" she asked as she spooned sugar into their cups.

"Though some practitioners believe they must use the laying on of hands as Christ was known to do, I've discovered that a soothing cadence of voice and, most importantly, steady eye contact is the key."

"How very fascinating," Elena's lips twitched with humor as she gave Lenore a knowing look. "I must say that I am not surprised that my cousin has an aptitude for such a thing."

Elliotson smiled, oblivious to the vampire's hint of mockery. "I believe her talent lies in the fact that aside from her quick wit, she has a calming, trustworthy air about her."

This time, Elena appeared to be teetering on the verge of hysterical laughter as she hid her smile behind her tea cup. "Yes, that must be the reason."

Oblivious to the vampire's amusement, the doctor turned back to Lenore. "Tomorrow we must look in on the less fortunate women in the village and see if they require our aid. I have been developing a new technique and cannot wait to try an experiment. To do so, we must cultivate their trust."

Lenore nibbled on a biscuit as she floundered for a response. "Well, tomorrow…"

Elena spoke before she could. "Tomorrow Miss Graves and I have errands and then a supper to attend."

"Perhaps you could look in on them for me," Lenore said, slightly irritated that Elena wouldn't let her speak for herself. "And then I will call on you as soon as I can to find out what you've discovered. Likely they would be more receptive to a doctor on the initial encounter anyway."

Elena clucked her tongue like a matron. "I'm not certain it would be appropriate for an unwed miss to call upon a man. What would Lord Darkwood think?"

"Then perhaps we can see if he may accompany us to the Bromley's supper," Lenore countered, unable to conceal a note of challenge in her voice.

Elliotson's grin returned. "I've already received an invitation. Lady Bromley is my second cousin once removed."

Elena's eyes blazed with virulent hostility for a second before features smoothed in a placid smile. "Oh, how delightful. What a small world we live in."

Lenore couldn't hold back a triumphant grin. "Then we shall see you tomorrow night. I am so happy you've come, dear friend."

Elliotson inclined his head before finishing his tea and rising from the table. "My delight in seeing you is far greater, Miss Graves. You seem to be thriving in the country. Now I must go. We shall speak again on the morrow."

The moment the doctor departed, Elena rounded on her with narrowed eyes. "You've been associating with a human? Do you have any idea how dangerous that is?"

"He helped me in ways no one else could," Lenore said firmly, gripping her teacup. "When I learned how to help heal other women, it healed me. I don't know how else to explain it."

"But what if he discovers why your so-called mesmerism abilities are so effective?" the vampire pressed.

"He won't," Lenore said with complete confidence. "He's a man, so he thinks my skill is due to his teachings."

Elena chuckled. "You have a valid point. But what of his talents? Surely he cannot do what we do."

"Actually, he can, in a way. I do not know if it is because he possesses a unique power, or if it is simply due to people believing he can put them in a trance." She couldn't fight a smile of admiration as she related what she'd learned from the doctor. "Dr. Elliotson was correct in his estimations of the power of the human imagination. Just as a bored noblewoman can convince herself that she is ill all of the time, with a nudge in the correct direction, a person can be persuaded to be well again."

"Surely not with a true physical malady," Elena argued with a dubious frown.

"True, I do not believe he can cure genuine illness," Lenore admitted, feeling somewhat traitorous to her friend. "Though he posits otherwise. However, I *do* believe that sometimes people think their conditions, such as aches from old injuries and arthritis, may not be as severe as they imagine. Mesmerism can ease those symptoms."

"That does hold a touch of logic," the vampire conceded. Her expression abruptly turned dark and grave. "He did not place *you* in a trance, did he?" Her voice rose in a panicked note.

"No," Lenore assured her. "He does not have that much power. I placed him in one, though he does not remember me doing so. That is how I am confident that he truly desires to help people."

Elena's shoulders relaxed. "Good, because if he was one of those rare mortals with psychic abilities, he would have to be killed or Changed. And as he is a prominent figure in Society, I'm afraid the former would be the only viable option."

Lenore shuddered at the thought of her dear friend being put to death. And it would be all her fault. "I vow that he knows nothing of our kind. In fact, despite some of his eccentric inclinations, Dr. Elliotson is still firmly grounded in science and does not believe in ghosts, mysticism, or beings such as ourselves. I am perfectly safe, I promise."

Elena frowned. "And you are hell-bent on continuing your association with him?"

Biting her lip, Lenore nodded. Even if she could free one other woman from depression or nightmares, she would count her blessings. Once more, remorse at forgetting her mission weighted her soul.

Would Gavin be angry that she wished to continue her work? In the rules he'd given her when she first arrived, he never said that helping mortals was forbidden.

Of course, she'd never asked him either.

Fifteen

Gavin looked up from his ledger at a knock on his study door. Frowning in irritation, he set down his glass of brandy. "Yes?"

Daniel, a vampire he'd hired to serve as his butler, opened the door. "My lord, Lady Broussant is here. She wishes to speak to you about an urgent matter."

Panic crawled over his flesh like spiders made of ice. Had something happened to Lenore? "Bring her in at once!" he said more loudly than he intended.

Mere seconds passed like hours as a hundred dreadful scenarios flashed through his mind in a waking nightmare. Had his kiss frightened her so badly that she fled? Had she taken ill? Had she somehow been burned by the sun?

Or worse, had that roaming gang of rogues captured her? Cecil had nearly captured one during his absence... within a stone's throw of Elena's cottage. Gavin had nearly gone mad with rage when he'd received the report. Could the rogues be pursuing Lenore directly? The thought sickened him. Although Elena was powerful enough to fight a rogue, Gavin couldn't help but wish Lenore was safe under his roof and his protection.

He frowned as he turned his glass, watching the firelight gleam in the amber liquid. Perhaps two months was too long to wait.

The second Elena's shadow fell across his desk, his eyes scanned hers. "What is it? Is Lenore well?"

"Oh yes, she's in perfect health," Elena reassured as she helped herself to his decanter of brandy. "However, there is a matter of concern. A human man called upon her tonight."

Gavin laughed in potent relief. Such was to be expected after he'd paid her such fervent attention. Doubtless some hot-headed buck wanted a spot of competition. "I don't see that to be too worrisome. If he gets to be too much of a nuisance, she can always bite the chap."

"He's not a chap," Elena said with a dour frown at odds with her youthful features. "That is, he's a physician she'd befriended in London. Apparently he practices some sort of treatment called 'mesmerism' and Lenore was his student."

"Yes, I've heard of that practice. Sheer quackery, albeit harmless." Gavin didn't care what the man did. What bothered him was that Lenore had a friendship with this man. For a vampire to associate too closely with a mortal was to invite untold danger. Was it possible that she'd loved the doctor before her abduction? Had the doctor arrived in Rochester in hopes to win her away from Gavin?

Although such a thing would be ludicrous, and furthermore not allowed by vampire law, the notion rankled all the same. How was Lenore to learn to trust him if she was still clinging to her past? And the last thing he needed was for her to renew this friendship and endanger herself and his people.

Elena brought him back to the matter at hand. "Quackery or not, Lenore insists that he can perform such a feat. And either way, she is able to entrance mortals even if he cannot. She wishes to use her abilities to help them."

"I see," he said levelly. Indeed he did. After the suffering she'd endured, it came as no surprise that Lenore would wish to ease the pain of others. But whether such a thing was wise or not, he could not yet say. He was still too disturbed by the notion of an intrusion of another who held her affections. Even more disturbed that he cared. It wasn't that he didn't want her to have friends. He merely wanted her to consider *him* as a friend. Or something more.

Finishing his brandy in a long draught that promised to give him a bellyache, Gavin carefully formulated a more concise response. "I will speak to her later about the doctor. Yet I do not think there is much to be concerned with. Her duties as my baroness will keep her too occupied to continue to associate with him overmuch."

Elena nodded, though a thin line of tension had formed between her brows, promising that she was not fully satisfied. "He will be at the Bromleys' supper tomorrow. I do hope you will evaluate him thoroughly."

"Oh, I intend to," he said silkily. "Thank you for bringing this matter to my attention. Now if you do not mind, I would like to be left alone to think about what you have told me."

Elena bowed deeply. "Of course, my lord. But please, do not be too harsh with Lenore. She cannot help her kind nature."

"I will be gentle with her, I promise." As for the already irksome doctor, he could not promise.

One thing was certain, though. Their engagement would be shorter than he'd originally intended. The sooner she was under his roof, the safer she'd be from the dangers of associating with mortals... and from the rogues.

***

Lenore fidgeted with her wrap, unable to fight off waves of trepidation and she and Elena made their way through the crush to greet their hostess. What would Gavin think of Dr. Elliotson?

Already gossip had spread through every corner of the drawing room that the physician had paid her a call.

"Was she ill?" one matron whispered to her husband.

"If so, why would she be here tonight? Besides, she looks positively blooming," he countered.

"You don't think it could be another sort of health issue, do you?" the matron pressed. "You know, the type that lasts about nine months."

"Now Madge, do not be unkind," the man chided.

Despite the gentleman's defense, that unkind speculation continued to circulate, though it did not carry too much weight as most acknowledged that Dr. Elliotson was not well known for overseeing pregnancies.

"I heard they were acquainted in London. Perhaps they'd had an understanding," Miss Chatterton whispered to her friends. "Though the Doctor is quite short and not at all comely."

"If that is true, how very sad that must be. For her to throw him over for a baron. Could she truly be so fickle and heartless?"

"Indeed. Also foolish. A doctor is a much more suitable match for one of her station. To pursue a title over comfort, well I hope the girl knows what she is doing. With Darkwood's limited staff and the rarity in which he holds balls and such, his income must be very low."

As the whispers swirled around her, Lenore's gaze landed upon Lord Darkwood. From the ominous scowl upon his countenance, there was no doubt that he heard the gossip as well. She rushed forward to assure him that Elliotson was merely a friend, but Lady Bromley intercepted her. And Elliotson stood beside her.

"Miss Graves," Lady Bromley began as all eyes swiveled to her. "I am so glad you were able to come. My cousin has been telling me about your acquaintanceship in London and that you were a student of his. I had no idea you were such a bluestocking."

Titters erupted around her, making her ears burn. Lenore took a deep breath and curtsied as she fumbled for the proper response. "I am glad to be here as well, my lady. And I am even more overjoyed that my friend and mentor has arrived in time to hear of my engagement."

Elena gave her a slight nod of approval and the laughter died down to hushed murmurs.

"Ah yes," Elliotson said with a bow. "I am anxious to meet the man who has captured the heart of my sharp-witted friend."

Lenore once more looked at Gavin and fought back a sigh of relief as she noticed that his features had softened. Though there was still a tightness to his lips that made her nervous. Hundreds of eyes bored into her back as Lady Chatterton led her and the doctor to the vampire baron.

"Lord Darkwood," the squire's wife began with more enthusiasm than was seemly. "Allow me to introduce you to my cousin, Doctor John Elliotson. Apparently he was a *close* friend of Miss Graves while she was in London."

Gavin's eyes swept down, regarding the short doctor without expression before he inclined his head in a slight bow. "Pleased to make your acquaintance, doctor. A friend of my dear Lenore is a friend of mine."

A few slight gasps sounded behind them at Darkwood's use of her Christian name in polite company. Had he done so to further press the point that they were engaged? Or was it merely a slip?

The Lord Vampire of Rochester did not make slips, if half of what Lenore had heard of him were true.

Ignoring the scrutiny of the spectators, Gavin extended his arm. "Shall I escort you to the dining room?"

Lenore gripped his bicep, squeezing it slightly in reassurance, though reassurance of what, she could not say. Surely he could not believe that she held any romantic affection for the doctor. And even then, why would he be jealous? Unless he had grown to care for her. Her heart clenched with futile hope.

During dinner, she watched Gavin's face carefully while Elliotson chattered about mesmerism and his other studies. Her future husband appeared skeptical, but he did not seem to be annoyed, or bear any envy toward the man.

"Have you set the date for the nuptials yet?" Lady Chatterton asked as they were served a berry soufflé.

Gavin stabbed his dessert with a fork. "Two weeks should be sufficient to have everything in order."

Lenore nearly choked on her spoon. *Two weeks?* But before he'd said their engagement would be two months or so. Why the sudden change?

Thankfully, the guests' surprise prevented them from noticing her own.

Lady Chatterton gasped. "But… you won't have time to have the banns read, or to plan a proper ceremony."

"I am procuring a special license." Gavin said, eyeing her blandly over the rim of his glass of sherry. He did not look at Lenore. "I cannot bear to wait any longer to make Miss Graves my bride."

More whispers broke out behind fans and glasses. "A special license? How romantic. Just like a Jane Austen novel."

Lenore managed a wan smile. If only romance were the reason for Gavin's sudden decision to rush.

Before the murmured speculations rose to a fevered pitch, Lord Bromley rose from his seat. "I propose a toast. To Lord Darkwood and his soon to be baroness, Miss Graves."

After they drank to Lord Bromley's toast, the servants cleared the desserts from the table and the ladies retired to the drawing room while the men enjoyed their cigars and port.

The young, unmarried women clustered around her, all prying for information about Lord Darkwood's sudden hurry to wed. Her stomach twisted and knotted as she covered her ignorance with platitudes.

"I am happy to defer to His Lordship's wishes." She fluttered her fan and managed a girlish titter. "I only hope I have time to procure a proper wedding gown."

The other young ladies smiled in approval before launching into a debate on the latest fashion plates for Paris. Meanwhile, the gossip continued to circulate around her. Some opined that perhaps Lord Darkwood felt threatened by the reemergence of her old gentleman friend. Others were now fully convinced that Gavin had indeed gotten her with child.

By the time the men returned to the drawing room to listen to Miss Bromley play the pianoforte, Lenore was half mad with the need for the real explanation.

Gavin took his place beside her and her heart once more skipped a beat at how imposingly beautiful he was. She licked dry lips and whispered behind her fan. "Why *do* you wanting to move the wedding date sooner?"

He shrugged, face expressionless. "Does there need to be a reason?"

Yes! She wanted to insist, but did not know if it was right to make demands of her Lord Vampire. "I suppose not, but some say your hurry has something to do with Dr. Elliotson's arrival. I hope that is not the reason, for I only feel friendship for him."

His lips twisted in a sneer. "That boisterous dwarf? Certainly not." At her intake of breath, his tone gentled. "He is an affable fellow, I give you that. As for wedding you sooner, I simply see no reason to play out the courtship any longer than necessary. The matrons have ceased pestering me and thrusting their milksop daughters at me, so I consider the endeavor a fait accompli."

"I see," she said softly and turned her face back to the performance.

Her eyes burned with what felt like impending tears as the reason behind his words struck her like a spear to the heart.

He truly didn't care about Elliotson's arrival at all. Not that she wanted him to be jealous or anything so foolish. But that would be better than the truth.

He had already grown bored with pretending to like her.

Sixteen
Two Weeks later

Over half of the village seemed to be in attendance within the large cathedral. Gavin stood beside his groomsmen, the priest behind him, and smiled with satisfaction. Despite his impulsive rush, this may be the finest wedding he'd ever had.

Hundreds of candles decorated the nave, reflecting off of the stained glass, gleaming candelabra, and marble statues of saints. A shaft of moonlight shone through the hole in the roof, adding a touch of silver to everything.

Gavin wondered why he'd chosen the cathedral. In his mortal years, the place had been his life. And though memories both wonderful and terrible haunted him to the point where he couldn't go more than a few months without walking beneath these hallowed vaults and arches— though not the cloisters, never that place— the thought of wedding one of his vampire brides here had never occurred to him.

But there was something about Lenore that made him want to provide the best for her. Maybe it was because she had lived all of her life in poverty. Maybe it was because he rather enjoyed the bright light that came into her eyes at what seemed to be the most trivial things.

No matter the reason, he could not wait to see her in the wedding gown he'd commissioned from the Siddons sisters. Thankfully that had been delivered on time, along with the trousseau and a third of the wardrobe he'd ordered. The rest would be ready in only a month. Lord Deveril had been vexed at the sudden request to deliver the gowns sooner, though he had been somewhat placated when Gavin offered to pay double the previously agreed price.

Lord Deveril himself sat near the front beside his wife as well as Lord and Lady Villar. Lord Villar had wanted to give the bride away, but that had been out of the question.

"Your connection to Miss Graves would raise unnecessary questions," Gavin had told him. "It is only out of respect to Lenore's wishes and your status that you were invited at all."

Villar had scowled, before nodding in grudging acknowledgment of Gavin's logic.

Yet the matter of who exactly would escort Lenore down the aisle remained a problem. At first he considered hiring a man from London to pretend to be her father, but then he realized that would take too much work and entail too many risks.

The issue was resolved when Dr. Elliotson begged for the honor. Gavin had been at the verge of refusing until the man pointed out that taking the role of fatherly figure would dispel any rumors that he held any romantic interest in Miss Graves. Gavin reluctantly agreed.

Still, he did not like it one bit. To be friends with a mortal invited countless risks.

His ire eased as the organ resonated throughout the cathedral, heralding the bride's approach.

She wore a gown of silver, embroidered with flowers threaded with what looked like diamonds. The moonlight danced on the silk and flashed on the jewels. Instead of pearls, loops of crystals twined through her hair, culminating in a little crown from which hung a gossamer veil.

Unbidden, Gavin's lips parted as he drank in the sight of her, an angel drifted down from heaven, or perhaps a goddess from the moon. A shy smile played across her lips, ethereal and fey. He suddenly wished all the guests would go to the devil and leave them alone so his eyes could drink in her beauty to his heart's content.

An unfamiliar ache tightened his chest as Lenore took her place by his side and turned to face the priest. Gavin held his breath, unable to determine what she was feeling at the moment. Did she like her dress? Was she pleased with the large attendance of guests? Or did the crowds frighten her? Did *he* frighten her?

Father Blatty opened the prayer book and began the ceremony. "Dearly beloved, we are gathered together here in the sight of God, and in the face of this congregation, to join together this man and this woman in holy matrimony…"

The droning words faded from his awareness as her dark eyes met his, so large he could drown in their depths. She looked so solemn, so nervous, he wished he could interrupt the priest and assure her that everything would be all right.

When the priest spoke of procreation being one of the primary purposes of marriage, Gavin watched Lenore closely. Would she have wanted children, had it been possible? He'd heard of some female vampires plunging into deep depressions because they could not conceive.

Thankfully, Lenore did not appear saddened. In fact, her lips twitched with wry amusement.

"Secondly," Father Blatty continued, "It was ordained for a remedy against sin, and to avoid fornication…"

Now it was Gavin's turn to bite back laughter. His sins were so extensive there was no remedy. As for fornication, he'd done plenty of that. Adultery? Bigamy? Perhaps he was guilty of those as well since he'd never divorced any of his previous wives. He frowned. Since when did that matter?

"Thirdly, it was ordained for the mutual society, help, and comfort, that the one ought to have of the other, both in prosperity and adversity. Into which holy estate these two persons present come now to be joined. Therefore if any man can show any just cause, why they may not lawfully be joined together, let him now speak, or else hereafter forever hold his peace." Father Blatty glanced around.

Gavin held his breath waiting for someone, perhaps Lord Villar, to object. His gaze scanned the crowd with such sudden worry that for a moment he imagined Justus in the masses. When blessed silence permeated the cathedral, he let out a sigh and chided himself for being so daft.

The priest then asked Gavin and Lenore if there were any impediments to their marriage. Once satisfied, he turned to Gavin.

"Gavin Drake, wilt thou have this woman to thy wedded wife, to live together after God's ordinance in the holy estate of matrimony? Wilt thou love her, comfort her, honor, and keep her in sickness and in health; and, forsaking all other, keep thee only unto her, so long as ye both shall live?"

"I will," he answered, taken aback by the conviction in his voice.

Father Blatty then turner to Lenore. "Lenore Graves, wilt thou have this man to thy wedded husband, to live together after God's ordinance in the holy estate of matrimony? Wilt thou obey him, and serve him, love, honor, and keep him in sickness and in health; and, forsaking all other, keep thee only unto him, so long as ye both shall live?"

"I will," Lenore's voice quavered slightly. Gavin could hardly blame her. *Serve and obey* were certainly more daunting than *love and comfort.*

"Who giveth this woman to be married to this man?" the priest inquired.

Dr. Elliotson placed Lenore's hand in Father Blatty's, who in turn placed her hand in Gavin's.

After directed by the priest, Gavin recited the vow he'd made at least once a century. "I, Gavin Drake, take thee, Lenore, to my wedded wife, to have and to hold from this day forward, for better for worse, for richer for poorer, in sickness and in health, to love and to cherish, till death us do part, according to God's holy ordinance; and thereto I plight thee my troth."

Lenore repeated the vow to take him as husband, voice soft as a whisper. Gavin squeezed her hand in reassurance.

Father Blatty then placed the ring upon the prayer book. Gavin took the small golden circlet adorned with a diamond surrounded by glittering black opals. He never gave any of his wives, even the ones who'd wed him more than once, the same ring.

Gratified at the awe in Lenore's eyes, he slipped the ring on her third finger and recited, "With this ring I thee wed, with my body I thee worship, and with all my worldly goods I thee endow: In the Name of the Father, and of the Son, and of the Holy Ghost. Amen." He bit back a bitter laugh. How long had it been since he'd believed in the trinity?

His gaze lingered on his new wife's lush lips and Gavin suddenly wished he'd opted to take her to Gretna Green and wed her over the anvil instead. Those brief ceremonies concluded with a kiss. What he would give to kiss her now.

The appeal of an elopement intensified as the priest launched into an endless recitation of psalms. By the time the litany ended, Gavin was grinding his teeth in impatience and Lenore appeared to be holding back a yawn.

At last Father Blatty turned and presented them man and wife. Lord and Lady Darkwood.

Gavin's mission had been accomplished.

Then why did everything feel so incomplete?

***

Justus ducked out of view of Rochester's second in command. The son of a bitch had already nearly caught wind of him twice. Taking a circuitous route, he finally made his way back to the castle ruins where his band waited.

Rolfe grinned when he entered the chamber they'd appropriated for their day rest. "Did you learn anything new?"

Justus nodded. "The wedding was a joyous affair. Odd that he chose to hold such an elaborate ceremony." And in the cathedral, no less. The implications of that were not lost on him, nor the look in Gavin's eyes when he beheld his bride. Sneaking into the ceremony had been risky, but what Justus had discovered had been worth the danger. His fists clenched at his sides as he forced an indifferent tone. "They'll enjoy a supper with dancing before spending the remainder of their wedding night at the manor, unable to hunt. I overheard Cecil saying there will be another Gathering next Sunday, so we'll have to disperse for that night." He smiled at his cohorts. "Did you all secure the items I requested?"

Rolfe nodded and fetched a stack of slim booklets from a large square stone they used as a table. "I found five copies of 'Wake not the Dead.' I wish I could have gotten more, but I had a tussle with one of the Maidstone vampires. Blimey, it's difficult getting into a bookshop at night as it is."

Justus took the volumes and smiled. "Five should do. The village is small enough." He looked to Will and Charlie. "And what were you able to come up with?"

Will withdrew a stack of pamphlets from his jacket. "You must read these. Some are absolutely preposterous. This one says that we cannot cross running water!" He laughed and handed them over.

Charlie shifted on his feet before handing Justus a few more pamphlets. "I can't rightly say what I got. I can't read, so I just went from the pictures."

Justus took the pamphlets and glared at the others, silencing their mocking laughter. As he skimmed through subjects such as ghosts, witches, riots in London, and one crumbling piece that might have been about vampires, he smiled. "Actually, a little variety would be beneficial. We don't want to be too obvious. And we certainly don't need to stir up a full-fledged panic."

"I think a panic would be good," Rolfe said, taking a knife from his pocket and tossing it in the air. "Have His High and Mighty Lordship quivering in his bed in fear of a stake."

"No," Justus said firmly, slapping the pamphlets on his thigh. "We would be even more vulnerable in that case. All we need is to rouse enough suspicion to make Rochester be forced to step down." He set down the stack of vampire literature and crossed his arms. "Actually, I would prefer for the suspicions to be directed at his bride. Let *her* be the cause of his downfall."

As the rogues nodded, Justus bared his fangs in a grim smirk. His spying on Gavin had at last revealed the reason for why the youngling had been chosen to be the next Baroness of Darkwood. The way Gavin had looked at Lenore, like she was an angel descended from heaven made Justus feel as if he were peering into a mirror. For that was how he'd looked at Bethany.

At long last, Gavin had fallen in love.

Justus clenched his fists in determination. Rochester had taken Justus's love from him. Now it was time for Justus to take his.

Seventeen

Lenore attempted to shield her hair as she and Gavin exited the church while people cheered and threw rice and flower petals. Part of her wanted simply to depart for her new home, weary of being the center of attention. The other half wanted to further prolong the moment when she'd be alone with her new husband.

No matter her wishes, it seemed she'd be granted a reprieve.

Traditionally, after a marriage ceremony was a wedding breakfast, held at a hall or by the bride's parents. Since it was night, there would be a wedding supper instead, hosted by Elena in lieu of Lenore's parents. The following week, Lenore would host a ball at Darkwood Manor. The thought filled her with palpable dread. What if she did everything wrong?

Gavin pulled her back to the present as he pulled grains of rice from her curls and the lace of her veil. "An abominable tradition," he said with a grin. "Being treated like pigeons in a park. My lady should be regarded with more respect."

Her scalp tingled with his touch. Suddenly she became aware that this was the first time she'd ridden in a carriage alone with Gavin.

Her husband. The word echoed in her mind with heavy finality. In the days leading up to the event, he came in and out of Elena's home like a dervish, quickly clipping out orders for the time and place of the nuptials. Elena took it all calmly, though with a degree of amusement as she reminded him of details such as flowers, the guest list, and the wedding supper. As the planning raced along, Lenore remained frozen in a state of confusion, wanting to contribute, but so overwhelmed with the rapid pace and details that she did not know where to begin, except to say she rather fancied jasmine and lavender.

Gone was the charming gentleman caller, in his place stood a pragmatic, impatient businessman, eager to conclude a bargain and move onto the next venture. In fact, Gavin hadn't smiled at her or laughed with her in over a week.

And he hadn't kissed her. The lump in her throat tightened every time he bid her goodnight with only a bow and a squeeze to her hand.

The only time he'd shown her a glimpse of his former affection was two nights ago, when he'd delivered her wedding gown. When she'd pulled the exquisite silver creation out of the carefully packed tissue paper, her breath had halted at the sight of such finery.

"Do you like it?" he'd asked, sounding nervous as she struggled to find the words.

Tears had burned behind her eyes as she caressed the elaborately embroidered silk. "It's— it's the most beautiful gown I've ever seen."

His usually firm lips curved in a radiant smile, reaching his eyes as they roved over her. "It is only fitting for your beauty." He rose from the settee, his features once more stern and composed. "The first portion of your new wardrobe has been delivered to our home. I trust that you've begun packing what you have here?"

Lenore carefully packed away the gown and nodded.

"Good. I have some matters to attend to, so I shall leave you." He gave her a quick, perfunctory kiss on the forehead and departed.

She didn't see him again until the ceremony.

And now she would be at his side for the next half century.

She glanced at him through the corners of her eyes, scanning the sharp angles of his cheekbones, the gleam of his black eyes… the angles of his lips. His rich dark curls were tied back with a burgundy ribbon that matched his waistcoat beneath his formal black jacket and trousers. While most of upper class vampires preferred subdued blacks and grays, Gavin favored a splash of color. She couldn't help but notice that it was very becoming.

And his hands, the first time in ages that she'd seen them without gloves, she'd forgotten how large and strong they were, how long and supple his fingers. She remembered how they'd felt entwined with hers in the church. The heat of his bare palm against hers, the strength of his grip, made her so dizzy she could barely follow the priest's words and recite her own in time.

Looking down at her own hands, so small and pale compared to his, she couldn't stop staring at her ring. The diamond was nearly as large as her thumbnail. The frame of glittering black stones reminded her of his eyes. But no matter how beautiful the ring, or how well it fit her finger, she couldn't stop wondering how many other fingers it had adorned.

The carriage rolled to a halt in Elena's drive behind a line of dozens of phaetons and barouches. Hanging lanterns illuminated the paths and gardens and a hired butler guarded the door to make certain only invited guests passed through.

A staff of borrowed servants carried trays of champagne flutes to refresh the guests while greeting the bride and groom in the receiving line where Elena led Lenore and Gavin to take their places.

"Lady Darkwood." Elena curtsied deeply. "Let me be the first to offer my congratulations."

Lady. After so many years of wanting to be one, Lenore felt like a sham. Yet here she was, and it was her duty to play her part.

"Thank you so much for the lovely supper. I can't believe you put this together so beautifully."

"And right beneath your nose," Elena grinned. "Now let me have a look at your ring before you are swarmed by the others."

Lenore blinked as she extended her hand. Hadn't she seen it before?

Elena gazed at the ring for a long moment, her thumb grazing the diamond. "Simply stunning. Mine was not so fine." Her lips curved in an impish smile. "Though at least it was better than Anne's."

"He doesn't use the same ring?" Lenore whispered with surprise.

"Of course not! Lord Rochester would never be such a cad to part a woman from her jewels." The vampire laughed as if Lenore had asked if the moon was made of cheese. "And your diamond is the largest of them all. I cannot contain my envy."

Unable to hide her shame at her churlish assumption, Lenore gazed back down at the ring. The first piece of jewelry she'd ever owned, and it was uniquely hers.

Alas, she did not get to savor the moment. Just as Elena predicted, nearly every female in attendance surrounded her, examining every facet of her ring. Unbidden, she looked to Gavin. There would be no help from that quarter as he was equally flocked by gentlemen clapping him on the back and shaking his hand.

Lord and Lady Villar were the next to greet her. "Is he treating you well?" Cassandra asked softly.

Lenore nodded. "Thus far he has been the epitome of kindness."

"Good," Rafael scowled. "Because if he is not…" he let the words hang in ominous promise.

"He is, I swear," Lenore quickly reassured him. The last thing she needed was to be the cause of a war.

The Lord Vampire of Cornwall and his bride were the next to greet her. Lady Deveril's golden eyes danced with merriment as she admired Lenore's wedding gown. "It is even more beautiful than when our seamstresses packed it away," she drawled in her American accent. "You look like a fairy princess."

By the time the receiving line ended, Lenore's legs ached and her mouth was dry from thanking everyone.

The supper itself passed in a whirl. Lenore was so dazed by the new deference everyone showed her that it was all she could do to follow the conversations around her and make the proper responses before the dishes were cleared away.

Elena had cleared her drawing room for dancing and hired musicians. Lenore and Gavin led the first waltz.

As he turned her on the floor, Lenore looked up at him, somewhat nervous. "Th-the ceremony was beautiful." Biting her lip, she cursed herself for stammering.

He nodded. "Yes, it was, rather. I am glad everything went according to plan." He remained silent for the remainder of the dance, though he kept looking down at her with a strange expression as if he had more to say.

To her surprise, after only the second dance, Gavin declared that it was time to depart.

"But won't that be rude?" she asked as he led her from the floor.

"On the contrary, it would be rude for us to linger… as well as imply that I am not eager to have my bride to myself." He leaned in closer, studying her face. "Besides, you look a little fatigued. Did you sleep at all during the day?"

Lenore shook her head. "Not really."

"Me neither," he confessed. "One would think after getting leg shackled once every century, I'd be accustomed to weddings. Yet this one seems to be different, somehow."

Before she could ask him to elaborate, he led her to Elena to announce their departure.

When they said their farewells, Lord Villar leaned in close and whispered, "Remember, if he mistreats you in any way, send me a message, and I will do all I can to bring you back home."

The vampire's whisper was not quiet enough. Gavin seized Lenore's arm and glared at Lord Villar with malevolent black eyes. "My wife *is* home now," he growled low, and led her away.

A heavy silence hung inside the carriage on their ride to Darkwood Manor. Lenore fought the urge to fidget with her skirts or ask if anything was amiss. A million questions caught in her throat.

When Gavin helped her out of the carriage, Lenore's eyes widened at the sight of the servants lined up in front of the manse, standing ramrod straight in their starched livery. Like the gossips said, there were only ten, a paltry amount for such a large house, though she knew that the sparse staff was not due to Gavin lacking funds, but to minimize the risk of mortals discovering what he was.

"My loyal servants, please welcome my bride and your new mistress, Lenore Drake, Baroness of Darkwood. I know that you will all serve her faithfully and see to her every comfort." As they all smiled and nodded, Gavin led her to each in turn, introducing the butler, the housekeeper, the cook, the housemaids, the gardener, and the carriage driver, and the footman. Nearly all were elderly, or had vision or hearing impediments, just like Elena's servants.

Each one bowed and curtsied before her. Some regarded her warmly, while others eyed her with trepidation. From her own brief stint in service, Lenore knew what they were thinking. Would she be a kind mistress, or a tyrannical shrew? Though she vowed to be the former, it wouldn't make a lick of difference if they knew she was a blood drinking monster.

"Mrs. Crain," Gavin addressed the housekeeper as the butler and footman opened the door. "My lady wife has eschewed a lady's maid. However, she does require a deft hand to attend to her magnificent hair. I recall that you used to serve as lady's maid to the Duchess of Grantham."

"I did, my lord."

"Very good. Would it be an imposition to ask you to care for Her Ladyship's hair? You would see an increase in your wages, of course."

The elderly housekeeper beamed at Lenore. "I would be honored, my lady."

"Thank you, Mrs. Crain," Lenore said, trying to hide her puzzlement that her hair was Gavin's first concern. Did he not like the way Elena had arranged it for the wedding? She thought it had never looked more beautiful.

"I am happy that's settled. I am going to show my baroness to our chambers. She will ring for you when she's ready to retire."

Mrs. Crain bobbed a curtsy. "Yes, my lord."

As Lenore walked with Gavin up the spiral staircase, her heart sped up with every step. He was taking her to their chambers. This was their wedding night. What would it be like to share a bed with him? Would he be able to keep his promise to not force her to submit to her wifely duties?

Memories of overhearing her mother and father echoed in her mind like ghosts from the past. *Her pleading that she was tired, his insistence that he had needs and it was her duty to submit to them. Her whimpers of pain. The thumping of the bedposts against the wall.*

But surely Gavin had more restraint than that. And sharing a bed with him, lying next to him during their day rest, perhaps that would be nice. She hadn't had company during those vulnerable hours since Blanche disappeared. Elena had slept in a separate chamber from hers. Oftentimes she grew lonely.

He opened the door to reveal the massive bedchamber that had haunted her memories since she'd first awakened months ago in his bed to the taste of his healing blood. The slight spicy masculine smell was the same, as was the massive oak bed and its thick crimson coverlet.

Gavin then crossed the room and opened another door. "This will be your bedchamber. Your gowns should already be in the wardrobe."

Lenore couldn't help but gape at the elegant, feminine chamber. The bed was a pale maple four poster with powder blue hangings and coverlets. A dainty secretoire sat in one corner, while another corner was dominated by a large vanity with a gilded mirror and dozens of cunning little drawers.

Lanterns stood on carved stands, lighting the windowless room bright as day. It then occurred to her that Gavin's chamber lacked windows as well.

"So will we spend our day sleep here?" she asked. Even Elena had outfitted her cellar with secure bedchambers.

"*You* will sleep in here. I will be in my adjoining room if you require anything." He took her hands and stepped closer. "Though this is usually forbidden, tonight you will have to feed on Mrs. Crain. We cannot risk being seen out hunting tonight and cause needless gossip." Leaning down, his lips brushed her cheek. "I'll leave you now to get settled. Remember, if you need anything, simply knock."

Lenore stared at his broad back as he left the room, closing the door behind him. Sinking down on the soft bed, she did not know whether to be relieved at the prospect of spending the day in it alone, or disappointed.

Eighteen

Gavin lay on his bed staring at the ceiling. The sun had risen hours ago, he could feel it in his bones. And yet he couldn't sleep. This was his wedding night, or rather, wedding day, and he was alone. True, he hadn't always consummated his marriages, but at least his brides had still lain beside him, talking and providing company, sometimes driving him to madness with their talk of all the changes they'd impose on his household. Elena had been the best, laughing with him and entertaining him with tales of her adventures and rise in society.

Though Lenore was a youngling, he still wanted to hear her stories, to know how she was Changed, what became of her maker, where she'd found the strength to survive the great adversity she'd endured the previous year. What were her hopes and dreams?

But instead of insisting she share his bed, he sent her to her own chamber. Because he didn't want to frighten her. And, he admitted the despicable truth to himself, because he did not want to be tempted.

Instead of being a lark at best, and a tiresome chore at worst, their courtship had turned into something else. Something that felt real, and frightening all at once. The mere touch of her hands, the taste of her lips had awoken a desire that shook him to the core.

He wanted her, plain and simple. Yet he'd promised never to take her. Their kisses in the gardens and the carriage had been safe, but here, in his bed? That was a completely different matter.

Yet there was no way in the fabled circles of hell that he would become one of those beasts who'd hurt her. It may be his legal right to take her, but if he did, she would see him as a monster. And he couldn't bear that. She'd already seen enough monsters in her short life. Thanks to his reputation, she already feared him. Usually that was the desired result, however, in her case, the way she trembled around him made a deep ache in his chest.

Tomorrow night he would do his best to ease her fears, assure her that she held a great amount of power in this marriage. And he would keep his hands to himself while he was at it.

Just as his eyes drifted closed, a scream rent the air.

Gavin threw back the bedcovers, hastily yanked on his bed robe, and charged into Lenore's chamber, fangs bared and ready to drain the life out of whoever dared intrude upon her.

Instead of a thief or vampire hunter, he saw his young bride thrashing on the bed, trapped in the throes of some nightmare.

***

Lenore struggled against the steel manacles, metal biting into her wrists as they came closer. Cruel hands grasped her legs wrenching them apart. The slobbering rogue bared his fangs in a leering grin as he knelt and unfastened his trousers. She whimpered in dread at the pain that was to come and—

"Lenore," a gentle voice rumbled over her.

The rogues looked up at the voice and dissolved as if cast into the sunlight.

Warm hands grasped her shoulders, snapping the manacles, freeing her from her prison. "Lenore," that warm, strong voice repeated. "You're all right. It was just a dream."

Slowly her eyes opened to see Gavin standing over her bed. Even in the darkness, she could see the worry and compassion in his dark eyes.

"I-I'm sorry I disturbed your rest," she stammered, still shaking from the nightmare.

"Think nothing of it," he said softly. "I vowed to comfort you."

A knock sounded on the door, followed by the sound of Mrs. Crain's voice. "My lady, I heard a scream."

"It's all right, I only had a bad dream," she called out, hoping the housekeeper wouldn't open the door. "You may go back to bed, Mrs. Crain."

"Very well, my lady. If you need anything, do not hesitate to ring for me."

After the housekeeper's footsteps faded away, Gavin released Lenore's shoulders and turned away. "I'll let you get your rest."

"No." The word tore from her throat in a desperate whimper. "Please don't leave me. I'm afraid if I close my eyes, I'll go back there."

His shoulders stiffened, and for a moment she thought he would refuse, but then he nodded and turned back to her bed. "As you wish."

Quickly she scooted over and lifted the covers to make room for him. As his weight dipped down on the mattress, her staccato heartbeat slowed to a more even tempo, but she still couldn't stop shivering from a chill that seemed to radiate outward from her bones.

"Are you cold?" he asked with aching concern. "I could build up the fire."

"It's not that sort of cold," she whispered. "It's inside, somehow. Could you, I mean, would you... hold me?" Humiliation churned in her belly that he'd witnessed one of her episodes, along with fear that she'd committed some sort of marital gaffe by asking such a thing.

"Are you certain that is what you want?" His voice sounded husky and worried. "I don't want to make your memories return."

"They won't. A comforting embrace is completely different than what those... *monsters* did to me." The affirmation in those words made her pause with myriad realizations. When she'd first awakened in his bed with him, a powerful vampire who had been a stranger to her, she hadn't been afraid... or at least not afraid that he'd do what Clayton's rogues had done. Swallowing a lump in her throat, she explained. "You make me feel safe."

Slowly, Gavin's arms slipped around her waist. Then gently, as if she were made of glass, he pulled her close against his firmly muscled chest, and rested his chin on the top of her head. Soothing warmth seeped into her body.

Suddenly she felt his hardness pressing against her lower back. But instead of jolting in panic, her stomach quivered in an alarming manner, because the sensation was not unpleasant. Was his arousal a natural reaction from their intimate proximity? Or did he want her? Rather than the old terror surfacing at the thought, swirling confusion engulfed her mind.

Only one thing was certain. He wouldn't force her. She knew that wholly and completely. He'd even positioned himself so that his erection was nowhere near her loins.

The chill in her bones melted away as she slowly relaxed in his embrace. And for the first time in nearly a year, Lenore fell into a peaceful sleep, with dreams of happiness and hope, rather than horror and pain.

Nineteen

Gavin awoke to the most delicious warmth he'd ever experienced. This must be what it was like to hold an angel, he mused, as she made a satisfied little hum and cuddled closer to him. Unfortunately, her innocent movement awoke his manhood, his shaft lengthening and throbbing with need.

No, he would not frighten her.

Carefully, he disengaged himself from her, his heart clenching when she moaned as if in protest.

"Is it night already?" Her voice was muzzy from sleep.

"Yes. I had thought we could hunt as soon as we're dressed." His stomach growled in agreement as he rose from the bed.

"Oh good, I am starving." She turned over to look at him just as he was adjusting his bed robe to hide his raging erection. Her lips parted and her cheeks flushed, but unbelievably, she did not appear frightened. She looked down at her lap and blatantly changed the subject. "I felt so guilty feeding from Mrs. Crain. She is so kindly and…"

"I know." Gavin himself did not feed at all last night. At his age he could go without for a time or two. But a youngling could become dangerous if they went without feeding for too long. Not for the first time he wondered how any passing mortals had fared when she'd escaped captivity. Shaking off the thought, he placed his hand over hers. "We only drink from the servants when there is no other choice. I do not foresee such circumstances again, if that puts your conscience at ease."

"Thank goodness," she said and rose from the bed, pulling her nightgown tight over her breasts.

Gavin tore his gaze from the outline of her nipples through the thin fabric. "Well, I shall leave you to dress."

"Wait." She reached out and placed her hand on his arm. "I'm still unaccustomed to these new gowns. Elena helped me before, but now…" She peered up at him shyly beneath thick lashes. "Could you?"

"Certainly." Of course she wouldn't have learned how to dress in the complicated gowns of the upper classes. Hell, his former wives had required assistance. The prospect of touching her filled him with delight even as he groaned inwardly at the temptation she'd unknowingly roused.

Lenore opened the wardrobe and gasped. "My God, these are all so beautiful."

Gavin held his breath at the sight of the sparkle in her eyes as she ran her fingers along the delicate gowns he'd had made for her. "Do they please you?"

"Very much." Her lips parted in awe. "And you bought these all for me?"

He nodded. "Only the best for my baroness."

Her lips curled in a bewitching smile as she took out an emerald green velvet walking dress trimmed with lace. "So many have said that you are ruthless and cruel. But you have treated me more kindly than anyone."

"I'm only harsh with those who cross me." Avoiding her gaze, he fetched her stays and motioned for her to turn around. "Now do not go round ruining my reputation." He softened the admonition with a light kiss on her shoulder.

Once he finished helping her dress, he rang for Mrs. Crain to arrange her hair and saw to his own clothing.

They declined a feigned breakfast and decided to walk, or run, rather. Gavin savored the flush in her cheeks and unadulterated joy in her eyes as they conquered the miles in a burst of preternatural speed.

"How did you hunt before?" he asked as they slowed to a walk and approached the village.

"I didn't, rather," Lenore said. "Blanche instructed me to sit on a park bench or stand on a street corner. The sight of a woman alone at night is always bound to attract a meal."

Distaste roiled through him at that fact of life, along with a thread of admiration that she had been able to twist the inherent beastly qualities of men to her advantage. "So you turned would-be predators into prey."

"Not all of them approached me for nefarious reasons. Some thought I needed help." She looked down at her leather walking boots and frowned. "I confess, I always feel guilty feeding from someone trying to offer me a kindness."

Her tender heart warmed some deep dark pit in his black soul. Yet such tenderness could be a double-edged sword. On one hand, a vampire less inclined to brutishness tended to follow the rules better. On the other, it was never a good idea to become too close to a mortal. And her friendship with that quack of a doctor was a definite liability.

"Who was Blanche?" he asked, changing the subject.

"The vampire who made me. She was very kind, but low ranking. I did not know her for very long." Grief filled her dark eyes. "She was killed by a Hunter only months after she Changed me."

"Why did she change you?" He was surprised at how curious he was in regards to her past.

"I was dying from the same consumption that took my mother." She gave him a bitter look from the corner of her eyes. "To be honest, I think our lungs were full of lint dust from the factory. I know I coughed enough of that foul dreck out. Anyway, Blanche came to visit, claiming to be a friend of the family, though we never figured out which family. But that didn't matter. She brought us food, honey, tea, and sometimes even laudanum when mother's suffering was beyond help. We spent many hours talking, and by the time Mother took her last breath, Blanche told me what she was and offered to Change me. She saved my life." Before Gavin could fully process the dismal picture she'd painted, Lenore looked back at him, eyes pleading to drop the subject. "What about you? When were you Changed?"

"During the reign of Edward the Second," he answered, snapping a green bud from a hawthorn tree. "I was only months away from becoming an ordained priest, though I'd long since lost my faith." Long ago discovered that God's so called chosen were not the saints they pretended to be, and there was no divine intervention for those in despair.

"What year was that?" Lenore interrupted his haunting memories of pain and fear.

Gavin paused and cursed himself for a fool. Older vampires usually disclosed their ages with whichever monarch was ruling at the time they were Changed. As a youngling, and one from common stock at that, Lenore would have no point of reference from his answer. "Thirteen-twelve," he clarified.

Her eyes widened. "That means you're over five hundred years old. I thought the Lord of London, I mean, the Duke of Burnrath, was the oldest vampire in England."

"Not even close. Lord Villar is also at least a century older than him. However, Ian may be the most powerful. Power derives from one's sire as well as age. One of the Elders reputably Changed him."

Gavin struggled to hide his envy. Ian could fly. Gavin was only barely learning how.

"I suppose that explains why I am so weak then. Blanche was only around seventy-five." Her shoulders slumped a moment before she glanced back at him. "And the one who Changed you?"

"A vampire posing as a noblewoman from some exotic land. She was about two centuries old. All she wanted was to make a vampire who would be her obedient pet. I wanted to escape my servitude at the Church, so I embraced her offer gladly. Too late I discovered that life with her was merely a different sort of servitude. And I was *never* suited to that." He laughed bitterly, unable to conceal his disgust at the memory. "Thankfully she grew bored with me after only a half century and moved onto another toy."

"I cannot imagine you being anyone's toy," Lenore said solemnly. Her nose scrunched up in the most adorable manner. "How many times have you been married?"

Gavin chuckled. If he didn't know better, he'd think she sounded jealous. "Only five times. Twice to Elena and three times to Anne. She left Rochester about a century ago." He halted as he spotted two men stumbling out of the King's Arms Inn. "Ah, there is our meal. We will follow them until they are out of public view, and then we'll strike."

"Like we're actually hunting them?" she asked, sounding more intrigued than disapproving.

"Precisely." He bared his fangs and licked his lips. "There is no need for you to present yourself as a victim, or even a seductress, as Elena amuses herself with doing. I prefer this manner best. It will make you feel like a real vampire."

Keeping to the shadows, they stalked their prey through the winding streets. Gavin smiled in approval at Lenore's whisper-light footsteps.

When the louts left the village proper to cut through an orchard, Gavin gave the signal to attack. In tandem, he and Lenore seized the men by the shoulders. Gavin's victim made a small yip of terror before he managed to put the poor sod in a trance. He'd been distracted watching Lenore mesmerize the mortal she grasped.

Together they feasted until sated, then silently commanded the men to sleep, leaving them collapsed in a heap beneath an apple tree.

Taking Lenore's arm, he grinned down at his new bride as they walked back to the village. "You did very well. How did it feel? To feed that way?"

"I should feel like a vicious monster," she looked down at her boots as she stepped back up on the cobblestone street. "But instead, I liked it. I felt... powerful."

"Good." He nodded in satisfaction. From what he'd seen, every vampire Lenore had ever encountered seemed to do their utmost to convince her that she was weak. Yes, she was a youngling, and yes, she'd been Changed by a lesser vampire, but that did not mean that she was completely without strength. Gavin resolved to convince her of that fact.

As they neared the village square, he walked beside Lenore, watching her daintily dab her lips with a dark cloth, a disturbing scent reached his nostrils.

"Rogues," he growled aloud without thinking.

Lenore's face went pale, despite the hearty meal she'd just drank. Without another word, Gavin scooped her up in his arms and dashed back to his manor in a burst of preternatural speed. Cecil and John were on sentry duty at the borders of his estate.

"I smelled rogues near the village square. Come with me," he told Cecil. Turning to the other vampire, he commanded. "Guard the perimeter. I will be sending you help as soon as I can. Do not let anyone pass unless it is myself, Cecil, or Benson."

John bowed low. "Yes, my lord."

Without another word, he carried Lenore to the house, only depositing her on the chaise once the front door was closed behind them. "I must leave you now, my lady, while I see to this urgent matter."

Anger boiled within him as he strode out the front door. Bloody rogues. The terror in Lenore's eyes at the very mention of them exacerbated his fury. Just as she'd begun to feel at ease, even to the point where she welcomed affection from him, they had to come about and ruin it all.

Even worse, they'd been in the village square. A bold move, and not a usual behavior from their cowardly sort. Anger and unease curdled in his belly like sour milk. Not only did such a deep invasion directly challenge his power and authority, the fact that they'd been able to pass so far into his territory meant that his people were in even greater danger than he'd first presumed.

Cecil and Benson flanking him, they spread out through the square, tracking the intruder's scents and subtly questioning nearby innkeepers and harlots.

Unfortunately, the scents did not lead to a specific trail, veering off in all directions as if they'd known they would be tracked.

Gavin ground his teeth in irritation. Their leader was clever, whoever he was. Again, he wondered...

"I want scouting parties to patrol the village every hour," he told his second and third in command. "Choose at least twenty qualified vampires tonight and we shall meet at the castle ruins tomorrow night."

Cecil and Benson bowed and chorused, "Yes, my lord."

Benson looked furious as he spat on the ground. "We'll have these blasted curs rounded up and eliminated soon, I promise."

As Gavin turned to walk back to the manor, he heard the crackle of parchment beneath his boot. Bending down, he picked up a pamphlet.

A perplexed frown twisted his lips as he read a list of ways to fend off vampires. How had this gotten here? The pamphlet had been written in the mid 1700's. Although having rogues and a vampire hunter invade his territory at the same time was too much of a coincidence for him to swallow, he couldn't fathom what rogue vampires would be doing with such literature, much less leave it lying around so conspicuously.

His scowl deepened as the most likely implication came to mind. Perhaps one of the villagers had grown suspicious.

Gavin would have to warn his people to remain discreet and vigilant. The pamphlet crumbled in his fist and it took all of his will to shove it in his pocket rather than rip it into a hundred pieces and scatter it in the wind.

Twenty
Three nights later

Lenore dipped the quill in the ink, her hand cramping as she wrote the same lines for the twentieth time.

The Baron and Baroness of Darkwood request the pleasure of— she filled in another name—*company for the supper and ball at Darkwood Manor, Thursday evening, the Thirtieth of March, at five o'clock.*

It would be the first ball she'd ever hosted, and everything must be perfect, to make Gavin proud. Even though he'd been preoccupied meeting with his second and third in command and had barely spoken to her for the past three nights, she was still eternally grateful to him for holding and comforting her during their wedding night, or rather, day.

Although such intimacy must have tempted him, he'd resisted. Once more, the memory of the feel of his hard length against her haunted her imagination.

Not for the first time since that night, she began to wonder if she could ever try to be a true wife to him. Perhaps, with him, the act would not hurt so much. Perhaps it would even be possible for her to experience a semblance of pleasure.

Elena broke through her musings. "So, how is life as the Baroness of Darkwood?" she asked as she sealed another envelope.

"More pleasant than I'd anticipated," she replied. "The servants have been very kind and I am looking forward to a bit of redecorating." Suddenly remembering that Elena had once been mistress to this house, she quickly added, "I hope you do not mind."

Elena laughed. "I haven't been the mistress of this house for over a century. Anything I've done has to be dreadfully outdated. And that's if Anne allowed any of my additions to remain." She leaned forward and lowered her voice. "Oh please tell me that you're going to redo those hideous Rococo themed furnishings in the parlor."

Lenore nodded so vigorously that she nearly dislodged her hair pins. "That is the first thing on my list. I have an appointment with the village carpenter tomorrow." Her grin faded as she mustered up the courage to bring up a subject that had wormed its way into her mind. "What was Anne like?"

"A pleasant enough vampire, despite her dubious tastes in fashion and decor." Elena smirked, whether in gentle mockery of Gavin's other former wife, or in knowledge of the reason behind Lenore's concern, she could not tell.

Lenore fought off a twinge of unease at the vague answer. "How did she and Lord Darkwood get on?"

"As partners in an arranged marriage, fairly well, though His Lordship told me that I was more amusing company." She replied with a smug smile. "Anne certainly had the better benefit in the bargain."

"How so?" Lenore asked, no longer caring if she sounded like a jealous shrew.

"She was a lover of women," Elena said without the slightest hint of censure. "Her marriage to Lord Darkwood allowed her the perfect cover to pursue her affairs. And last century, Anne fell in love with the Lord of Salisbury, one of the few female Lord Vampires in Britain."

Lenore's shoulders relaxed in palpable relief that Rochester's other marriage also had not been love matches. A sudden wave of guilt washed over her, threatening to choke her. She shouldn't be happy that none of Gavin's wives had loved him. He deserved to be loved.

"What is amiss?" Elena's voice broke through her remorseful musings. "You look like someone ruined your favorite gown."

Lenore looked down and smoothed her skirts. "I am sad for His Lordship. Has he never had someone who loved him?"

Elena's eyes widened before her gaze turned distant and musing. "I'm not certain he has. If so, he's never spoken of such." She opened her mouth as if to say something else, and then she shook her head. "Do not worry overmuch. If he wanted love, he wouldn't persist in making his marriages business arrangements."

"Well, I want to do something kind for him." The intensity of that desire tugged at her heart. "He's shown me so many kindnesses."

Elena shrugged, though a mysterious smile played across her lips. "Simply be a kind and obedient wife, care for his home, keep his secrets, and he will be happy."

Lenore nodded, though that hardly felt like it was enough. She wanted to make him smile, give him comfort, ease his loneliness. But the only wifely thing she knew how to do was mending and housework.

Mrs. Crain and her maids appeared to have the cleaning well in hand, so after Elena left, Lenore went up to Gavin's bedchamber and threw open the wardrobe. As she searched his garments for stains or tears, Gavin's masculine scent permeated her senses, making her dizzy as things tightened in her lower body.

What was it about him that made her react so oddly?

Before she could ponder the question further, the butler knocked on the door. "I beg your pardon, my lady. A Doctor Elliotson is here to see you. I had him wait in the parlor."

"Thank you, Finch," Lenore replied and closed Gavin's wardrobe. "I shall be right down. Please tell Mrs. Strout that we'd like some tea."

Elliotson stood when she entered the parlor and bowed lower than necessary. "It is wonderful to see you, Lady Darkwood. Marriage agrees with you."

"Thank you, Doctor," she said.

After the tea was served, they talked of inconsequential matters such as the upcoming ball and her plans to redecorate. When they finished, Elliotson set down his cup and gave her a level gaze. "I am so pleased to hear of all the wonderful things you plan as a new baroness, and I am very impressed with your rise in rank."

"And?" she prodded, knowing him well enough to know there would be more.

"I do not wish to be impertinent." He tugged at his neck cloth. "But I do hope you don't think you are above working with the commoners."

Lenore shook her head with an indelicate snort. "Certainly not!" she retorted louder than intended. "I mean, the question was a trifle impertinent, though I can understand why you were concerned. So many of the noble class believe they are too good to help those less fortunate. I do not. In fact, my resolve is stronger than ever."

"Splendid," Elliotson rubbed his hands together with glee. "Now hopefully you may not think me too forward in that I have already arranged a meeting with a few women in the village tomorrow evening at seven. I do hope you will be able to join me."

"Nothing could keep me from it." Even as the bold words slipped from her mouth, an inner voice warned, *Rochester could.*

Not if I do not tell him, she countered inwardly.

***

Gavin headed up the stairs after another long night of hunting rogues. There had been traces of them everywhere, it seemed, but no definitive trail.

And they had come across more pamphlets about vampires. Even worse, he'd overheard villagers muttering about them over pints of ale. Wondering perhaps if such creatures were real. Gavin had been certain to feed on anyone voicing such dangerous speculations, leaving the conviction that there were no such things as vampires before releasing them from their trances.

Once more, he considered telling Lenore more about the rogues, as well as the possibility that there could be a vampire hunter in the area. But he held off, not wanting to frighten her for one thing, for another, he wanted to know more about the situation before he said anything.

Perhaps if there was a hunter about, he would solve Gavin's problem and kill the rogues.

He sneered. If only he would be so lucky.

He found Lenore in the parlor, sitting by the fire with one of his shirts on her lap. Her deft fingers wielded a needle, mending a tear with diligent care.

The picture of tranquil domesticity she presented made his heart ache. None of his previous brides had bothered to do something so simple and thoughtful as to mend his clothes. Why would they, when he could always buy new garments?

"How was your evening?" she asked, her needle poised between her tiny fingers.

"Not as successful as I would have liked." Before she could prod, he looked at the clock. "It will be dawn in little more than an hour. We had best hunt now."

As they ventured outside, Lenore gave him constant inquiring glances, as if she wanted to ask him a question. Gavin held back from asking her to come out with whatever was on her mind, despite his curiosity. If she wanted to know more about the rogues, that would have to wait.

They found their prey with a young couple just finishing a tumble in a barn. Gavin recognized the man as Lady Chatterton's stable master. The young miss appeared to be a maid of some sort.

By the time they were sated and returned home, exhaustion weighted his muscles like lead. Rogues invading his lands, some mysterious person or persons attempting to stir up hysteria on vampires… his maddening attraction to his baroness, and myriad thoughts tumbled in his head to the point where there was nothing he wanted to do but escape the torment in sleep.

Leading Lenore to their adjoining chambers, he resisted the urge to claim her lips in a mindless kiss. Instead, he gave her a chaste peck on her smooth brow and shrugged out of his coat. "I will see you at dusk, my lady wife."

Once more, a question flared in her large eyes, but still she did not ask. Perhaps it could wait until nightfall. "Goodnight, my lord." She curtsied and left his room, closing the door behind her.

The separation felt like miles.

Before he gave in to the temptation to follow her, Gavin undressed and went to bed.

His eyelids were just drifting shut when he heard the sound of a doorknob turning. Gavin opened his eyes to see Lenore standing in the doorway of their adjoining rooms. In the dark chamber, he could barely make out the shape of her. But what a beautiful shape it was, all the same. An angel in a long white night gown, dark hair tumbled around her shoulders.

"I cannot sleep," she said softly, clasping her arms and looking achingly vulnerable. "May I... that is, would it be all right if I..."

"Stay with me," he finished, pulling the coverlet aside and making room for her.

"Thank you," she whispered, slipping into bed beside him, filling the former emptiness with her warmth.

Gavin reached over and lit a candle on the bedside. Likely she'd been locked up in the darkness during her captivity, so perhaps a little light would give her comfort.

That, and he could see her beauty more clearly. With that silken mahogany hair, dark, soulful eyes, and decadent, full lips, he wanted to throttle all those who had called her mousy and plain.

Slowly, to give her time to pull away, he took her into his arms, inhaling her soft hair that smelled like lavender. Lenore's contented sigh made warmth flow through his heart. But the feel of her body pressed close to his made rampant lust unfurl within him.

She shifted back, close to him and he sucked in a breath as her rounded backside brushed against his hardness.

"Does it hurt?" she asked with touching worry.

"Yes," he admitted before thinking better of it. "But I can take care of it myself later." Truly he was a fool for not having done so before she'd come to his bed.

"How do you... take care of it?" She rolled over to face him, her eyes wide and curious in the candlelight.

"With my hand," he answered plainly, not knowing what else to say but the truth.

Silence stretched the air between them until she spoke again. "Well, why don't you?"

His jaw dropped and it took a moment to recover his words. "I beg your pardon?"

"Why don't you ah, take care of your ache now? I do not wish for you to remain in pain."

"I do not think that would be proper," he said. "To do that in front of you." Though he could not deny the appeal. To behold her while he pleasured himself would be the next best thing to touching her.

Unbelievably, Lenore chuckled. "You used to take pride in impropriety. Why the sudden modesty?" Her eyes glittered as she peered at him through a curtain of dark hair. "Besides, we're married. We were supposed to be engaging in activities that are far more intimate."

He bit back a groan as her words intensified his aching lust.

"I can, ah, turn away if that makes you more comfortable," she said quietly.

Cursing himself for a reprehensible beast, he slowly lowered the coverlet, exposing the outline of his turgid length beneath his bedclothes. He knew he should make her look away, but instead, he voiced his desires aloud. Grasping himself, he said, "I want to look upon you."

As he gripped himself through the satin of his bed robe, Lenore sat up and then knelt beside him. The sight of her tousled hair and her high rounded breasts at the verge of spilling from the low cut night dress was certainly arousing, but it was the rapt fascination in her large dark eyes and lush parted lips, which was so erotic, that made his blood sing.

"I want to look upon you as well," she whispered. "I've never seen a man's form… that is…" she trailed off with a furious blush.

"Very well, I shall indulge your curiosity." He fought to keep his voice level even as trepidation coursed through his veins. What if she recoiled at the sight of his swollen length? Would it bring to mind the ones that had violated her?

Slowly, he untied the sash on his robe. He used to take pride in the fact that all of his lovers always declared him to be well endowed. But now he wished that he was not so large and intimidating.

Her audible intake of breath made him move to cover himself once more, but she stopped him, placing her hand on his.

"You're... beautiful." She studied his body as if it were a rare work of art. "Like that painting in the library, except for..." Her gaze trailed down to his erect cock and her blush deepened. "Well, that."

Unable to stop himself, his fingers wrapped around his shaft, squeezing and stroking. His gaze held Lenore's daring her to look away, at the same time, pleading her not to.

"Would you like me to help?" she asked.

Help? Oh yes, she could help by lying down and hiking her nightdress up to her waist. "Sweet Christ, woman! Are you trying to torment me?"

She shook her head. "No. You have done so much to please me that I only want to please you in return."

He seized her hand, gripping it tightly. "If you think to do this as some misplaced sense of obligation—"

"No." She shook her head vigorously, making her breasts quiver in the most delightful manner. "That is, I do wish to please you as you've pleased me, but I also wish to touch you, to know what you feel like."

Her words shocked him to the core. As he considered her offer, a tendril of hope curled within his heart. Could it be possible to undo the damage that had been done to her? Gavin hid his dangerous thoughts with a languid smile. "Ah, but nothing pleases me more than *your* pleasure. So you may touch me, but only if you also touch yourself." *Or let me touch you*, he almost added.

She blinked. "Do you mean…" She looked down at her lap. "There?"

"Yes, there." Still holding her hand, he guided her fingers between her thighs and pressed them against her mons, searching until he found that special spot. Her pupils dilated and she let out a small gasp that hardened him further. "Now did that please you?"

"I think so," she panted, reaching for him with her free hand. As her delicate fingers curled around his shaft, it was his turn to gasp. "Did that please you?"

"God, yes," he groaned as she gently squeezed and stroked his full length. While he still maintained a semblance of sense, he quickly reassured her. "Remember, you hold all of the power. If you become uncomfortable, you may stop at any time."

In answer, she quickened her strokes, a small gasp escaping her lips as she continued to fondle herself. The raw pleasure on her countenance pleasured him almost more than her touch. Unable to stop himself, he thrust himself into her hand.

Lenore echoed his movements, her hips undulating as she found a rhythm that tantalized them both. Her shallow pants quickly turned to moans, sensual music to his ears.

As they moved together, Gavin couldn't stop watching her. She looked like a nymph, a patron goddess of lust. His breath quickened as her soft hands wrought unfathomable ecstasy to his body.

Suddenly, her hips quivered and fine trembles wracked her form. Lenore's eyes opened wide in astonishment, and for a moment she froze.

"Don't stop," he rasped. "Let it happen."

Trust and reassurance filled her eyes before she resumed her intoxicating strokes. She threw back her head and cried out as the climax overtook her. The sight of her above him with one hand between her thighs and the other wrapped around his cock was so erotic that Gavin couldn't hold back his own orgasm any longer.

Only after his release spilled on his belly did he worry that she might be repulsed.

And she had frozen, but not with horror. Instead, her face was rapt with awe and fascination.

"I never knew…" she gasped, "that it could be so…"

"Yes," he finished, cleaning himself with his robe. He reached for her hand to wipe it as well, but she snatched it back, looking at it with curiosity.

Though he was relieved to see no hint of revulsion in her eyes, his face still burned with embarrassment as he grabbed a handkerchief from the bedside table and handed it to her.

Once she was cleaned up, he snuffed the candle and gathered her in his arms.

"Did I please you?" she asked.

"Only if you were pleased," he answered.

"Oh, I was," she whispered, cuddling closer to him. "I'd never imagined such sensations were possible."

"They are." He placed a gentle kiss on the back of her neck. "And so many more."

As they drifted off to sleep, he prayed he would be able to show her more.

Twenty-one

Lenore awoke with a languorous stretch, a smile tugging at her lips. Gavin was already awake and dressed, looking devastatingly handsome in a charcoal gray frock coat and a navy waistcoat.

"I must meet with my tenants," he said, tying his cravat. "Perhaps you can hunt with Elena."

"I planned on paying a few calls," she said evasively. "I can hunt then."

"Very well, as long as you are sated. I will count the hours until I see you again" He bent down and his lips claimed hers in a gentle, teasing kiss.

Immediately, frissons of electric heat flared between her thighs, leaving her breathless and unable to form the words for a simple goodbye.

When he closed the door, she fell back on the bed with wide eyes, gasping as her female center continued to throb, a faint echo of the cataclysmic sensations she'd experienced before their day sleep.

He'd awoken something within her, a strange hunger that was exhilarating and frightening all at once. Yet in the throes of their simultaneous pleasure, Lenore learned the truth of Gavin's words. She *was* powerful. To give and receive such pleasure made her feel like a mighty sorceress.

Momentarily, her hand crept between her thighs before she snatched it back, feeling shamefully naughty. She would be late meeting Dr. Elliotson if she indulged in such antics. Besides, it would be much better to savor the anticipation for the dawn. Would Gavin want to do that again? She hoped so. And to her surprise, she most fervently hoped that this time, he would touch her.

A voice deep within asked a question she'd long suppressed. Would she be able to abide with more than that?

The usual terror did not surface at the thought. Only a maddening uncertainty. She wanted more of what she'd experienced with Gavin last night… but she didn't want him to hurt her.

Lenore closed her eyes and took a deep breath. She would think of Gavin later. Now there were women who needed her help.

She met Dr. Elliotson at the village market, which was closed, aside from a few vendors selling hot pies, ale, and some other ware cried out in such gibberish she could not discern what the toothless man was selling.

Four women sat across from the doctor on a table reserved for the market-goers to take luncheon. From their chapped hands and faint aroma of hay, they seemed to be farmers' wives. When they saw Lenore, they rose from the bench and curtsied reverently, though she could see suspicion glinting in their weary eyes. However, there was something else, a faint glimmer of hope.

"Lady Darkwood," Elliotson bowed and extended his hand for her to shake. "I am so happy you were able to come. Allow me to introduce you to Mrs. Crawley, Mrs. Reed, Mrs. Woodward, and Miss Thompson. I have been telling all of them about your great talent with this new way of healing."

"It's not healing," she said quickly, ignoring Elliotson's frown of disapproval. Lifting her chin, she clarified. "One cannot heal instantly from this treatment. However, it most certainly can help you heal over time. And this treatment is most effective for ailments of the mind and heart. I'm afraid we cannot mend broken legs or cure disease or anything of that nature."

The women nodded in approval at her candid explanation. She understood their skepticism. Anyone promising a fast cure would be assumed to be a quack or a snake oil salesman. And most times they were right. She'd long wanted to dissuade Elliotson from even referring to mesmerism as healing or worse, a cure, but hadn't mustered to courage to say so. Until now.

"Did the doctor heal you, my lady?" Mrs. Woodward asked pointedly.

Elliotson's eyes widened with worry. He had never been able to mesmerize her. However, Lenore was able to give an honest answer. "My time with Doctor Elliotson has helped me overcome my own troubles in ways I'd thought unfathomable."

The women glanced at each other in silent consideration before Mrs. Woodward, the apparent designated leader, stepped forward. "How does the treatment work?"

Lenore took a seat on the bench and gestured for the others to do the same. "First, we talk. You would tell Dr. Elliotson or me about anything that plagues your mind to the point where you have trouble sleeping, or your day to day life suffers. Then either the doctor or I will place you in a trance, a sort of waking dream, for lack of a better word."

Mrs. Woodward's frown deepened. "And what do you do to us once we're in this trance?"

"We would encourage you not to allow your troubles to burden you, to guide you in gathering strength and peace." Lenore kept her tone soothing and level. "You will finish the session feeling calm and relaxed."

The farmer's wife raised a brow. "How would that heal us?"

Elliotson answered. "The power of the mind is a marvelous thing. We'll convince it to heal you."

Mrs. Woodward leaned back with narrowed eyes. "And how do we know you won't trick us instead? Steal our coin or make us bark like dogs like a magician at the fair?"

"It doesn't work that way," Lenore hastily assured them. "As the good doctor said, the mind is powerful. We can't make it do anything you don't truly want." Well, Elliotson couldn't. Lenore could, though she only utilized that power for her own safety. "Also, you may have a friend or more with you during the session to make certain of your well being."

The last bit convinced them and all four women nodded. Mrs. Woodward offered to go first. "I would prefer to do this with Her Ladyship, if that is all right."

Elliotson frowned for a moment, his pique at being rejected vanishing quickly with a broad smile. "Of course."

"Well, I want Dr. Elliotson to do my treatment," Mrs. Crawley said. "After all, he is a real doctor and surely has more experience."

"You will be in good hands," Elliotson assured, visibly placated.

Mrs. Woodward sniffed and rose from the bench. "I feel more comfortable speaking to another woman about my troubles." Her shrewd blue eyes shifted back to Lenore. "May we speak in private at that table under the yew tree? Gwen will come with me."

Lenore nodded even though she had no idea which of them was Gwen until Miss Thompson stood and joined her friend. Once they were seated at the other table, out of any man's hearing, Mrs. Woodward, who implored Lenore to call her Alice, told her that she was a widow, managing the farm herself. A gentleman had begun calling on her, and though Alice had grown fond of him, her late husband had beat her so frequently that she couldn't be near a man for very long before she had trouble breathing.

"I know exactly what that's like," Lenore told her, heart aching in sympathy.

Alice stared, slack jawed. "You do, my lady?"

"Well, I used to," she said quickly, not wanting the woman to assume that Gavin abused her. Before Alice could inquire further, Lenore pressed forward. "Have you told your new beau about your former husband?"

"Beau?" Alice giggled. "You make me sound like a young Society miss. I'm nearly forty years old." Her expression sobered. "No, I haven't told Sam about what Frank was like. I'm afraid to. What if he thinks I deserved it? What if he thinks I was a bad wife and decides he no longer wants to see me?"

"You did not deserve such treatment." Outrage filled Lenore to the point where she had to resist the urge to bare her fangs. Taking a deep breath, she spoke more levelly. "If this Sam truly cares for you, he will do all he can to reassure you and be willing to promise never to hurt you."

Alice sighed, brow furrowed with doubt. "You sound so sure."

"From what I've learned, most men see hurting women as repugnant." She'd gained that knowledge from reading the minds of men when she fed on them. And knowing that not every male she encountered was a monster made it easier to sleep during the day. "Also, I had some misgivings of my own before I wed Lord Darkwood. Discussing my worries did much to alleviate them."

Alice nodded, eyes wide in understanding. "Discussing them has done much to help them already. Sometimes that's all somebody needs. A sympathetic ear and sound advice. I may not even need you to do your hocus pocus."

"I agree that talking helps." Though Dr. Elliotson did not when Lenore broached the possibility that perhaps talking with their patients helped them just as much, if not more, than mesmerizing them. "And I will not mesmerize you if you don't want me to."

Alice shook her head. "No, I want to try it. Maybe you can tell my mind to make me brave. Give me courage before I tell Sam."

"Very well. Now look into my eyes and take ten even breaths…"

Gwen looked on with a combination of concern and curiosity as Lenore willed Alice to be full of confidence and courage. After that Alice thanked her with teary eyes and she helped Gwen overcome heartache from a jilted lover.

That was a little more tricky, since love was such a complicated matter, and broken hearts were hard to heal. Not for the first time did Lenore wonder if she'd ever fall in love… or if she already had. Whenever she thought of Gavin, her chest tightened, her stomach quivered, and she had an unreasonable urge to do everything in her power to make him happy. Was that love?

Lenore shied from the question and focused on Gwen.

Despite Lenore's ignorance on matters of the heart, her efforts must have been sufficient, since Gwen and Alice praised her and vowed to tell their friends about her healing. The other two women appeared to be just as pleased with Elliotson's treatments.

After the women departed, Elliotson clasped his hands together. "Splendid work, my lady. I vow we'll have twice as many patients next time. And we're one step closer to opening our own clinic."

"Splendid," Lenore tried to sound enthusiastic, but almost couldn't manage. She knew Elliotson's primary goal was to open his own mesmerism clinic to treat the upper classes and generate a tidy profit, but even though she knew he would need such profit to expand the parameters of his research and treatments, she couldn't help feeling reluctant at the prospect of abandoning the common women who needed help the most.

Though she understood the practicality of his aims, Lenore took so much joy in helping the poor that it would break her heart for treatments and care to no longer be available to them. Not only that, but as a baroness... not to mention a vampire, her circumstances prevented her from doing more than she already was. "I must go home now. His Lordship may be waiting for me."

Elliotson nodded. "Shall I walk you home?"

"No, my carriage has come." Actually, Chandler would be meeting her in the village square in a half hour. Just enough time for her to find her prey and feed. Lenore captured Elliotson's gaze. "You see my carriage. We say goodbye."

"Goodbye," Elliotson said dutifully.

"You see me get inside and drive away," she willed the image into his mind. "You will wake up in thirty seconds and go home."

The doctor nodded. "Home."

After looking around for witnesses, Lenore took off in a flash. In London she'd hardly ever utilized her supernatural speed, but here in the country, she couldn't fathom why she'd gone so long without it.

She found a quick meal in a farmhand walking to the nearest pub, jingling coins in his pocket as he whistled. By the time she made it to the square, Chandler was waiting for her with the carriage.

When she arrived home, Gavin had not yet returned. She couldn't hold back the crushing tide of disappointment. Was this what he'd intended their marriage to be like? Him taking off to Lord knew where, leaving her alone until nearly dawn? Where had all the dancing, laughter, and smiles of their courtship gone?

He'd said the marriage was to be in name only, she reminded herself. And the courtship had been a display for the Quality's benefit. It had all been false.

But that didn't stop her from missing it. Especially when he was so warm and affectionate when they shared a bed. Surely that had not been feigned. Memories of what they'd done this morning flitted through her mind, the intent way he'd looked at her when she'd touched herself, his hardness in her hand when she'd stroked him, the mind bending pleasure.

A pang of longing flared in her loins. Surely that couldn't have been a farce. After all, she knew he had something on his mind. He'd been distracted ever since he'd smelled rogues in the area. A tendril of unease coiled in her belly. Why hadn't he told her what had come of his search? His anger last night made it clear that he hadn't found them, but surely he could have confided in her.

Her lips curved in a knowing smile as it all became clear. Of course Ruthless Rochester would be reluctant to admit to any sort of failure. All Lord Vampires were proud, and he was the proudest she'd known.

Besides, she hadn't told him about her meetings with Dr. Elliotson. Perhaps secrets in a marriage were normal. A light laugh trickled from her throat. *Nothing* was normal about this marriage.

Still chuckling, she headed to the parlor and went back to her mending, fighting the urge to glance at the clock every other minute.

It was almost dawn by the time Gavin returned. He froze in the doorway, eyeing her as she stitched his trousers with an unreadable expression. Just as Lenore began to ask what was amiss, that dark cloud returned to his countenance.

"I am sorry I am late." His expression remained unreadable. "Do you need to hunt?"

She shook her head. "I've already fed twice. Once before paying calls and once before I returned home." *Home.* She was growing to love the sound of that word.

"Shall we retire for the day then?" His voice sounded forced and somehow flat.

Studying the lines of stress and fatigue ravaging his noble features, she nodded.

Her breath caught in anticipation as they entered the bedchamber. Would she join him in his bed? Would he want her to pleasure him again? Liquid heat flowed through her body, accompanied by a shiver.

Gavin shrugged out of his coat and turned to her. "Do you need help with your gown?"

She nodded and turned around before he could see the naked anticipation in her eyes. Even the light motions of his fingers as he unfastened the buttons made her pulse quicken. And when he loosened her stays, every inch of her flesh came alive, crying out for his touch.

She could feel the heat radiating from his body across the mere inches that separated them. When he'd removed everything but her chemise, she was unable to resist the temptation any longer. Tentatively, she leaned back to press against his chest.

Gavin hissed as if burned. His hands grasped her shoulders, pulling her closer until she could feel his hardness. This time it didn't frighten her. This time—

Abruptly, he released her and stepped back. "I can't tonight. I…"

When he trailed off, she turned to face him. "Why not? Did I displease you last time when I…" Now it was her turn to trail off, unable to find words for what they'd done.

"No." He shook his head vehemently, yet some hidden shadow remained in his eyes. "You pleased me *too* much. I merely have a great deal on my mind and need some time by myself."

You've had the last eight hours to yourself, she protested inwardly.

"Although if you do have another nightmare, I will be there in an instant, I promise." He walked past her to open her door.

The distance stretched between them with every step. When the door closed, she felt like it severed one of her heartstrings.

***

Justus flipped through the pages of notes penned by Dr. Elliotson, the quack that Rochester's bride had been associating with. He'd filched them after following the doctor home and feeding on him. But the sloppily scrawled words were nearly as incomprehensible as what he'd seen in the man's mind when drinking his blood.

The most interesting thing he'd discovered from his first glimpse in Elliotson's memories was the fact that Lenore had been a student of his in London, while together they... did whatever it was they had been doing tonight when he'd watched them.

He'd hidden in the shadows of a vacant market stall while Lady Darkwood and the doctor spoke with a group of peasant women. His brow had creased in confusion as they'd spoken of mind control... something only vampires could do. Unless there truly was such a thing as witches, which he'd never believed.

When Lenore had led two of the women to another table and placed one of them in a trance, Justus's jaw had dropped. What in the name of God did she think she was doing? Vampires were never supposed to reveal any of their secrets to mortals.

Rather than feeding on either of the women, Lenore had then commanded them to feel good about themselves, to have courage and feel peace. Why?

So captivated with the conundrum before him, he nearly forgot about the doctor. Justus had to clap a hand over his mouth to muffle his gasp when he saw that somehow, Elliotson had managed to place his companions in a trance as well. Surely it had to be a parlor trick, but from the glazed look he'd seen in the woman's eyes, the same rapt look of countless mortals he'd captured, his skepticism wavered. Were witches real after all?

The foolishness of the thought irritated him even as his curiosity rose. After the women left, Lenore once more used her preternatural abilities to convince Elliotson that she'd departed in a carriage when she truly ran off to hunt.

Instead of following Lady Darkwood, Justus stalked after Elliotson. Lenore hadn't bothered to take a bite. What a waste. Well, he would be certain to rectify that.

The moment Elliotson unlocked the front door of his cottage, Justus was on him in a flash. As the doctor's blood flowed in his mouth, words and images flashed behind Justus's eyes. What Elliotson and Lenore had been doing was some practice called mesmerism. They truly believed they could heal people with mental commands. Justus would have laughed if his mouth hadn't been full. He didn't know whether to be relieved or disappointed.

If Lenore had let her mortal friend know what she was, he would have the perfect means to destroy her and discredit Rochester. Finishing his meal, he shrugged. It was no matter. What Gavin's wife was doing was dangerous enough as it was. And Justus knew just how he'd use her actions to his advantage.

"Where are the notes you've taken on your experiments with Lady Darkwood?" he asked the brainwashed doctor.

"In my study," Elliotson droned.

"Bring them to me." Justus had commanded.

Now, back beneath the castle ruins, he flipped through the journal, searching for every bit of information that was incriminating, or at least could be construed that way.

Rolfe interrupted him with a tap on the shoulder. "It's my turn to take the watch."

"That's all right," Justus waved him off. "I'm still reading. Go back to sleep."

The vampire sat next to him. "What are you reading?"

Justus grinned. "It seems Lady Darkwood's friendship with that London doctor is even more interesting than we'd guessed."

Rolfe cocked his head to the side. "Is that ugly little troll truly her lover?"

Justus shook his head. "No, nothing so mundane."

After he finished telling his fellow rogue about Lenore's and Elliotson's experiments with the village women, Rolfe scowled. "This doctor can put humans in a trance?"

Justus nodded. "As hard to believe as it may be, I believe he can."

"In the old days, we killed mortals with such powers." Rolfe's voice shook with outrage tinged with fear. "In fact, I don't think it would be a bad idea if we disposed of this one."

Justus smirked. "No, I have a better idea."

Twenty-two

His wife was lying to him.

Gavin's fists clenched at his sides as he watched her enfold a mortal woman in a compassionate embrace. She'd told him that she was paying calls, which may not be a complete lie, depending on interpretation, but the deception weighed heavy all the same. Especially when no less than three society matrons had inquired as to why Lady Darkwood had *not* come round to pay a visit.

Grinding his teeth, he'd fobbed the noblewomen off with the excuse that his new baroness being too occupied with putting his sadly neglected household in order and preparing for her first ball.

Many had offered to come by Darkwood Manor to offer guidance. At first, Gavin had politely declined, but the more he thought about it, the more the idea appeared to offer a solution. If Lenore was occupied fulfilling her duties as a Lady, she'd be far too busy to continue this nonsense with the eccentric doctor.

No, that wasn't exactly true, he admitted reluctantly. Aside from neglecting to visit the local nobility, Lenore had been a dutiful wife. Together with Elena, all of the preparations for tomorrow's ball were underway, the ledgers had been combed through and balanced, and the house was well into the process of a much needed redecorating. *And* she mended his clothing. Something about that made him feel warm.

But that did not make her deception acceptable, or her association with these mortals safe in any way. Especially with the sudden prevalence of superstitious literature in the village. Which of course, he hadn't told her about. So perhaps he was deceiving her too.

Gavin shook his head. It wasn't the same. He was only concealing information to avoid causing her undue worry. She had no excuse for her flagrant mistruth.

He should march out from his hiding place, seize his wayward bride, throw her over his shoulder and carry her back home where she would be safe.

Yet he couldn't do it. The pure joy in her face as she helped those women, the tranquil confidence in her voice as she advised them with their troubles, and the shining gratitude in their eyes as they thanked her stayed his hand.

This made her happy. And he'd never seen her more aware of her own power as she was here in this place with these troubled peasants.

Besides, he reasoned, perhaps if Lenore improved the dispositions of the village folk, they'd be less apt to be susceptible to superstitious hysteria and embark on a witch hunt. Furthermore, frequenting such crowded public areas should ensure that she would be safe from that thrice damned band of rogues. Cecil had gotten the scent and look of one of them memorized. A big, barrel-chested male, with dirty brown hair, who he and Benson were now assuming to be the leader. *Not* Justus, to his everlasting relief.

He repeated those same rationalizations to Cecil later when his second asked why he was allowing Lenore to continue with her work with Elliotson.

"And speaking of those rogues," he continued, trying to hide his impotent fury. "Have you found any trace of them?"

"Actually, yes." Cecil's voice didn't sound as jubilant as one would expect. "We caught one, but the rest scattered."

"Wonderful." Fierce triumph welled in Gavin's chest... and a tremor of unease. What if it *was*... he broke off the thought. "After we question him, we will be able to find out where the rest have hidden."

His third in command looked down at his feet. "I don't think he'll be forthcoming."

"Why not?"

"He's dead," Cecil said quietly, still preoccupied with the dead grass.

"What?" Gavin growled. His lungs compressed. What if... *What if?* No, he told himself, Cecil would have said if it were Justus.

Cecil spread his hands helplessly. "The bloody cur attacked Benson, stabbed him in the chest. Missed his heart, thank whatever god looks down on our kind, but he also had him pinned on the ground, fangs buried in his neck, trying to drain him. I had to separate them with my sword."

"And you separated his head from his shoulders in the process," Gavin surmised, struggling to maintain his composure.

"Yes, my lord. I'm sorry." Abject shame shrunk the vampire's form. "I know you wanted them taken alive."

"Not at the cost of one of my people," Gavin placed a hand on Cecil's shoulder and spoke firmly. "You acted exactly as you should have. That is why you are my second." Though he meant his words, he couldn't help but think that Justus would have done things differently. None had been as quick and clever as Gavin's former second. Justus wouldn't have allowed anyone to catch him unawares.

Gavin closed his eyes, a wave of regret washing over him as he remembered the look of hurt betrayal in his former second's eyes when he'd been forced to exile him. Technically Justus's crime merited a death sentence, but he couldn't bear to kill his best friend. He shoved away the memory. "How is Benson?"

"At home, recovering. I carried him there myself and fed him from my own vein." Relief shone in Cecil's eyes that his compatriot had survived. "Jenny is there nursing him. I think she fancies him."

"That is a monumental relief. I will look in on him before dawn." Another thought occurred to him. He had to know. "Where is the rogue's body?"

"I placed it in the dungeons," Cecil said quickly. "I thought you might like to examine it for evidence and whatnot."

"Quick thinking." Gavin clapped him on the back, fighting his mounting anxiety. "Let's see to the body now. I do not want my wife to see it."

"Just as she does not want you to know what she's up to." His third's voice was so chiding, it rankled.

"Cecil," Gavin growled a warning.

"My apologies," Cecil said with a wry grin. "All I meant was that I am glad I don't have to suffer being leg shackled and all the inconvenience and deceit that one has to contend with."

"I am contending just fine." Gavin raised his gaze heavenward. "You forget that I have done this before."

"As you say." The skepticism in Cecil's tone was thick enough to choke on. "At least Elena was more obedient."

Gavin sighed. He would have to deal with Lenore's recalcitrance soon, or lose face among his people. His turmoil was forgotten as they entered the secret passage to his lower dungeons, where he kept rogues and traitors. When Cecil opened the cell to reveal the corpse, Gavin's gaze flew straight to the severed head… with its *yellow* hair.

Not red.

He released a breath he hadn't known he was holding. It wasn't Justus.

Only then did he realize how much he'd dreaded the prospect of seeing his friend dead. Shaking his head, Gavin returned his focus on the corpse. "Well, I suppose we should go through his pockets."

Unfortunately, there was little knowledge to be discerned from the corpse. All they found was ten quid, a tarnished brass pocket watch, and a tattered handkerchief.

Gavin's shoulders slumped as he crouched by the body, slightly queasy at the sight of the headless form. Just as he was about to rise and issue a command to dispose of it, his gaze lighted on a strand of hair on the rogue's ragged coat.

Throat tight, he plucked the strand from the corpse and held it to the light. It was long and glinted with crimson fire... just like Justus's fiery locks.

Could it be? He wondered, even as he dismissed the notion, contemplating more plausible sources. A woman most likely, given the length. Probably a mortal he'd drank from.

Justus *couldn't* be here, leading a group of rogues. Although he was an excellent leader. But Gavin could not fathom Justus being so foolish as to return to Rochester.

Because then Gavin would have to kill him.

***

With a heavy heart, Justus slowly walked back to the hidden lair under the catacombs of the cathedral. They'd killed Charlie.

But as much as he wanted to curse Benson and Cecil to the deepest pit of hell, he couldn't. Charlie's death had been a natural consequence of his own stupidity. Damn the fool, what had he been thinking, not only attacking one vampire who was thrice his age and power, but with another right there as well?

But Charlie had always been impulsive to the point of hazard. That was why he'd been exiled in the first place only last year for killing a mortal in sight of others. The foolish lad had been lucky his former Lord hadn't put him out in the sun the next day.

And now his luck had run out.

The moment Justus entered the chamber where they spent their day rest, Rolfe, who was on guard, took one look at his stricken face and his brow furrowed in concern.

"What happened?" Rolfe demanded.

"They caught Charlie."

"Bloody hell!" Rolfe's eyes widened in shock, outrage, and finally fear. "Do you think he'll tell them where we are?"

Justus sighed and spoke through a lump in his throat. "No chance of that. They killed him."

"My God," Rolfe gasped. He remained silent and trembling, a suspicious sheen that looked like tears gleamed in his eyes, reflecting the lantern light. Then his eyes began to glow in unholy rage. "Those blasted curs, I'll kill them with my bare hands when I get the chance!"

"No," Justus commanded soft, but firm. "It was Charlie's damned fault."

Even after he explained, Rolfe remained quivering in anger. "That doesn't change the fact that Charlie was one of ours. Rochester and his accursed third must pay."

"Don't you dare do anything foolish. I do not wish to lose you too." Justus placed a firm hand on Rolfe's shoulder, willing him to listen. "What happened was Charlie's own fault. We should at least be grateful that he wasn't captured and interrogated. And that he had a quick death."

"They'd never take me alive," Rolfe growled. "I've fought that dandy, Cecil. I know the range of his power. I could make short work of him."

"You will do nothing without my leave. I am the leader here." Justus bared his fangs in warning. "Or have you forgotten that?"

"No, my lord," Rolfe said sullenly. "It's just that—"

"Enough!" Justus sighed in exasperation. Rolfe's hot temper would get him in trouble one day. Hoping to calm him, he changed the subject. "Has Will returned yet?"

"No, my lord," Rolfe continued to avoid his gaze, and then stiffened as if a thought occurred to him. "Do you think Rochester's vampires got him too?"

Justus shook his head. "I'd commanded him to flee the moment Cecil and Benson came upon us. He's to hide somewhere past the border of Rochester's territory and not return until an hour before dawn."

They waited in tense silence until Will cautiously made his way back to their hidden lair. Both Justus and Rolfe exhaled audible sighs of gratitude to see their cohort unharmed.

Once more, Justus relayed the painful news of the loss of Charlie, feeling like a heartless bastard at his relief that at least his immediate death meant they were not in danger of exposure.

Justus didn't want Rochester to know who was responsible for his downfall. Not until Gavin had been cast down, his love destroyed, and all that was his stripped away.

Only then did he wish for Gavin to look him in the face and know the consequences of betraying one's best friend.

Twenty-three

Lenore thanked Finch as he took her cloak. Tonight's sessions had gone well, as the village women and farmer's wives had grown to trust her. She learned about sick children, abusive husbands, stillborn babies, and endless heartache. And though she'd felt good about cheering them and helping them find the strength to endure, some dark shadow of melancholy seemed to engulf her. She was lonely, though it made no sense, as she'd had company with Elliotson and made new friends almost every night. And when she wasn't working with the women, she and Elena worked on preparations for tomorrow's ball.

She bit back a sigh. That dratted ball.

The butler bowed. "Ah, his lordship wanted me to inform you that he is waiting for you in the library."

Her heart leapt in a combination of nervousness and joy. For so long he'd been neglecting her, and now he wanted to speak with her. Was it about the ball? Her stomach had been so knotted with worry that she might have missed some crucial detail that it had been nearly impossible to concentrate on her work with the village women tonight.

Or did he merely miss her and wish to enjoy her company again? He hadn't shared a bed with her since the night she'd touched him intimately. Not for the first time did she wonder if she'd either done it wrong, or if she'd done it too right and tempted him. Did he wish for her to do it again? Hope flared within her heart at the thought. But it was quickly doused with her third supposition. What if he'd learned about her work with Elliotson?

Fidgeting with her gloves as she walked up the curved staircase, she willed herself to appear calm. After all, he hadn't expressly forbidden her from seeing Elliotson.

But if he did now? Lenore didn't know if she could bear it. Although the doctor had been growing slightly fanatical of late and wanting to delve into some odd treatments, such as diagnosing illnesses by feeling the bumps on patients' heads, she didn't know what she'd do if she couldn't help all those women.

What would she do in this house while Gavin chased rogues and oversaw his territory while she remained here alone?

When she opened the door, she saw Gavin facing the fire, his hand behind his back. From the slight lift of his broad shoulders, she knew he'd heard her come in.

"How was your evening, my darling wife?" His voice was so level she couldn't tell if the inquiry was polite or suspicious.

"Very well, thank you," she managed to answer just as mildly. "How was yours?"

He turned around to face her, his gaze sweeping up and down her form, devouring every inch of her. "Oh I'd much rather talk about *yours*." He cocked his head to the side, regarding her with a smile that didn't reach his eyes. "Where were you?"

She swallowed. "In the village." There was no point in lying. *He knew.*

He stalked closer to her, like a cat on the verge of trapping a mouse. "And what were you doing there?"

"I think you already know that." Though she longed to look away from those penetrating black eyes, she held his gaze.

His chin lifted in a semblance of a nod. "Although it is true that I've been watching you, no, I don't know exactly what you were doing." His brows lowered and his scowl returned. "Though I would if you had told me in the first place." He seized her hands and held her gaze. "Why did you lie to me? Just what did you think you would accomplish telling me you were paying calls, only to sneak off and perform some sort of cabal with a gathering of peasants?"

Lifting her chin, she retorted, "You haven't told me where you've been going every night either."

"That's different. I am the Lord of this borough and I decide what is your business to know. Furthermore, I never told an outright lie." His eyes narrowed dangerously. "So why did you?"

She sucked in a breath and confessed the dreaded truth. "Because I thought you would forbid me from doing it."

For a moment, he just stared at her. Silence hung in the air thick enough to cut. Finally, he ran a hand through his thick curls and sighed. "Aside from that being the most foolish reasoning I've heard in ages, how were you supposed to know what I would or would not have done?" His brow rose in challenge, but she was too speechless to form a response. He eyed her intently before continuing. "The only thing of which you can be certain is that I am vexed with your deception."

This time, Lenore couldn't fight the quaver in her voice. "What are you going to do?"

"That all depends on you." Still holding her hands, he led her to the burgundy velvet loveseat by the fire. "I'm going to give you one more chance to tell me what exactly it is you are doing with those women. I've seen you speaking with them and placing them in trances, but I do not know why, or what you hope to accomplish. Explain everything as you should have in the first place, and I will weigh my decision accordingly."

Rather than being merciless as she'd feared, thus far he was being more than fair. Shame roiled through her at her ignorant assumption and cowardice. Why couldn't she have had enough of a backbone to talk to him?

Taking a deep breath, she carefully pled her case. As she often told the women she helped, sometimes it was best to begin at the beginning. "I'd been introduced to Elliotson by Cassandra, I mean, Lady Villar's physician friend, Thomas Wakley, after she was unable to help me with my nightmares and, well, episodes."

"Episodes?" The inquiry sounded more curious than hostile.

"Sometimes I am overwhelmed with the memories of what happened last year. I freeze like a rabbit and cannot breathe. Or I shake uncontrollably, like when I had that bad dream." Humiliation burned her face at the admission of weakness. She prayed he wouldn't laugh, or look at her like he had when he'd first encountered her, like she was pitiful and weak. "Since Cassandra and Dr. Wakley only work with matters of the body, they referred me to Dr. Elliotson, who specializes in matters of the mind. Though he was unable to mesmerize me—"

Gavin interrupted her. "And a damn good thing he couldn't, or he would have been hunted down and killed." When she shivered, he squeezed her hand. "I apologize for my interruption. Please, go on."

Lenore closed her eyes as the firm, warm grip of his hand jumbled her thoughts. "It helped me greatly to talk to Elliotson about my problems. Though I never specified what had happened to put me in such a state, I'm sure he could guess. He then took me on as a student and brought me to the East End, where he mesmerized poor women who worked in factories, women like I had been before I was Changed." A small smile curled her lips. "He was very impressed when he saw that I could do it too. He now sees himself as the greatest teacher in the world."

Gavin laughed lightly before his features sobered. He cocked his head to the side, peering at her with implacable curiosity. "What exactly do you do with their minds when you have the women under your power?"

Lenore explained the entire process, studying his face for any indication of anger or disapproval. Trepidation bubbled in her stomach as she slid off the loveseat and sank to her knees as the lower caste vampires did when pleading to their lord. "Please, my lord. Let me continue my work. Helping those women helps me. And I do not want to spend my nights here in a veritably empty house."

Still grasping her hand, he pulled her back onto the loveseat. "Do *not* grovel," he bit out through clenched teeth. "You are my *wife*, no longer an underling, and I will not have my wife on her knees in supplication."

The thunderous command seemed to reverberate in her bones.

Gavin's gaze raked across her before he heaved a sigh. "Now, as for your second complaint, if you feel lonely, you could begin making those calls you'd claimed to be paying."

Lenore shook her head, recoiling in disgust at the thought of chatting over tea with expensively dressed maidens and matrons who tittered at her from behind their fans. "It's not the same. I will never fit in with those indolent, spoilt society ladies." She'd abandoned her dreams of being a lady once she realized how dismal a prospect it was.

"Well, you do not fit with the lower classes, either," Gavin countered. "You are a baroness now, not a commoner, and baronesses typically do not socialize with the lower classes. Furthermore, you are also now the wife of the Lord Vampire in this city, so you are no longer a lower ranking vampire, either."

Her shoulders slumped in dismay. "So that is it then? Taking teas with women I have nothing in common with and, what is that fancy word they use… rusticating?" *Rotting* was more apt.

He stroked his chin, looking perplexed and contemplative. "You did not seem to be troubled with this when we first made our bargain. And unless you are an accomplished actress, I would say you enjoyed our courtship."

"Our *courtship*?" Unconcealed scorn dripped from her tone as she pulled her hand away. "I would say you were the better performer."

He raised a brow. "What do you mean?"

Unable to look at him, she struggled to list his transgressions as an accusation, rather than a confession of all the things she missed about him. "Your great pretense of fondness for me. Your dancing attendance on me, laughing and talking with me as if you had any interest in anything I had to say. Dancing with me... kissing me." Her face flamed at the last.

"Are you saying you enjoyed my attentions?" His fingers grasped her chin, tilting her head to meet his potent gaze. "And you've missed me?"

"Yes." The admission tore from her throat.

Something in his stern countenance softened. "I confess that I have been neglectful of late. I did not think much of it, as Elena and Anne were occupied with their own pursuits." His fingers lightly caressed her cheek. "I'll endeavor to spend more time with you."

"I don't want to inconvenience you," she said, mortified at the prospect of him keeping her company out of pity. "Besides, I still wish to continue my work." She froze in realization that in the haze of Gavin's devouring gaze and gentle touch, she'd momentarily forgotten all about her work.

"I *will* allow you to continue to do so, for now." Before she could graciously thank him and inwardly rejoice, he held up a hand. "However, you must reduce your meetings to only once a week. Also, you must do your duty and pay your calls. Tell them your activities in the village are a sort of charitable pursuit so you don't draw dangerous gossip."

She nodded gratefully. "Yes, my lord. Thank you, I—"

"What did I tell you about groveling?" he said softly as his thumb caressed her wrist in soothing strokes. "As I told you before, you are no longer an underling. And if there is something you want, *please* have the spine and dignity to ask me."

She inclined her head in what she hoped was a regal manner. "I will."

But he wasn't finished. Gavin grasped her shoulders, holding her gaze. "However, even with your newly elevated status, if you deceive me again, I will have no choice but to punish you. And by God, I do not want to, but it would be my duty as Lord."

Closing her eyes, she nodded, remembering the vampire he'd imprisoned and only released early as a wedding gift to her. "I understand."

When she opened her eyes, his shoulders relaxed as if eased by a heavy burden. "Now that we have that settled, let us move onto other matters. I am home for the remainder of the night and I will also be here for tomorrow's ball, naturally."

"Heavens!" Lenore's hand flew up to her mouth. "I'd forgotten all about the ball."

Gavin laughed. "You do not seem to have forgotten anything. The ballroom is decorated, the meal is well planned, the flowers were delivered and all the guests have been invited and seated accordingly for the supper. I am proud of your hard work."

Her belly turned over at the compliment. "Thank you, but much of the preparations were Elena's doing."

"Do not presume to think I cannot detect which details you had your hand in." He smiled. "Oh, you did forget one thing, though."

Her stomach plummeted. "What?" And was it something she could rectify in time?

"Your ball gown."

Lenore sighed in abject relief. "I didn't forget. I'm wearing the one that you ordered for me."

Gavin shook his head, a playful smile curving his lips. "That is not good enough for your first ball. The other half of your wardrobe has been delivered this evening, including your gown for tomorrow."

He led her upstairs into her bedchamber and threw open her wardrobe with a flourish.

Lenore's eyes widened at the shimmering violet gown with a lace overskirt woven with gold thread, and a matching appliqué on the sleeves and bodice. With shaking hands, she lifted it from its hanger and held it to her chest.

"It looks like something a princess would wear," she breathed. Not wanting to risk damaging the tissue thin garment, she hung the gown back up.

"I am happy you are pleased," Gavin chuckled. "Hopefully your other garments will not pale in comparison."

Unable to resist, Lenore peered further into the wardrobe to see what else had arrived. Her gaze lit upon a dark green velvet riding habit. Her fingers trailed across the black trim. "It is so exquisite," she murmured. "It's a shame I do not know how to ride."

"Another oversight on my part," Gavin said. "I will teach you, starting tonight."

"Tonight?" she tore her attention from the riding habit. "But it's only a few hours before dawn."

"Plenty of time for the first step," he said cheerfully. "Tell me, have you ever been on a horse?"

"Only once, and I remember none of it." She shivered at the memory. "When you first found me on your land. I'd fainted before you took me up on your horse and brought me here."

Gavin chuckled. "Well, let's go for a quick ride on Edgar while we hunt."

"Edgar?" She couldn't help giggling. "What an odd name for a horse!"

He shrugged. "He looked like an Edgar."

Lenore remembered the massive black stallion towering over her. Honestly, "Nightmare" or "Grim Reaper" sounded more apt.

She quickly changed into the riding habit, turning a full circle in the mirror to enjoy the effect. It was a shame she could no longer go out in the daylight. The sun would reflect so prettily on the material.

Even with Gavin's assistance, mounting the horse was intimidating, despite knowing that if she fell, her preternatural body would heal any injuries. It was just that Edgar was so enormous, putting her high off the ground. When Edgar began walking in a slow gait that made the ground dip below her, Lenore clung to the pommel of the saddle with enough force to make the leather groan.

"Careful," Gavin's voice rumbled in her ear. "Remember your strength, and don't break my saddle."

Lenore took a deep breath and focused on the warmth of his chest against her back, the secure circle his arms formed around her as he held the reins. Awareness of Gavin's closeness replaced her trepidation. Though the saddle was large, she all but sat on his lap. She felt him grow harder against her backside, and the rocking motion of the horse's gait made her core ache with need.

Her low moan turned into a gasp as Edgar broke into a trot. Gavin's arms tightened around her. "Easy. He can sense your nervousness and that makes him anxious. Relax, and feel how I am guiding him."

Taking a deep breath, Lenore concentrated on following his advice. Her tension eased as she focused on the trail they took through the fields, and then down a cobblestone street to a nearby pub. Gavin helped her down, and she walked on shaky legs until the sound of crashing blows and painful grunts erupted behind the building.

Lenore didn't wait for Gavin to finish tying up Edgar before charging into the shadows. Two men punched and kicked a huddled form on the ground. The jingle of coins with every blow left little doubt as to what motivated the attack.

Quick as a cat, Lenore seized the man who'd lifted his foot for another kick and slammed him against the wall. Behind her she heard a yelp of surprise and smiled. Gavin had seized the other.

As her captive struggled against her iron grip, Lenore reveled in her preternatural strength. "Now you will learn what it is like to be victimized by someone stronger," she whispered before capturing him with her gaze and plunging her fangs in his throat.

She drank more than her usual amount, ensuring he'd be weak and dizzy for the next few days. By the time she released the man, Gavin had helped the one who'd been attacked off of the ground and cleared his memory. The other attacker lay slumped next to a pile of rubbish.

After giving the poor chap a guinea and walking him home, Lenore felt exultant... powerful.

Gavin grinned at her and pressed his lips to her temple. "Now *that* is the strong woman I married."

Though her primary motivations had been saving that poor man, his praise made a tremor of pleasure run through her body, which only intensified as he lifted her onto Edgar's back.

"Would you be willing to chance a gallop?" he asked, voice rife with exuberance.

She nodded. After defeating that massive bloke, riding on horseback was far less intimidating.

In fact, as the landscape raced beneath her and the wind whipped her cheeks, she decided that riding was exhilarating. When would be a good time to ask Gavin to buy her a horse?

Twenty-four

When they returned home, Gavin helped her dismount and led Edgar to the stables, where he showed her how to rub him down. After they left the horse comfortably munching on oats, he ordered a hot bath for her.

Lenore couldn't fight a smile as she sank into the blissfully hot water. Not only had Gavin granted her the permission to continue her work, but they'd talked more this night than they had since before they were married. And that horse ride, combined with rescuing someone in danger made her feel more confident and stronger than when Gavin declared that she wasn't weak.

After finishing her bath and dressing in a silken night dress that looked far too provocative for sleeping, a measure of her joy bled into nervous anticipation. Would she and Gavin share a bed tonight? She missed his presence with such intensity that it was like a physical ache.

Just as she was considering the shamefully immoral idea of feigning a nightmare, Gavin knocked on her door before entering.

Running a hand through his hair, he suddenly looked boyish and nervous. "Would you ah, prefer my company this day?"

Her nipples hardened for some inexplicable reason and she covered her breasts with her robe. "Yes," she whispered, hoping she didn't sound too eager.

They slipped into her bed together and extinguished all of the lights except for one small lantern on the table beside her bed.

For a while, an awkward silence stretched between them before he spoke. "Remember when you said that talking about your troubles helped you feel better?"

"Yes," she replied cautiously. *Did he mean—*

"Why not talk to me?" He leaned up on his elbow and regarded her intently.

Nervousness snaked in her belly. "Because you're my husband."

"What do you mean?" he prodded with a soft tone.

"I mean, it took a long time not to feel… dirty after what those rogues did to me… I still feel used... and like a part of me is missing." She shuddered at the memory. "I don't want you to see me that way." Before he could respond she gathered her courage and pressed forward. "When you first found me, you didn't press me on the details of why I was starved and weak. You have no notion of how grateful I was for that. And when the horrid truth of what happened was revealed in front of all the vampires of London, I was most humiliated because you were there too. I don't know why. Maybe because you were the first vampire since Blanche to treat me with kindness."

"I'd hardly call my capturing and interrogating you kind," he said drily. "Furthermore, I did not see you as dirty or used when I first learned what those vermin had done to you, and I do not see you that way now." His knuckles brushed her cheek. "You are not less for what you endured, you are more. You are not a victim, you are a survivor."

Tears filled her eyes at his kind words. Could she come to believe them? "I wish surviving didn't hurt so much."

His fingers cradled her face. "Me too. And I will do all I can to ease your hurts." Gavin's voice was soft with compassion she never would have suspected he'd possess. "You'd said that you feel as if a part of you is missing. Perhaps you can find it."

A surge of hope rose up in her heart at his words. "What do you mean?"

To her astonishment, Gavin appeared shy as he spoke. "Since you told me that you do not wish to engage in the physical side of marriage, I am led to believe that those rogues took away your pleasure in lovemaking... or your contentment in chastity, whichever you'd enjoyed before you were captured."

Cheeks heating again, Lenore nodded. "Yes." He was right. Not for the first time did she wonder what it could have been like if she'd never been assaulted. If this could have been a normal marriage.

Gavin continued in a slow, cautious tone as if expecting her to bolt from the bed. "Well, you *can* get that back. They are all dead, remember that. They do not have control over your body or how you feel anymore."

Lenore closed her eyes, hiding from his scrutiny for a moment. "I do not know which I would have wanted in the first place. Aside from what you had me do to myself the other night, I've never experienced the pleasure you speak of, but I also do not know whether or not I am or would have been happy remaining chaste either."

"Were you a virgin before... ah..."

She opened her eyes to see him blushing. "No." She took a ragged breath and explained. "There was a boy I walked out with when I was fifteen. One night we got drunk on a jug of his father's ale and he said he would marry me, so I let him." She chuckled lightly at how foolish she'd been. "I honestly cannot remember a thing about it. Except for two terrifying weeks of worrying that he'd gotten me with child, and a few months of heartbreak when he'd married a butcher's daughter instead."

"If you would like to know what true pleasure feels like, I would be honored to show you. But," he added quickly, "it doesn't have to be me. I will honor the original terms of our arrangement if you choose."

Heavens, she mused. He now appeared more nervous than she had been when she decided to become his wife.

As if taking her silence as a rejection, he continued almost apologetically. "And if you choose to remain chaste, I will ensure that no man touches you for the rest of your days, even after our arrangement has ended. I'll—"

She placed her finger over his lips, gathering the courage to talk about what had been on her mind for some time. "I don't think I want to be chaste. And I don't think I want another man to show me pleasure. After all, I love your kisses, and how I feel when you hold me in your arms." Saying those words aloud lifted a heavy weight from her heart. "I enjoyed touching you, that other night. I also enjoyed touching myself." The admission came with no shame. "Now I want *you* to touch me."

Gavin's eyes widened. Desire and uncertainty radiated from their black depths. "Are you certain?"

"Yes." To prove her words, she took his hand and placed it on her breast.

"God, Lenore..." His harsh intake of breath made her tremble with anticipation.

It was her turn to gasp as his fingers gently caressed her through the thin fabric of her night dress. Her nipples hardened once more, but the sensation wasn't unpleasant. A tingling heat coursed through her veins in a direct path from her breasts to the aching place between her thighs.

Then Gavin leaned forward and kissed her. Whisper soft at first, the light touch of his lips made her tingle all over, a surge of longing, begging for more. She reached out and grasped his shoulder, pulling him closer. He obliged her, deepening the kiss. Heady bliss swirled around her, and when she thought the exquisite feeling had peaked, his tongue delved into her mouth, sending an arc of electric pleasure down her spine.

A low moan escaped her throat as his fingers tangled in her hair, and his other hand wrought magic on her body, caressing and exploring as if she were a priceless treasure.

When he broke the kiss, Lenore whimpered, bereft, until his lips found the hollow of her neck. The whimper turned into a gasp as a new awareness flooded her being. She trembled as he kissed and nibbled her sensitive flesh. Every time his fangs grazed her skin, she jolted with awareness.

Then he moved lower, looking up at her with a question in his gaze.

"Yes," she breathed.

Gavin lowered his head, his mouth closing on her breast through the nightgown. Lenore moaned at the intensity of what he was doing. His fingers tugged lightly at her bodice until one of her breasts was revealed.

"Absolute perfection," he murmured before flicking his tongue across her nipple. His other hand stroked her left breast as if not wanting to neglect any part of her.

Lenore writhed beneath his attentions, marveling that anything could feel so good. When he suckled her nipples, bolts of sensation shot straight to her core, making it throb and ache with need. Unbelievably, he moved even lower, kissing her ribcage, her belly, her hips.

His hands slid up her thighs, caressing her flesh with slow, soft strokes. "Your body is so beautiful. Let me kiss the pain away." Gavin's voice was husky and pleading.

Lenore looked down at him in wonder. Did he know how much his ministrations had made her ache? Or was he referring to how she'd been hurt in that place before? It didn't matter. Need consumed her, and she reached down to run her fingers through his curls.

"Yes, she gasped raggedly.

Hunger flashed in his eyes as he hiked her skirts up, kissing her hips as his hands gripped her thighs and gently eased them apart.

Lenore stiffened a moment as bad memories threatened to intrude, but when his lips pressed almost reverently to her mons, her inner demons fled away and her entire awareness encompassed him. He kissed her again, making liquid heat flood her core.

For a brief moment, she worried that he'd find her wetness unseemly. But then his tongue flicked across her damp flesh and she lost all coherent thoughts. Electric jolts of ecstasy ignited the sensitive bud between her thighs, rippling surges of pleasure that built and built until her whole body shuddered.

Gavin was merciless, gripping her thighs so she couldn't wiggle away from his ministrations. Instead of fighting against the restraint, she knew he'd release her if she asked him to. The realization of that trust made her tangle her hands in his hair, pulling him closer.

The moment she surrendered, the orgasm rushed through her, more powerful than what she'd wrought by hand.

"Please, please," someone cried out, and she realized it was her. Incandescent sparks flashed before her eyes as her climax reached a new plateau.

By the time Gavin lifted his head, Lenore was limp and quivering.

A ragged gasp escaped her lips. "Gavin, please, take me…"

Licking his lips, he shook his head. "I think we'd be best to be cautious and progress slowly. I don't want to do anything to risk destroying your pleasure."

He scooted back up next to her on the bed and Lenore's eyes widened as she glimpsed his large erection. "But what about you?"

"My discomfort is well worth what you allowed me to do." He licked his lips and regarded her with a smile that made her quiver anew. "Though if it would please you to touch me as you did the other night…"

With a wicked smile rife with new knowledge, she reached for him. "I would be delighted."

Twenty-five

Gavin stood next to Lenore to greet their guests as they filed into the manor for the ball after the Chatterton's butler announced them. Gavin's butler, Finch, had at first been peeved at the duty going to someone else, but the old man's voice was far too faint and raspy. Gavin had eased his pride by reminding him that it was his responsibility to oversee all of these temporary servants.

Now he caught constant glimpses of Finch trailing after myriad footmen with an eagle eye and thumping his cane if someone incurred his disapproval. Lenore also watched the stooped butler from the corner of her eye and hid a smile with her fan.

Lenore looked so exquisite that Gavin's breath fled his body every time he looked upon her. Too bad he would only be able to enjoy one dance with her without causing undue talk. While they'd been able to dance to their heart's content during their engagement, it was considered unseemly for a married couple to dance together. Gavin cursed Society's ludicrous customs.

Still, he couldn't hold back his pride with Lenore at how superbly she'd arranged this ball. His house was immaculate and redecorated with so many different touches that it looked like a new place. Hundreds of candles lit the place as bright as day. The ballroom floor had been polished to a mirror finish and the borrowed kitchen staff had prepared a feast that tempted even him. All the while, every guest that entered looked at her with surprise as if they hadn't expected her to carry it off.

Gavin glanced at Lenore again, and once more memories flooded his mind of the night they'd shared. The way she'd tasted, the way she'd trembled beneath him... the way she'd trusted him.

Christ, he couldn't wait for all of these infernal people to leave so he could take his wife to bed. Perhaps tonight, he could finally make her his. A wave of primal lust rushed flared through him with such force it took all of his will to control his body and maintain decorum.

When at last he was able to take her into his arms for the waltz, Gavin couldn't stop smiling and devouring her with his eyes. "You have done splendidly, my dear. Though I confess, I do wish you wouldn't have ordered eight hour candles."

"I know," she said with matching regret in her eyes. "But Elena insisted that it was expected. She wanted this to be the greatest crush of the year."

"It may as well be," he replied. "For it will not be a habit, I can assure you." He cast an irritated look at the dancers beside them, who'd almost brushed against them. "And soon we'll be alone."

"Yes," she breathed, her eyes glowing with anticipation before melting further into his grip.

They enjoyed the remainder of their dance in silence, savoring their contact and the swaying of their bodies to the music, knowing that they would enjoy a deeper, more intimate dance later.

Still, when the notes of the music faded, parting from her was the hardest thing he'd done.

His next partner was Lady Chatterton. Gavin fought back a groan. "Lord Darkwood," she said with false cheer that belied the malice in her eyes. She still hadn't gotten over the fact that he hadn't wed her daughter. If she knew what he was, doubtless she would be thanking him. "Your home looks even lovelier than the last time I was here."

"You flatter me." He fought back a laugh.

The last time she was here was three months ago, when she'd been out walking with her daughter and they'd decided to pay a "neighborly" call. Though Finch had informed them that Gavin was abed, they'd insisted on waiting. Apparently, they'd remained for nearly two hours before giving up.

"…been feeling veritably snubbed," Lady Chatterton was saying. "Do tell Lady Darkwood that we have missed her and do look forward to her calling upon us."

"I will," Gavin said, wishing to be anywhere but in this simpering viper's presence. "I know she's been so busy continuing the charitable work she and Dr. Elliotson had begun in London."

"Oh, is *that* what they've been up to?" Lady Chatterton fluttered her lashes with exaggerated innocence. "I confess, from the talk I've heard, I thought they were doing something far more sinister. In fact, I'd begun to fear for your young bride's life."

"What do you mean?" Gavin's hands tightened on Lady Chatterton's fingers until she drew a pained breath. With a murmur of apology, he relaxed his grip. "What talk?"

The matron tittered. "Apparently some of the farmers and shop workers have said that Dr. Elliotson is a witch."

Gavin snorted in derision, though the implication of anything preternatural where Lenore was concerned filled him with unease. "Rot and nonsense. Didn't people dispense with witch hunts nearly two centuries ago?"

"Yes, but you know commoners. They can be so superstitious." Lady Chatterton laughed with him, though her mirth had a covert tinge, as if she were laughing at something else. "Some of them are even saying he's a vampire."

The floor seemed to dip beneath Gavin's feet. "I beg your pardon?"

"I'm afraid so. The poor dear man," she leaned forward and lowered her voice in a conspiratorial whisper. "In fact, the villagers have been stirred into such a frenzy that one of them dumped a bottle of holy water over Elliotson's head this afternoon. I heard it from my maid who had it from the cook who saw the whole thing when she was at market." Lady Chatterton feigned a melodramatic sigh. "That's why the good doctor did not make to the ball tonight. I would imagine he is too embarrassed. I must say that I am a trifle abashed myself. How backward we must seem to him."

"Quite," Gavin said through clenched teeth. When the music faded away, Gavin bowed to the gossipy matron before escorting her back to her husband, who was too infirm to dance. "If you will excuse me, I must inform Lady Darkwood of the reason for her friend's absence."

Panic and dread filled him as his gaze darted through the crowd, looking for Lenore. He now knew the reasoning for those occult pamphlets and stories being circulated around. Though the target seemed to be Elliotson, he was no less unnerved. How long would it be before people started to take note that Lenore was never seen during the day?

Among the upper classes, such habits went unnoticed, as many danced and drank until dawn, but the farmers and merchants were a different kettle of fish.

He finally spotted Lenore dancing with Lord Creely. Her nose was pinched in testament to the man's notorious odor. Gavin almost charged forward to pull her from the dance floor, but stopped with an inward curse. If he hauled her away in front of everyone, he'd only incite more gossip.

Taking a glass of champagne from a passing footman, he watched her switch to her next partner in the quadrille. Her flushed cheeks and brilliant smile as she noticed him watching her made his heart twist.

Last night she'd been so happy when he told her that she could continue her work. Now he'd have to break her heart and go back on his word.

But he had no choice. There was no way he could allow Lenore to endanger herself by continuing her association with Elliotson and his mesmerism. And even if he could ensure her safety and rid his territory of all suspicion, it was too late. The gossip she'd unwittingly incurred could endanger his position as Lord of this territory.

She would be furious and accuse him of betraying her, he knew it. Gavin sighed and decided to hold off talking with her until the ball was over. Best to avoid a scene. Or perhaps he just wanted to see her happy for a little while longer.

Rather than making the remainder of the evening drag, his decision seemed to accelerate the clock. In what felt like mere minutes, the guests said their farewells and drifted away.

When the last person departed, Lenore turned to him, eyes glittering with palpable cheer. "I cannot believe I carried this off. Are you proud of me, lord husband?"

Husband... Gavin's gut twisted in agony. It was the first time she'd called him that in an affectionate manner. And now it would be the last.

"Yes, I am proud of you." His voice cracked.

She looked up at him, her eyes widening with concern. "Are you all right?"

"No," he said tightly. "Come upstairs with me. There is something I must speak to you about."

As he followed her up the stairs, his chest grew heavier with each worried glance she darted his way. By the time they entered his bedchamber, where only hours ago, he'd anticipated making love to her all day long, Gavin couldn't breathe.

Lenore sat on the bed that Gavin now knew they wouldn't be sharing. She fidgeted with her skirts while he paced in front of her.

"What is it?" she demanded, dark eyes full of growing unease. "Are you unwell?"

Unable to stop pacing, he ran a hand through his hair. "There was a disturbing incident in the village today, involving your friend, Doctor Elliotson."

She bolted to her feet. "Good heavens! I'd been wondering why he did not come tonight. What happened? We must go to him at once."

"Sit down, please." He rubbed his arms in futile effort to warm a chill that emanated from within. "The doctor is fine, albeit undoubtedly embarrassed." Taking a deep breath, he explained. "One of the villagers doused him with holy water, accusing him of being a vampire."

Lenore gasped. "Oh my God. That poor man. I'm glad he wasn't hurt. But you're right, he must be humiliated. Tomorrow I'll have to—"

"You don't understand the severity of the situation," Gavin cut her off before she could speak more of what was now impossible. "Someone has been spreading pamphlets and stories about vampires for some time now. And tonight I'd discovered that rumors about Elliotson, and possibly you as well, have been circulating for some time."

"Oh…" she said numbly, her face growing pale.

"Therefore," he forced the words past the guilty bile which seemed to coat his throat. "I have no choice but to forbid you from seeing Elliotson or performing mesmerism on the village women."

Her jaw dropped, lower lip quivering. "But you told me last night that I could continue my work!"

"I know I did," he said quietly. "That was before I learned about the danger you're in. Not to mention the fact that such speculations not only place all of my people at risk, they endanger my position as Lord of this territory. If the Elders caught wind of this—"

"But I can stop the rumors!" She cried out in an agonizing plea. "I can—"

"Enough!" he snapped before his voice broke. The betrayal in her large eyes too much to bear, he looked away. "My decision is final. My first priority is ensuring our safety and seeking out the source of these suspicions. After all risk is eliminated, perhaps in a few years…"

He trailed off as Lenore rose from the bed, marched to her bedchamber, and slammed the door behind her.

Not even bothering to remove his clothes, Gavin fell back on his bed with a sigh. His cold, empty bed.

All of the trust he'd worked to build with Lenore was now shattered. The tentative bond they'd forged had snapped.

And he knew their relationship was only going to deteriorate further. Because he knew she'd find some way to disobey his orders.

A bitter laugh escaped his lips. He'd originally wanted her for his wife due to her loyalty, obedience, and being less inclined to cause a scandal. God, he'd been wrong on every count.

And yet, he didn't want her any other way.

***

Justus ground his teeth as he listened to the men in the pub laughing over the eccentric doctor being doused with holy water. The foolish mortals had cast their suspicions on the wrong man.

Meanwhile, the rich were dancing and gallivanting under the roof of a real vampire and they were to mutton-headed to realize it.

Oh yes, he'd heard plenty about the big celebration at "the big house," from what dishes were allegedly being served—of which neither Rochester nor his bride could partake much— to an item by item account of what all of the guests had been wearing.

Odd how things like that hadn't bothered him before, when he'd been Gavin's second and had attended many balls and musicales. He'd loved watching beautiful women alight from their carriages, their gowns making them resemble brilliantly colored birds from far off lands. He'd savored holding them close in a dance and the challenge of persuading a pretty young thing to allow him to lure her to a secluded area long enough for him to steal a kiss and a pint or two of blood.

Until he'd met Bethany. Until his world and heart had been turned upside down, and ultimately crushed. Until he'd lost her and everything else he'd ever known and loved.

And now that he was constantly on the run with no home and the only money he had was what he stole from the mortals he fed on— very little of whom were heavy in the pockets— hearing of the doings of the rich only served to disgust him. But he couldn't get close enough to the upper crust to steal from them, much less feed on them.

And due to his own diminished circumstances, he was unable to bring himself to take too much from the poor folk he fed on, blood or money. Which didn't seem to bother his compatriots, if their healthy color was any indicator.

Why did the poor carry so much fascination with the rich? Why did they love them when the wealthy didn't give a fig about them, except to make their fortunes on their backs?

Justus shook his head and turned his attention back to the conversations as he sipped his ale.

"It is a good thing they didn't try such a thing on Lady Darkwood," Rolfe said. "His Lordship would have skinned their hides!"

Justus caught his eye and gave him a slight nod. This was what they were here for. To spread the seeds of suspicion, but to do it so subtly the people would think they came up with the notions on their own.

"Her Ladyship is no vampire!" a tavern wench yelled shrilly. "She is the kindest, gentlest soul I've ever met. She's helped so many women in this village when the other noblewomen don't pay us any notice!"

Oh good Lord. Justus rolled his eyes. Just because vampires were monsters, that didn't make them bad people.

"Aye," another man said. "She helped my wife overcome her grief from losing our firstborn. Now we're going to try again."

"I heard she might be with child 'erself," someone else said with a salacious laugh. "And that's why His Lordship wed her in such a hurry."

No she's not! He wanted to shout. *He only wanted to spirit her away before you lackwits noticed her particular aversion to daylight.*

"Well, the good doctor helped people too," an old man said. "And today's foolishness proved that he's not some mythical blood drinking monster either, so let's drop the matter and focus on more sensible subjects, like Saturday's cricket match."

Most of the men nodded, but a few were too deep in their cups to countenance a diversion.

"Maybe the doctor's a witch!" a nearly toothless man suggested.

"I thought vampires couldn't venture out during the day," Rolfe said.

Justus resisted the urge to nod in agreement and instead shook his head in silent command. They didn't want to draw too much attention to themselves. Strangers in the village were always met with suspicion. Let it remain on the doctor.

"They can't," a voice said with such cold surety that the hairs on Justus's neck stood on end.

Slowly he turned his head to see who had spoken, and frowned at a large, muscled man with the most pitiless gray eyes he'd ever beheld.

Another stranger in the village.

Twenty-six

Lenore fought the urge to glance over her shoulder for the fifth time as she headed up the path to Dr. Elliotson's rented cottage. She just couldn't abandon her friend. She had to say goodbye.

Taking a deep breath, she fought to keep the memories of last night from rendering her into a helpless mass of grief. She'd spent her entire day rest curled into a ball of impotent fury and grief as it was, only drifting in and out of a troubled sleep.

Last night had been so perfect, her first ball she'd hosted as Lady Darkwood, her dance with her husband, basking under his adoring gaze, full of promise. She'd veritably quivered with anticipation for him to make her his wife in truth. A perfect culmination for the gift he'd bestowed upon her before, showing her how much pleasure they could give each other.

Then the guests had left, she'd walked to him demurely, when all she'd longed to do was throw her arms around him and pull his head down for another of his spellbinding kisses. Everything had been perfect. She had her work to fulfill her soul and a man to heal her heart and body.

Then everything had been ripped asunder. Instead of giving her all of the joy and comfort he'd promised, Gavin took away everything that brought her happiness. The betrayal speared her like a blade through her heart. For a moment she'd even wondered if his previous permission to continue her work had been a lie to seduce her, just like that nearly forgotten boy had lied about marriage to get under her skirts. She'd quickly rejected such pettiness. For one thing, Ruthless Rochester was too powerful and handsome to resort to such tricks to bed a woman, and for another, the dangers he'd presented were all too real.

But that did not mean she could forgive him. Especially with his refusal to give her a chance to say goodbye to her friends and patients.

She'd spent her day rest huddled on her bed in grief and anger. And after night had fallen, and Gavin rapped on her door to offer to take her to hunt, she'd told him to go away, still unable to bear looking at him.

"Very well," he'd said. "But you do need to eat. I need to look in on my people, and when I return, if you refuse to come out, I'll break down the door. And don't think of running off while I'm gone. I have guards surrounding the manor."

The cold, commanding tone heated her blood with anger. How dare he speak to her like she was a child? And since her captivity and escape from Clayton's rogues, she'd become adept at evading other vampires.

After his footsteps faded, she rolled out of bed and donned a gown, boots and cloak. Then she crossed the room and lifted the edge of a tapestry that concealed a boarded up window. Using her preternatural strength, she worked the board loose and quietly eased the window open, cringing as it creaked in protest.

She paused and listened. No one came to investigate the noise, and she was free.

Lenore *would* obey Gavin's orders, but only after she said goodbye. After all, she reasoned as she made her way up the steps to

Elliotson's cottage, she didn't want the doctor to be in danger if he came to the manor to inquire about her absence.

With a heavy heart, she rapped on his door, her thoughts in a jumbled vortex as she struggled to decide what to say.

Elliotson opened the door, his eyes widening in shock to see her. "Lady Darkwood. What a pleasant surprise!" Yet there was a wary look in his eyes that belied his words.

"May I come in?" Lenore said quickly. "I must speak to you."

"Yes, of course." He opened the door wider and ushered her inside. "I'll put the kettle on for some tea."

She shook her head, drowning in sadness. "I'm sorry, I have no time for that."

He raised a brow. "That urgent, eh?"

"I'm afraid so." Grief radiated from her in waves.

"Very well, let us have a seat anyway." He led her into a small sitting room overflowing with piles of books, parchment and dirty tea cups. "I apologize for this abysmal mess. I've been too consumed with my research. I lost one of my journals and have been turning the place upside down to find it."

"That is quite all right," she said impatiently. Her nerves jangled with fearful urgency. If Gavin or one of his vampires saw her here... she couldn't finish the thought.

Elliotson cleared a stack of books from a chair and she sat, her legs shaky. "Are you certain you don't wish for a cup of tea? You look pale."

She shook her head.

He sat across from her on a sofa next to a jumble of papers. "What is it that you wanted to speak to me about?"

"My husband disapproves of my work." Her words came out flat as tears burned her eyes. It wasn't exactly a lie. "So he has commanded me not to see you again."

Was it a trick of the light, or did he look happy? Or perhaps he was only relieved that she did not bring up yesterday's incident in the village? "I am sorry to hear that. You were the finest student I've ever had. Though I suppose this was to be expected. No man would be elated to hear that his wife was associating so closely with another man, much less mingling with those below her station." His brows lowered in censure. "Have you disobeyed him now by coming here?"

She nodded, concealing a frown. What had happened to his pressing her to use her station to help? "I had to say goodbye."

He made an odd harrumphing sound, whether in understanding or disapproval, she could not tell. "While I appreciate your kind heart, I do not want to be subject to Lord Darkwood's wrath." He rose from his seat. "Come, I'll let you out back so you are not seen."

"Tell our patients that I wish them well and that I will miss them," she spoke through the lump in her throat as she rose to follow him.

"I will." He patted her shoulder. "I am quite sure they'll be just fine. I'll see to their treatments, don't you worry." Again, that suspicious look of happiness flickered in his gaze. "Or at least I shall until I depart."

Her steps halted. "Oh, you're leaving?"

"Yes. The people here are too backward and superstitious to accept the full scope of my treatments." The way his expression darkened made Lenore certain that he was referring to his abrupt baptism. "Not to mention the fact that I've neglected my responsibilities in London for far too long. I only have a few more experiments to conduct before I'm off for home. Now come along, you must leave before your husband finds you missing." He grabbed her elbow and quickly marched her out the rear door.

"Goodbye, John," she addressed him by his Christian name for the first time, and the last. "You were the best friend I've ever had and I'll never forget everything you've done for me."

"Yes, yes," he replied in a clipped voice as he led her out the back door. "It has been a delight to know you as well, my dear."

"Thank you," she began, but he'd already closed the door.

His abruptness and seeming lack of concern for the fact that they would never see each other again stung. The tears that had burned her eyes fell freely now, chilling her face in the cool night air. Once more she remembered the gleeful twinkle in his eyes... and then his petulant frown when the village women chose to have Lenore treat them instead.

He'd been jealous. Why hadn't she seen that before? He'd also been peeved when she'd expressed reluctance for some of his more outrageous experiments. And with her out of the way, he'd have free reign to indulge in them. No wonder he'd seemed pleased with her departure. And to think she'd thought him to be a close friend.

At least the women would miss her when she was gone, she sniffled as she walked down the road to her next destination. It broke her heart that she wouldn't be able to tell all of them goodbye. However, she resolved to tell Alice and Mrs. Hanson, the two largest gossips in the county. And she had more than one reason for those choices.

Avoiding the market and village square, which Gavin's vampires were doubtless guarding like hawks, Lenore instead went to the Woodward farm, where she found Alice closing her barn door for the night.

"My lady!" her new friend shouted, picking up her skirts and running to her.

This was no cold greeting, Lenore thought with a tremulous smile as Alice embraced her. This time her words of farewell were difficult as she choked them out. The farmer's wife nodded in sympathetic understanding.

"Rubbing elbows with our sort never was proper," Alice said firmly, patting Lenore's hand. "It was only a matter of time before your husband decided that. You have a household to run and heirs to birth."

They exchanged a tearful farewell before Lenore performed the most difficult part of this visit. Grasping Alice's shoulders, she captured her gaze. Then, with guilt choking her, Lenore sank her fangs into the woman's throat and opened her mind to Alice's memories. After only three swallows, she withdrew and healed her friend's wound with her blood. Still holding Alice entranced, she filled her mind with images of seeing Lenore when she went to market, and of walking beside her to the meetings before dusk fell.

Releasing Alice's mind, she fought back tears once more as she embraced her friend one last time and headed off to bid Mrs. Hanson goodbye... and to fill her mind with false memories.

As much as she hated toying with their minds like that, Gavin was right about the risks of the speculations that had been circulating about her and Elliotson. Hopefully her efforts would help mitigate the danger. After all, though vampires were just as immune to holy water as humans, they were not immune to sunlight. She'd be certain to convince Mrs. Hanson that she glimpsed Gavin in the daylight as well.

Once her heartbreaking mission was complete, Lenore hurried back to Darkwood Manor, evading detection from the vampires guarding the place. She made her way back up the tree as quietly as possible and back to her bedchamber, replacing the board over the window and covering it with the tapestry.

Quickly, she changed her clothes and lay back on her bed. It seemed she'd gotten away with her deception after all, since her door remained intact.

Moments after she closed her eyes, she heard footsteps coming up the stairs, down the hall, and finally to her door.

"Are you quite finished starving yourself?" Gavin's voice rang with contempt.

For a moment Lenore was tempted to say no and remain in her room, but then she realized that if she hadn't gone out and fed already, she would have been famished. There was no need to draw suspicion.

"Yes," she called back sullenly. "Allow me to dress and I shall be down."

When she opened her door, she saw that he hadn't moved from his post in the hall. He stood rigid and stern, with his arms crossed, yet there was an odd glimmer of some indiscernible emotion to his gaze. Was it remorse?

He didn't say a word as he offered his arm. Lenore took it and couldn't fight a flare of heat at his touch. A lump formed in her throat. Why did they have to be at odds with each other? Why couldn't all the painful tragedy of last night never have happened?

Once they were outside, Gavin cleared his throat. "I apologize for being so harsh last eve. If you want to bid your doctor friend farewell, I'll take you tomorrow night."

He gave her a long, penetrating look as something like guilt crawled over her like an army of ants. Lowering her head to hide her gaze, she nodded. "Th-thank you."

Again silence enveloped them, thick and choking before he inclined his head. "We must find our meals quickly and then go to the castle ruins. I've arranged a Gathering to tell our people about this new danger."

Our people. The words simultaneously filled her with longing and remorse. They were her people now… and how much of this danger had been her doing? Would Gavin tell them about her deeds? Or did they already know? Would they hate her?

They found their meal quickly in a pair of pickpockets before Gavin took her hand, once more imbuing her with unfulfilled need. Then they ran. As the world dissolved into a blur when they covered the miles in ground devouring speed, Lenore's heart lightened for a precious moment. No matter how badly he'd hurt her, she'd always be grateful to him for showing her what she could do with her meager power.

Too soon they arrived at the castle, its crumbled walls and parapets standing like a sentinel under the moonlight.

Heart in her throat, she allowed herself to take comfort in the strength of Gavin's grip as he led her through the concealed tunnel and down to the gathering area deep within the bowels of the castle.

Oh how she hated these Gatherings, being surrounded by dozens of more powerful vampires, enduring their looks of scorn as they smelled her weakness.

This time, something was different. The Rochester vampires all bowed slightly to her after acknowledging their lord. This time, as the Lord Vampire's wife, she garnered respect.

Yet she did not deserve it.

"People of Rochester," Gavin's voice boomed with authority. "I've gathered you here tonight to inform you of a new danger in our midst. Someone has been spreading vampire literature throughout the village."

Countless mutters of startled surprise reverberated from the chamber.

Gavin surveyed his people, his face grave. "The superstitions appear to have returned, as Doctor Elliotson, my lady wife's mortal friend, was doused with holy water yesterday afternoon."

Their collective gasp made Lenore's chest tighten.

"Thankfully whoever did it is clearly ignorant of what will hurt our kind, but that does not make the incident any less grave. Cecil, Benson, and I have been trying to discern the source of sudden influx of fear mongering. My lady wife has also been doing her part, in searching the minds of the village women while she performed her mesmerism with the doctor."

Lenore sucked in a breath as the vampires' eyes widened and they nodded in comprehension. Fighting to keep her face stoic, she wondered why Gavin had told them such a lie to justify her actions. Was it to keep them from censuring her? Or to prevent embarrassment to himself?

Of course, if any of her patients had suspected anything pertaining to the supernatural she *would* have erased it from their minds and she *would* have told Gavin. The reasoning gave her some comfort and justification to the ruse.

"Given our investigations," Gavin continued. "The only thing that seems to have any relation to this influx of hysteria is the infiltration of rogues in our lands. The vampire propaganda appeared shortly after they did."

As the audience gasped and muttered, Lenore also started in shock. In the midst of her preoccupation with her work and growing captivation with her husband, she'd nearly forgotten all about the rogues. A ball of ice formed in her belly. Biting back a whimper, she focused on Gavin's words. Could they have truly been responsible for spreading rumors about vampires?

Gavin paced back and forth before his people, his brows knitted together in contemplative consternation. "Though I confess, I do not know what motives they would have for bringing such danger to us, as it would pose greater risks to themselves, but there is no other explanation." His eyes glowed with wicked fury as he bared his fangs in a deadly smile. "Perhaps they'll explain themselves when we round them up and interrogate them." He glanced over at Cecil with a smirk. "That is, if Cecil is able to have some restraint and not slay them on the spot like the last one."

Lenore glanced at Cecil in astonishment. He'd killed a rogue? Gavin *had* truly been busy when he'd left her alone all those nights. Fresh guilt gnawed at her as she remembered accusing him of neglect, along with a tinge of relief that at least one rogue was dead.

"Speaking of, you will be pleased to know that Benson has recovered from being attacked, though I've still ordered him to rest for another night or two," Gavin told them all. "So I know he would greatly appreciate visitors to ease his boredom."

Oh God, Lenore's stomach clenched. Gavin's second had been attacked? Why hadn't he told her? If she'd known the danger had escalated that far, she would have ceased her work in the village on her own.

Anger welled in her stomach at Gavin for leaving her ignorant.

Gavin's voice rang out in severe command. "In the light of these new dangers, not only do I reiterate my command to always hunt in pairs…"

Lenore's heart constricted, remembering all the times she'd gone alone. Why hadn't Gavin told her?

"But also do your best to subtly dissuade everyone you feed on that our kind is but a foolish myth." Gavin's expression softened into an amused smirk. "Eating garlic, crossing running water, carrying a bible, and other such nonsense should help as well. And I don't need to tell you to destroy any book or pamphlet you encounter."

The vampires chuckled a moment before Gavin held up a hand. "Before we disperse for the night, there is one more matter I must address. Lenore, come here."

Lenore flinched at the sudden coolness in his tone.

Lifting her skirts, she tentatively approached him. "Yes, my lord?"

"You have disobeyed me," he said coldly. This wasn't her husband's voice. This was his lord's voice. "Cecil saw you visiting the doctor without my leave."

He knew, she realized with little surprise. His talk of taking her to visit Elliotson had only been a test, to see if she'd come clean. How could she have been so foolish as to think her venture had been unnoticed? Gasps and whispers erupted around her, the scrutiny of the audience palpable as a swarm of insects.

Although she was humiliated at having her transgression made public, she couldn't hold Gavin at fault. With his third in command reporting the incident, he had no choice but to do this, or risk losing face. Though if he'd told her about the rogues in the first place, she wouldn't be in this position. However, she wouldn't dare argue with him in front of their people.

Lenore remembered his earlier command. *Do not grovel.* Instead, she raised her gaze to his, humble but not entreating. "I did, my lord. I am sorry."

Was it her imagination, or did some of the vampires nod in approval?

"I told you to stay away from Elliotson, but you did not listen to me." Gavin stalked around her like a lion cornering a gazelle. "You give me no choice but to punish you."

The memory of Myrtle's terrified eyes as Cecil and Benson dragged her off, her abject pleas for mercy, made shudders wrack her form so severely, she nearly collapsed on the platform.

Echoing the fearsome memory, Cecil and another vampire moved forward to seize her.

Gavin held up a hand, freezing them mid-step. "I will address this matter myself." He grasped Lenore's arm, though not ungently. "This gathering is now adjourned."

The Rochester vampires' eyes bored through her back as he led her out of the chamber.

Twenty-seven

Once they returned to Darkwood Manor, it took all of Lenore's will not to struggle and try to flee. The only thing that stopped her was the knowledge that Gavin would certainly catch her and increase her punishment.

"Sleep," Gavin commanded the servants, leaving them to shamble like automatons up to their quarters.

To her surprise, he did not haul her down to his dungeons. Instead, he led her up to their bedchamber.

Closing the door behind them, he locked the door with an ominous click and paced in front of her.

"What am I to do with you, Lenore?" His voice rang with frustration and regret. "I promised I would never hurt you the way Clayton and his rogues did, so that means I cannot shackle you, or lock you away. I cannot starve you. I could discipline you in the manner that many husbands do with their wives…"

She sucked in an outraged gasp.

"But I find the idea repugnant," he finished.

She relaxed slightly at the news that she wouldn't be beaten or imprisoned, but her trepidation remained as he stalked around her like a ravenous wolf.

Straightening her spine, she stared back at him. "If you'd told me what had occurred with your second, or even that the rogues were spreading vampire literature, I never would have gone to see Elliotson alone."

To her surprise, his shoulders slumped in defeat. "I should have told you. I only kept the information from you because I was afraid it would make your nightmares return." He sighed. "However, that still does not give you the right to disobey your lord, especially so flagrantly in front of a witness."

"What are you going to do?" she whispered past the thudding of her heart.

"First, you are not to leave this house without me for the next month," he told her, then shook his head before she could say a word. "But there must also be an immediate consequence, though as some of the fault is mine, it won't be too severe." His long fingers grasped her chin. "Do you know why vampires sometimes feed on each other?"

She shook her head. "I only fed from the rogue for the strength to escape."

"Strength." Gavin nodded. "That is precisely it. With permission, it is a great honor."

Again, the memory of him feeding her from his own vein, bestowing his power upon her flashed through her mind with aching clarity.

"Without permission, it is considered a demonstration of superiority." Gavin's voice grew husky and ominous. "I've heard tales of a vampire who only feeds on other vampires, draining their power, taking it for his own. I'm quite certain they're Banburry tales to frighten younglings like you into not straying from their masters, but that does not make the idea any less disconcerting."

He sat on the bed and patted the place on the mattress beside him. "Come here."

As Lenore met his gaze, she realized two things. Firstly, despite his firm voice and stern expression, there was a hollow grief in his eyes stating that he clearly didn't want to do this, for fear of hurting her, no matter his talk of this being less severe.

Secondly, she'd often imagined what it would be like to have his mouth on her neck, his fangs piercing her flesh. Perhaps it was a morbid desire. His words about the reasoning behind vampires feeding on each other gave credence to that question, but Lenore could not help desiring his bite all the same.

However, she could not reveal her happiness that what was to be a punishment was a reward in her eyes.

Yet she still wanted to assure him that this would not make her fear or loathe him.

Looking down at her feet to hide the myriad expressions playing across her face, she slowly approached the bed. She didn't have to fake the quaver in her voice. "I understand that I have done wrong and I will accept the consequences."

Squaring her shoulders, she lifted her chin and met his gaze.

The admiration in his black eyes made her belly flutter. "I am proud of your dignity and responsibility." His hand slid up her back, as if in a soothing caress, before his fingers grasped her shoulder, turning to face him. Gently, he brushed her loose strands of hair away from her exposed neck. His touch made goose bumps rise on her flesh. "Tilt your head." His voice came in a husky rasp and his eyes glowed with unholy hunger.

Rather than fear at the sight of his savage thirst, her belly quivered with warmth. Heart pounding, she obeyed.

"I will try to make it as quick and painless as possible," he whispered before his arm locked around her, pulling her close.

Contrary to his words, he did not strike immediately. Instead, his head dipped down and his warm breath grazed lightly across her skin, making her shiver, though not from cold. Then his silken lips pressed against her neck in a kiss that should have been chaste, yet was not.

Unbidden, her arms slipped around his powerful frame, drawing him closer. When his fangs pierced her flesh, she bit back a cry. Yes, there was pain, but there was also an electric jolt of wicked pleasure arcing a direct path from her throat to the tender place between her thighs.

The pleasure increased with the pulling pressure against her skin as he drank from her, ecstatic heat pulsing within her core with every swallow. Lenore clasped him tighter, unable to hold back her moans. As if they had a mind of their own, her hips undulated towards him, seeking relief from the ache he'd caused.

Just when a wave of dizziness made her grip on him weaken, Gavin withdrew his fangs and gently lowered her until her head rested against the pillows.

Nourished from her blood, weak as it was, it was still more potent than a human's, and Gavin blazed with life and power. His face glowed with vitality, his eyes glittered with untold power. He looked so beautiful that she momentarily lost the ability to breathe.

With a tentative hand, he lightly brushed her hair from her face, worry creasing his brow. "Did I hurt you too much?"

"No," she whispered, blinking as a fresh wave of dizziness made the room tilt.

Gavin's eyes narrowed. "Damn it, I knew I took too much. You tasted so good, it was hard to stop. I am sorry."

"No, it was my punishment. I deserved far worse. In fact," Shame coursed through her veins as she confessed the truth. "I enjoyed it."

He chucked her under the chin. "You should not have admitted that to me. All the same, I fear I must reduce your penance even further."

She couldn't hold back a half-smile. "What do you mean?"

He lay down beside her, gathered her in his arms and rolled until she lay atop him. "As I said, I took too much. Now I must give some back."

Instead of offering his wrist, Gavin brushed his long dark curls to the side, baring his neck. Lenore sucked in a breath as feral hunger engulfed her... along with a pang of desire.

Tentatively, she lowered her head and brushed her lips across his pulsing vein, taking forbidden satisfaction at his quick intake of breath. Gently, her fangs pierced his neck. His hips arched upward, his hardness pressing against her sensitive core.

When his potent blood flowed into her mouth, Lenore growled with uncontrollable bliss. Her hips rode him, seeking release from the ache between her thighs, her hunger feeding into lust as his power renewed her and awoke every inch of her body.

"Enough," he rasped, rolling them both until she was pinned and forced to withdraw.

A whimper tore from her at the sudden break from the source of such intoxicating nourishment. Unable to help herself, her tongue darted up and licked his wound.

"I should punish you for that as well," he chided, though eyes were heavy-lidded with satiation.

She closed her eyes, unable to muster remorse. "Yes, you probably should," she admitted.

Gavin sighed and released her, flopping on his back. "Why do you have to make this so difficult? I know I told you not to grovel, but that does not mean I want you to be so shameless either."

"I know." Her sigh echoed his. "But I could not pretend to dislike your feeding from me. I-I am done with pretending."

He leaned up on his elbow. "What do you mean?"

Maybe it was the mercy he'd shown tonight, or the fact that he was the one who'd helped her stop being ashamed, but the confession bubbled to the surface. "When I was imprisoned by Clayton's vampires, I ah, pretended to enjoy their attentions to lure them close enough to give me the opportunity to escape." She closed her eyes as humiliation burned her face. "And I hate myself for it."

"Why?" he asked quietly.

"Because it's disgusting and shameful." She continued to avoid meeting his eyes. "I invited him to touch me. I touched him back. And when my fangs sank into his neck, I *did* enjoy the taste."

"Lenore." His voice rang with abject command, and when he placed his hand on her shoulder, only then did she realize that she was shaking again. Only when she stilled did he continue. "There is no shame in any of that. You did what you had to do to survive and escape."

The utter confidence in his words made her turn her head to face him. "How can you be so sure?"

"Because I've had to do my own pretending." Self-revulsion and vulnerability slashed across his normally confident face.

"What do you mean?" she prodded carefully.

"When I was a boy training for the clergy, there was a priest who... well, had a taste for such boys." He closed his eyes, cringing with pain.

Lenore shuddered as she grasped the implication of his words. "My God, do you mean he—"

Gavin nodded. "Every night after the midnight prayers, he'd stop me on my way back to my room and take me to his chambers in the cloisters. He told me I should be honored by his attentions to be so chosen by one of God's ordained messengers... that it was a secret and I'd be cast out if I told anyone." He sucked in a ragged breath. "That he'd beat me if I did not let him touch me... or touch him back."

The painful horror of his words rendered her speechless. All Lenore could do was slip her hand into his and squeeze.

He took another breath and continued in a flat, detached voice that belied the agony in his gaze. "Eventually he was transferred to another parish, promoted to a bishop. He'd grown tired of me anyway as I'd become a man, but that didn't stop me from thanking Christ that he was gone. It also didn't stop me from tracking him down and showing him my fangs. Then I drained him dry after he pissed himself." Cold satisfaction blazed through his words. "That was back when we were permitted to kill mortals."

"Good," Lenore said harshly. Then the pain and horror of what he'd suffered clenched her heart like a fist. Slowly, she reached out and placed a comforting hand on his shoulder. "That was why you understood what I'd been through. You'd suffered even worse."

"I would not call it worse," Gavin said with a dismissive shrug. "More enduring, certainly, but it does not negate the savagery inflicted on you."

His understanding made a lump rise in her throat. "That is how you knew what my attackers had stolen from me even when I didn't." She couldn't withhold her awe. "How did you manage to..." she swallowed, searching for the right words... "To find pleasure after what happened to you?"

"The vampire who'd made me. She'd been a slave before she was Changed. She taught me how to take control over my body, to give myself pleasure and bestow it upon others." His lip curved up in another bitter smile. "Though I suppose it was easier for me, given that my sensual attention is inclined to females. And despite the fact that she only wanted me to be her slave, I remain grateful to her for that at least." His expression sobered. "To be honest, I wasn't certain

I'd be able to give you any pleasure. I was afraid I'd frighten or hurt you." He met her gaze and stroked her hair. "I still am," he said quietly.

Lenore's chest tightened at his profound regard for her feelings. "You've given me more pleasure than I could ever fathom. And I trust you to give me more." She closed her eyes shyly, before opening them again to face him. "That is, if you still want me."

"I think I've wanted you from the moment you first awoke in my bed." The blazing hunger in his onyx eyes made her heart skip a beat.

"I meant," she struggled to speak, "that after talking of such painful memories, you might not want—"

"Oh, I do want." He rolled on top of her, lifting up on his elbows before lowering his face inches above hers. "Very much."

Then his lips came down on hers, the kiss deep and searching. Hot desire flared in her belly as she melted under his weight, tangling her hands in his silken hair to bring him closer, entreating him for more.

He kissed her until she was dizzy, tasting her mouth and tongue as if he couldn't get enough. When his mouth at last drew away from hers, Lenore was gasping with need. He then trailed his mouth down her jaw and to her neck, scraping her skin with his fangs, before soothing the grazes with light flicks of his tongue.

Before he could move down further, Lenore grasped his jacket and tugged on it with a pleading murmur. The moment Gavin shrugged out the garment and tossed it over the bed, she tore the buttons of his waistcoat, needing to see and feel his bare flesh.

Gavin laughed and chucked her under the chin. "I do hope you'll mend that."

"Of course," she said with a smile. "I'll mend this too." And she ripped his shirt open, scattering buttons all over the bed.

Then her hands spread across the breadth of his bare chest, savoring the heat and firmness of his muscles.

Suddenly, he drew back and rolled her over onto her stomach. "Now it is my turn."

Lenore sucked in a breath and braced herself for him to tear off her dress, but instead he unbuttoned the gown with torturous slowness. She shivered at each light touch of his fingers along her spine and sighed in anticipation as he slowly slid her gown down her body and tossed it aside. Then he lowered his head and unlaced her stays with his teeth.

By the time he'd undressed her, she was writhing with the need to touch him, to feel all of him. She started to roll over, but Gavin pinned her down, his thighs pressing against her bare legs. Brushing her hair to the side, he covered her body with whisper soft kisses, from the back of her neck all the way down to her ankles. Lenore couldn't hold back small sounds of surprised delight at the feel of his lips grazing her back, her thighs, and even her rear.

At last, he allowed her to turn over while he removed his trousers. Lenore lay back on the pillows and drank in the sight of his beautiful, powerful body. She didn't care if it was improper to stare, she wanted to savor every detail of his bare muscled chest, the ridged planes of his stomach, his corded thighs, and the length of his cock.

She blushed at the sight of it, remembering how he felt in her hand, its curves and ridges, the surprisingly soft head, the way it spasmed when she'd stroked him. She then remembered how he'd kissed and licked her female center and wondered what it would be like to lick and kiss him. She almost rose up to offer, but then Gavin climbed back onto the bed and covered her lips with his.

Lenore marveled at the magic of it all. Ever since she'd confessed to enjoying his kisses, Gavin had made sure to do it often and in ways she'd never dreamed of. Her thoughts fled as he once more kissed the spot on her neck that made her toes curl.

Then just as he'd lavished attention on her back, he proceeded to kiss every inch of her exposed flesh, even her hands.

She suddenly remembered his wedding vow. *With my body, I thee worship.*

Was this what those words meant? She certainly felt cherished. Her fingers caressed his back and shoulders before tangling in his hair. Oh, how she loved his hair.

Then his fingers explored that hot, aching place between her thighs. Lenore arched her back with a moan. When his thumb lightly circled her sensitive bud, she couldn't help crying out and wiggling her hips for more.

Just when the pleasure began to peak to an unbearable level, Lenore reached for him. "Please, take me."

With a low growl, he covered her body with his. She gasped at the delicious weight of him. "*Please.*"

Gavin lifted his hips and poised the tip of his length against her entrance. "Are you certain?"

Lenore stared into his black eyes for what felt like an eternity, overwhelmed by his caring. "You won't hurt me," she said with absolute confidence.

Something softened in his gaze. "Stop me if I do."

Slowly, he entered her, filling her with a lush, consuming sensation that took her breath away. This was no savage, tearing invasion. This was a loving joining that almost felt sacred. Each centimeter invoked a new sensation as she tightened around him and her body ached for more.

When at last he was fully inside her, Gavin released a breath in tandem with her own. Instead of pounding into her like she was an object to be subjected to his aggression, he remained still and leaned forward, looking deep into her eyes as if trying to communicate with her soul.

"Are you all right?" he asked.

"Yes," she whispered and wrapped her arms and legs around him, seating him even deeper before she pulled him down for another kiss.

As his lips moved over hers, their hips arched in a slow, tantalizing rhythm that replaced the ache with an intoxicating heat. Lenore clung to him tighter still, moving against him, feeling his heart pounding against hers as their breath quickened.

Closing her eyes, she concentrated on the feel of him moving inside her, the way their bodies moved in tandem like an age old dance. They were one now, flesh united, creating something that only they could experience. Something powerful... magical... ethereal.

Gavin's thrusts increased slightly in tempo, reaching a place deep inside that came alive with electric frissons that pulsed and grew. Lenore reached for it, clasping him tighter, arching upward, searching for more.

And then it happened. Gavin thrust deeper still, and her center erupted, pulsing and tingling until white light flashed beneath her eyelids. She shuddered beneath him, her entire being flaring with life and heat.

Gavin let out a low groan, his shaft quivering inside her with his release, multiplying her own. Lenore dug her nails into his back, crying out in incoherent bliss.

The intensity ebbed away, replaced by a languid contentment she could have never fathomed.

Gavin collapsed atop her, his heart pounding against hers, their heated skin radiating drowsy satiety. He nuzzled against her neck, still breathing raggedly. "My God," he gasped.

Lenore hummed in agreement. "Is it always like this?"

She immediately regretted her words as it brought back the realization that he'd done this with others. Still, she was glad to have experienced this wonder as well.

"No," he said, his voice thoughtful. "This was... different... and incredible."

Her heart bloomed with elation. Somehow, with her lack of experience and crippling past, she'd become something special to him.

"How was it for you?" he asked almost worriedly.

"Wonderful." She held him tighter, reluctant for the moment when their bodies would part. "I..." *Love you,* she almost said. "Th-thank you."

He kissed her long and lingering before rolling over onto his back with a satisfied hum and pulled her close. A sudden weariness weighted her body as he stroked her back. The sun had risen, but they were safe, cocooned in the darkness of his bedchamber, husband and wife in truth.

As she rested her head on his chest and closed her eyes, she knew that this day, there would be no bad dreams. Because Gavin was there to protect her.

Twenty-eight

Gavin awoke with the most satisfied smile ever to cross his face. Lenore remained tucked under his arm, looking relaxed and sated. Not wanting to wake her yet, he was content to just look at her. She was so small and fragile in appearance, yet capable of such courage, strength, and will. Even the will to defy him.

His grin broadened. Instead of punishing her, somehow he'd found himself feeling guilty for enjoying her taste so damned much that he offered his own vein... for the second time. Ever since he'd first met her, he had an irrefutable urge to protect her. Even from himself, it seemed.

Lenore's lashes fluttered as she opened her eyes and gave him a sleepy smile.

His heart stuttered. Never before had a woman affected him so deeply. Was it love? He'd been infatuated a time or two, but he'd never fallen in love. But as she reached forward to brush a stray curl from his face, he knew he wanted to wake up to her every night.

"Good evening," she said softly, the covers slipping from her shoulder to reveal one perfect breast. "What are your plans for the evening?"

He leaned forward and claimed her lips in a kiss that radiated warmth all the way down to his toes. "Cecil and Benson will be here around midnight to discuss a new strategy for hunting down the rogues. And then of course we need to patrol. You will stay here and Elena will come to watch over you." When she smiled, he tapped her on the nose with a scolding finger. "You are still being punished, so be sure to appear humbled and repentant." He growled as she grinned. "That means stop smiling."

"But it's hard not to smile when you've made me so happy." She laid her head on his chest, snuggling against him.

He fought the urge to smile back. "I am being serious. You are not to go anywhere without supervision until these rogues are found and people in the village stop talking about the existence of vampires."

She stiffened and raised her head. A thousand thoughts seemed to flicker in the depths of her dark eyes before she gave him a solemn nod. "Yes, my lord." Her voice rang with painful humility. "And I truly am sorry for disobeying you. I had little regard for the danger. I did try to rectify some of that when I stole away and told Dr. Elliotson and two of the village women goodbye."

He cocked his head to the side, his grip tightening on her arms. "What do you mean?"

Her lips curled up in a satisfied smile. "I convinced the two biggest gossips in the village that they'd seen me during the day."

For a moment all he could do was stare. "How?"

"When we feed on humans, we can see their memories." When he nodded, she continued. "So after I fed, I kept them in the mesmeric trance and placed images of myself in their memories."

Gavin's jaw dropped as he digested the implications of her words. "You gave them false memories? That is... brilliant." He would have to discuss it with his people. This was something they all should do.

Then he frowned. Could any vampire do such a thing? Or was it an ability unique to Lenore? He would have to find out. And most certainly discuss her tactic with Cecil and Benson.

"Is anything wrong?" Lenore asked worriedly.

He shook his head. "No. You've only given me much to think about, that is all." Reaching forward, he cupped her face, stroking her cheek with his thumb. "Wit and beauty. What more could I ask for in a bride?"

She blushed a delightful pink. "Obedience, perhaps."

"Yes, that reminds me of your punishment." He lowered the coverlet and devoured her body with his eyes. "Perhaps I should keep you confined to this bed."

Her blush deepened, but her eyes took on a wicked gleam as she slid her hand down to wrap around his erect shaft, making him gasp. "That sounds like *such* a hardship."

His hands slid down to do some exploring of his own before he pulled her close to him and melded his mouth to hers.

After another invigorating bout of lovemaking, he assisted her in dressing in a pretty peach confection that set off her blushes quite nicely. They then set out on Edgar's back to seek their meal.

"I think we should call upon Lord and Lady Chatterton," he whispered against her neck, reveling in the way she shivered in his arms. "Her gossip could be very inconvenient for us if we do not act."

Lenore cringed in revulsion at the prospect of meeting with the odious woman, but nodded in reluctant resolve. "Which of us shall bite her?"

"Perhaps we should draw lots." He nipped her ear, turning her laughter into a gasp.

In the end, Lenore claimed the dubious honor when Lady Chatterton led her off alone to the hothouse to show off her prized roses, while Gavin feasted on Lord Chatterton when they shared a cigar. Gavin did his best to persuade the viscount that they'd hunted fox only last week. He hoped the implanted memory was effective.

Lenore appeared to be more confident when they reunited and bade their farewells.

By the time they returned home, it was a quarter to midnight. To Gavin's surprise, Benson was already waiting for them in the library, his face pale as if he hadn't fed in several nights. At first Gavin thought his second's haggard appearance was due to his near fatal attack from the rogue, but then Benson spoke.

"Cecil is dead." The vampire's voice was hollow with shock and grief.

The floor seemed to drop beneath Gavin's feet and he nearly collapsed. "What?" Agony and fury warred within him until a roar tore from his throat. "I'm going to tear those bloody rogues limb from limb."

Benson shook his head, his eyes wide with unadulterated terror. "It wasn't the rogues. It was a Hunter."

Shock and terror struck Gavin like a musket blast. On legs that felt like custard, he shambled to a chair and sat down hard. "A Hunter?" he repeated like a babbling half-wit. "How do you know?"

Benson shivered before answering. "When he did not arrive at our arranged meeting place for patrol, I went to his home. He wasn't there, so I checked the root cellar out back where he spends his day rest. The door was splintered open and his bed stained with blood." The whites of his eyes stood out in stark clarity. "I followed the trail and came upon a section of burnt grass that matched the length of his body perfectly." Tears spilled down his cheeks and he wiped them away with his sleeve. "In the center, a charred stake was driven into the ground."

"My God," Gavin breathed past the lump in his throat. For a long time he couldn't grasp any rational thought as his world spiraled out of control. Gripping the arms of his chair until the wood cracked beneath the baize, he finally managed to speak. "We must gather the others, warn them."

Benson nodded, looking spent and numb.

"My lady wife must not remain alone, not with a Hunter prowling about." Not to mention the fact that she was already under restrictive supervision.

Only then did he remember that Lenore was in the room and had heard everything. He looked over at her. She remained where she'd first stood, just inside the entrance to the library. Her face had gone chalk-white and she shook like a frightened rabbit. Gavin cursed inwardly. Another of her episodes.

Her maker had been slain by a Hunter. He remembered that now. Slowly Gavin rose on weakened legs and crossed the room to take her into his arms, wanting nothing more than to soothe and protect her. Her shaking eased to a light tremor as he stroked her hair.

"It's going to be all right," he whispered, trying to comfort her. "I'll keep you safe, I promise."

"But what about you?" she choked out a sob. "It's all my fault. I put everyone in danger!"

"You did no such thing," he told her sharply, guilt strangling him. He'd certainly made it sound that way earlier. "The fault is mine for keeping you ignorant."

And Lenore hadn't forgotten that. "But if I hadn't continued my work with Dr. Elliotson…"

"His Lordship is right," Benson interjected. "You did not cause this. We found the vampire literature before your eccentric friend started your odd little public meetings."

Lenore's gaze darted to Gavin's second. "You did?"

"Yes." Benson assured her. "Now I wonder if the Hunter was the one spreading the literature about in the first place."

Gavin shook his head slowly. It was the most logical explanation… yet it did not feel right. "I can't explain it, but I still think the rogues are involved."

"Why?" Benson's voice rang with disbelief. "With their constant movement, they'd be the most vulnerable. Hell, maybe if we're lucky, the Hunter already eliminated them." He shrugged. "Did our work for us."

"It's only a feeling I have… and a strand of hair I found upon the rogue who attacked you the other night."

"A hair?" Benson raised a brow as if Gavin spoke in riddles.

"Long and red," Gavin admitted, hoping his omission hadn't caused Cecil's death.

"Lots of harlots have long red hair," Benson countered almost too sharply, as if in denial. "And those would be the easiest meal for their ilk."

"No, *dark* red," Gavin clarified. "Like it hadn't been exposed to the sun in years.

Benson's shoulders slumped even as his gaze still flashed with denial. "Justus?"

"Who is Justus?" Lenore asked.

Benson ignored her, still wide-eyed with disbelief. "But why would he do such a foolish thing?"

"Revenge," Gavin said quietly, drowning in old memories.

"You showed him mercy! You allowed him to live!" Benson argued, slamming his fist on the arm of his chair. "He should be grateful you didn't take his head!"

"Yes, but since he feels that I took away the love of his life, I doubt he has little thanks to offer for my lenience." Gavin sighed, regret weighting his heart. "Still, you may be correct. Luring a Hunter is too dangerous and foolish for his usual cold reasoning. He was the most clever of us."

Benson's eyes narrowed. "Are you saying I am not clever?"

"No, but you must admit that his flavor of wit was different than your own. That is why you worked so well together." Gavin willed himself to maintain patience as he reminded him.

Benson gave a reluctant nod. "You're right. And as much as it pains me to admit, he was far more intelligent than Cecil, God rest his soul. Cecil was too impulsive at times." His frown deepened. "What if Justus is pretending to be a Hunter to scare us?"

Gavin shook his head. "That doesn't sound like him. And I refuse to believe he'd kill Cecil. Not after all they'd been through together."

Lenore squirmed in Gavin's arms. "Who is Justus?" she repeated impatiently.

"I'll tell you the whole tragic tale later tonight, I promise." Though Gavin was not eager to reveal to Lenore that *he* had made a rogue. Not only that, but possibly one who was now leading a band to terrorize his people. After what she'd been through, he dreaded her reaction to *that* bit of information. Reluctantly, he released her. "Benson and I must go now to arrange another Gathering and try to find evidence of the Hunter. Elena should be here any moment to guard you."

Lenore shook her head. "I am going with you. You said these are now my people. I want to do what I can to help protect them."

"You'll do no such thing," Gavin growled.

A voice spoke behind them. "Yes, she will."

Elena entered the library and faced Gavin with a defiant glare. "If there is a Hunter about, there is no way I am remaining here while you men embark on another fruitless chase and waste time alerting our people just between the two of you. And since Lenore is not to be left alone, she will accompany me."

"Elena…" Gavin began. She had a point, but…

"Don't you 'Elena' me." The vampire drew herself up to her full height. "I am older and stronger than Cecil or Benson. And I've slain a few Hunters in my centuries. If you don't wish your wife to come with you, she can accompany Cecil and me." Her eyes scanned the room. "Where is he?"

The silence fell so heavy one could hear a mouse scuttle across the next floor.

"Cecil was slain," Gavin said through numb lips. "By the Hunter."

Elena drew back as if he'd slapped her. "Cecil?" Her voice cracked with sadness before her eyes glowed a fiery amber and her lip curled up to bare her fangs. "I'll drain the son of a bitch dry!" Picking up her skirts, she marched from the room, leaving everyone else no choice but to follow.

***

Justus entered the pub and his eyes lit with fury as he saw Rolfe speaking with the stranger who'd come here the night before. His gaze narrowed at the big leather bag at the man's feet, full of lumps as if carrying a plethora of items, and with a cross tooled on the front flap, above the clasp. Justus had seen a similar bag before.

Gathering his courage, he plastered a carefree smile on his face before taking a seat next to his friend.

"Justus, old chap!" Rolfe's eyes widened in surprise before he spoke with equally feigned cheer. "What brings you out and about? I'd thought your pockets were emptied by that tart you've taken a fancy to."

Justus blinked at the absurd lie, then smiled as he realized it would suit his purpose just fine. "Oh, they would be if you did not owe me five pounds for our wager." He chuckled at Rolfe's perplexed frown. "Though perhaps you'd prefer to discuss that in private? Your new friend does not need to know how poor a gambler you are."

"On the contrary." The stranger's voice had a raspy undertone, like the hiss of a snake. "Such information would be extremely useful to a gambling man."

Justus gave him a tight smile before clapping his arm on Rolfe's shoulder. "Now what kind of friend would I be if I allowed a stranger to take advantage of my mate's gullibility? Come now, Rolfe, the ale and wenches will still be here when you get back. I won't completely clean out your pockets. Only lighten them."

The stranger continued to study Justus with a thoroughness that made goose bumps rise on his arms. "I do hope you'll forgive my forwardness, but you have the most striking hair. I cannot say I've ever seen such a shade. It almost appears unnatural."

"I'm afraid it *is* indeed unnatural," Justus said with a tragic sigh. "I'd tried for a position at the mill, but the miller wouldn't hire Irishmen, so I tried to dye my hair brown." He managed a self-deprecating chuckle. "It did not take, as you can see. Rolfe here won that wager."

The stranger looked unimpressed with Justus's oft' used excuse. "You do not sound Irish."

"Better safe than sorry." Justus stood, pulling Rolfe with him. "Anyway, we must be going. Perhaps we may share a pint later."

"I certainly hope so." The stranger held out his hand. "My name is Walter Von Bronkhorst. Your friend Rolfe has been a fascinating drinking companion. I'd wager you would be even more interesting."

"Truly, I'm a dull sort," Justus kept his tone bland and indifferent. Quickly, he hauled Rolfe out of the pub, keeping his senses open in case Von Bronkhorst decided to follow.

"What is the matter with you?" Rolfe said, though Justus could hear a note of guilt in his tone.

"Be quiet until we return to our lair." He led them in a circuitous route, clamping his hand tighter on Rolfe when he tried to use his vampire speed. "Not now. I do not want us to be seen. Wait until we reach that copse of trees.

Once they returned to their chamber under the castle ruins, Justus's anger rose when they came upon Will stoking a small fire. "Idiot! Put that out immediately. Do you want someone to see the smoke?"

"But I'm tired of being cold," Will argued with a petulant frown. "And you said we'd be safe as long as we only come here after Rochester has had a Gathering."

"We can survive the cold," Justus snarled. "But we cannot survive a stake through the heart. Rolfe has lured a Hunter here."

"What?" Will leapt to his feet and quickly doused the fire with the last of their water, which they drank to feel full if they were not able to hunt.

"I don't know what you are going on about," Rolfe began indignantly, though his face gave away his guilt.

"Shut it, Rolfe," Justus snapped, rubbing the bridge of his nose. "I am the leader here, so that makes me the Lord Vampire of our little trio. Do you wish to learn the punishment of lying to your lord? If not, tell me the truth at once."

Rolfe sank to his knees. "All right! I saw his advertisement in the circular and wrote him an anonymous note asking him to come. I thought that if he heard all the talk we'd hinted about Rochester's bride, he would dispose of our problem."

"You fool!" Justus roared. "I don't want him dead. I want him exiled! Banished by the Elders, or better yet, cast out by those he calls friends. Besides, all you have done is make our situation more precarious. You heard the talk of Lady Darkwood's saintly deeds and how Elliotson was vindicated by his ability to walk about in the daylight. Not to mention the fact that Darkwood Manor is heavily guarded and no one knows exactly where he and his wife rest during the day. A Hunter couldn't get near them if he tried. That's why they always pick off the poor and the weak... such as ourselves."

"I'm sorry m' lord," Rolfe stammered, eyes wide with fear in the realization of what he'd done. "I was only—"

Justus held up a hand and crossed the length of the chamber to gather his things. "We must move at once. Back to the cathedral. For one thing, most Hunters still believe we cannot enter holy ground, for another, Rochester shall hear of this Hunter at any moment and call another Gathering."

As they scrambled out from the bowels of the castle and ran off like thieves in the night, Justus wondered if it would be better to take his comrades away from this place and abandon his quest for vengeance.

But when he closed his eyes and saw Bethany's angelic face, he knew he couldn't give up now. Not when he was so close.

Twenty-nine

Lenore clung to Gavin's hand as he warned the terrified vampires about the Hunter and the rogues. Her heart weighed heavy with pain at the sorrow in his voice when he told them about Cecil's death.

"Some people say that we have no souls," he said, eyes haunted and solemn. "But I don't believe that. We're also not reanimated corpses, after all, as many humans believe." He cracked a small smile, attempting to bring a touch of humor. Eyes glistening when he elicited a few chuckles, he continued. "I believe Cecil had a soul and was a good person. Brave, loyal, and kind. I believe he is in some sort of heaven, whether the one mentioned in the bible, where he is reunited with his mortal family, or perhaps one for our kind. As soon as the Hunter and rogues are eliminated, we shall gather together to honor and celebrate his memory."

Lenore watched her husband with comfort and awe at his touching speech. Both the Duke of Burnrath and Lord Villar had honored London vampires who had died, but never with such warm regard and comfort to those who'd known and mourned the fallen.

Gavin allowed a long moment of silence before he spoke again. "For our last order of business, I appoint Elena as my new third in command."

"Elena," the vampires chorused and bowed their heads in tandem as Elena knelt before Gavin.

"I will hold my post with honor and loyalty," she said solemnly before Gavin helped her to her feet.

"I know you will," he told her with a wan smile before turning back to his people. "This Gathering is adjourned. Remember, do not go anywhere alone until we've purged every threat from our land."

Two by two, the Rochester vampires filed out of the chamber through various tunnels, to avoid the attention a large group would draw.

Just as Gavin, Lenore, Benson, and Elena were about to head out, the sound of running footsteps skittered across the stone floor.

"My lord!" A slight, blonde female vampire burst into the chamber. "Someone else has been down here. I smelled a trace of fresh smoke."

Gavin's eyes widened before he regained his composure. "Thank you for informing me, Kate." His brows drew together. "Where is your companion for the night?"

Kate flushed. "Alan is at the entrance to the tunnel where we smelled the smoke."

Gavin sighed and rubbed the bridge of his nose. "Did I not just command you to stay together at all times?"

Her lips parted in fearful realization. "I'm sorry, my lord, I—"

"Never mind." He waved his hand impatiently. "Show me this tunnel."

Gavin tucked Lenore behind him, having Elena and Benson flank her as they followed Kate down a narrow corridor that branched off in three different directions. Kate pointed at the one to the left, thick with cobwebs and littered with rubble. As they proceeded down the treacherous path, Lenore detected the faint trace of smoke, as if a fire had recently been lit somewhere nearby.

They came upon a tall, lanky male vampire who stood with his fists slightly raised at his sides, as if expecting to fend off a sudden attack. When he saw Gavin, he dropped to his knees. "My lord."

"Alan." Gavin gestured for him to rise. "Kate said you found an entrance to another tunnel. Where is it?"

Lenore looked behind Alan, blinking in surprise to see nothing but a stone wall.

Then Alan turned and shoved his arm around it. What had looked to be a shadow was in fact a fissure. Gavin peered inside and sniffed. "The smoke definitely originated from here." He turned back to Benson and Elena. "Stay here."

"Not a chance, my lord," Benson argued.

"Very well," Gavin shrugged. "Kate and Alan, you may go home now. And stay together, for God's sake!"

As Benson followed Gavin into the dark, narrow passage, Lenore glanced back at Elena to see if she would stop her from following. Instead, Gavin's new third in command gave her a brisk nod, ushering her forward.

The tunnel was so dark that even with their preternatural senses, it was difficult to see much more than the outline of the vampire in front of her. Lenore's mouth went dry and her pulse accelerated with every step. What would they find at the end of the tunnel? Were the rogues hiding there, or the Hunter? Neither sounded appealing, though she'd somewhat prefer the latter as there was only one Hunter and four of them. Lord knew how many rogues were about. Lenore wished she could hold onto Gavin's arm, but Benson flanked him, as was his duty as second in command.

Finally, the tunnel widened so Gavin and Benson could walk abreast. Tentatively, Lenore reached out to place a hand on her husband's back, needing a touch of comfort. Enclosed places had bothered her ever since her captivity.

Gavin glanced over his shoulder and met her gaze. Whether or not he disapproved of her presence, she could not tell. Suddenly, he and Benson halted, causing her to bump into him.

"Vampires," he whispered, reaching back to steady her.

She shivered. It *was* the rogues. Were they still there? If so, could they hear Gavin and his companions approaching?

She held her breath as they crept forward. By the time they emerged in a somewhat large chamber, black spots danced before her vision. She'd heard that vampires could survive without breathing, well, *survive* wasn't the best term. They'd die, but revive again the moment they were exposed to the slightest bit of air.

Shaking off the macabre thought, she forced herself to let out the breath she held and breathe in slowly. The scent of strange vampires hung thickly in the chamber, along with the odor of a recently doused fire. Reluctantly, she took her hand from Gavin's back, allowing him to explore the area further... or fight if necessary.

Elena remained by her side, and for once, she did not mind being looked after. Memories of another underground chamber, where she'd been shackled and gagged and violated by a gang of hulking rogues, assaulted her mind. She wished she would have remained in the Gathering Hall and never considered coming down here.

"They must have left fairly recently," Benson's voice made her jump. "The wood is still warm, despite being wet."

"Something made them douse it quickly and flee." Gavin struck a match and lit a piece of wood that looked like a broken chair leg in a makeshift torch. "Likely the Gathering. Though I wonder when they decided to hide here... and why. Surely they could smell that this place is oft' frequented."

Lenore's shoulders relaxed at the assurance that the rogues were gone.

Elena made a clucking sound with her tongue. "Or maybe they know when it's usually frequented. We meet here monthly. Usually around the same time. Either they've been watching, or if Justus truly is part of this group, he already knows."

"And he would know where else he could hide," Benson added. "I know you don't want to consider that it could be him, but…"

"I didn't," Gavin said in a strange tone before he bent down and picked up something from the dusty stone floor. The object gleamed a dull silver in the light of his makeshift torch. "But now I have no choice but to face the fact that my former friend has indeed returned."

Benson strode over to him as Gavin held the object up to the light. "I remember when he started wearing that." He shook his head, eyes wide in awe. "So he never took it off in all this time."

Lenore saw that it was a locket and was curious to know what was inside. Apparently she wasn't the only one.

"How do you know it's his?" Elena asked. "Shouldn't you open it?"

"I *know* it's his, and I know what's inside," Gavin said quietly, and slipped the locket in his pocket before anyone could press him further.

Benson gave him a knowing look. "It's a miniature of *her*, isn't it? That mortal girl who caused his downfall."

"He caused his own downfall," Gavin countered, voice rough with anger. "If he'd handled things in a reasonable matter, he could have had her and remained with us. But yes, the locket holds her portrait and a lock of her hair. Justus showed it to me when he pleaded for me to allow him to Change her."

Elena's features softened with pity. "The things people will do when they're in love. I wonder where she is?"

"Shortly after the debacle, her parents packed her off to Manchester. I'd assumed Justus had tracked her down and Changed her." Gavin sighed and looked at the ground. "Now I am not so certain."

Benson stroked his chin with a pensive frown. "If that trinket is all he had of her, he will be missing it."

"Perhaps he can come and claim it from me," Gavin said coldly. "I will be glad to return it to him before I kill him."

"So you'll do it then?" Elena's voice was almost a whisper. "Execute your best friend?"

"If he's responsible for Cecil's death, he gives me no choice." Gavin kept his gaze to the floor for an interminable moment before he raised his head. "At any rate, we've identified one of our rogues. Let us leave this place and turn our attention on deducing where he is hiding."

"And the Hunter," Benson said with a scowl. "We must find him, or her, as well."

Gavin nodded. "Start with inquiries in the village. Find out what people know about strangers in town."

"Yes, my lord," Elena and Benson chorused.

They made their way out of the tunnel, Gavin reaching behind to clasp Lenore's hand. How did he know that she was still uneasy? She smiled. It didn't matter. She was only grateful that he gave her comfort.

Once they left the ruins, Benson departed for the village with Elena at his side. She had plans to round up some of the oldest vampires in Rochester and search out Justus's previous haunts.

As Gavin reached for Lenore's hand in preparation for their run, she wrapped her arms around him. "What are you going to do next?"

"I'm going to take you home. You were unsettled in that chamber." He held her tighter. "So we shall relax for a spell and then

I will write letters to the neighboring Lord Vampires and warn them about the Hunter, as well as the rogues."

Tension Lenore didn't know she had drained from her at the news that he would remain with her tonight.

Once they were settled in the library with a hot fire and cups of steaming tea, Gavin set his cup aside and rubbed Lenore's taut shoulders.

She leaned into his grip with a sigh and tried to hold onto her thoughts. "Tell me about Justus."

Gavin sighed. "He was my second in command and my greatest of friends. He was a tall chap, with hair of the darkest red I've ever seen and even longer than mine." His fingers worked a knot at the base of her neck. "He was extremely clever, and had the most uncanny way of prying information from the vaguest sources, and was the very best at hunting rogues." A bark of laughter startled her. "Which explains why he's been able to evade me for so long."

He fell silent, massaging her until she thought she'd melt in her chair, if it weren't for her rampant curiosity about the vampire who had been close to Gavin and was now his enemy.

"What happened to make you exile him?" She'd gathered that it was because of a woman. Had Gavin loved her too, and exiled Justus over jealousy? A sharp pang speared her heart at the thought. Or perhaps there was something more sinister? Not that she'd wish for that either.

Gavin withdrew his hands from her shoulders and walked around to sit in a chair next to hers. "Eight years ago, Justus met a young miss at the Ellingsworth ball and immediately became besotted. While that is not always a bad thing, and is the most common reason to Change someone, this case was dangerous for many reasons. Firstly, because she was the daughter of a prominent politician. We are forbidden to Change public figures for obvious reasons. Secondly, she hadn't even reached her age of majority. Though she was not a child, she was still a minor, and that is forbidden as well. Thirdly, she was already betrothed to another."

Lenore realized she didn't know any of the rules about Changing mortals, except that it was best for a vampire not to attempt it until he or she was at least a century old. She leaned forward with fascination... and a measure of dread as she knew this love story would not end well.

"I told him to avoid her," Gavin continued. "And when he wouldn't listen, I told him to be careful. And for a while, I thought he was at least doing that. After all, he did not Mark her, and from his scent, I do not think he went so far as to take her maidenhood." Self recrimination tightened his features. "But I was wrong. One night he came to me and begged me to allow him to Change her. I refused. I was going to have him moved to another Lord Vampire's territory for his own protection, but it was too late. Cecil informed me that Justus had told the girl what he was... even worse, she'd told her parents."

Lenore gasped. That was the most foolish, most forbidden thing one of their kind could do.

"The penalty for revealing ourselves to mortals is death," Gavin said, as if she did not know. "But I could not do it. I couldn't even report him to the Elders. Instead, I exiled him. Something, I rarely do, as I don't wish to create more rogues. Yet even that was preferable to slaying my dearest friend."

He covered his face with his hands, radiating painful grief. "This is all my fault. The rogues, the Hunter. Because of my weakness in giving Justus mercy, I got Cecil killed! And even still, I do not want to kill Justus."

Lenore rose from her seat and wrapped her arms around him, cradling his head to her breast. "Your mercy is not a weakness. You acted nobly, and wisely. You've done your best to keep your friend from breaking the law, your best to save his life. The fault is *his* for not accepting all you'd done for him. The fault is *his* that you will have to kill him." She paused as a thought struck her. "Do you think he went mad? I hear some of the old ones do and have to be put down."

"Perhaps. Though he is younger than me by fifty years, some do succumb early." A measure of anguish faded from his eyes at her words, whether her assertion that he was not to blame for Cecil's death, or the inherent justification in her speculation about his friend going mad, she could not say.

"Perhaps I am going mad as well," he murmured, kissing her neck. "I'm certainly mad about you."

He yanked her onto his lap, and for a brief time, their troubles faded into the ether.

Thirty

Gavin awoke the next evening, feeling unfathomably content despite all the turmoil unleashed upon him. Something about Lenore's heartfelt offer of comfort, her quiet faith in him to do what was right bolstered his confidence and compelled him to believe that all would work out in the end.

After climbing out of bed, he gazed at her in awe and hunger, remembering how she'd straddled him in that chair and ridden him until they were both mindless with pleasure. He longed for a repeat performance, but sadly acknowledged that there would be little time.

As if sensing his urgency, Lenore awoke with a languid stretch and blinked at him sleepily. "What is tonight's strategy?"

"We'll visit the Medway Inn, a favored establishment of indolent lordlings, and inquire if any of them have recognized Justus or seen a stranger in the area who could be the Hunter. He often played cards there and gathered information." Not only was it a ludicrously obvious idea that he should have thought of sooner, it also meant that Lenore could remain with him. With all that had transpired in the past three nights, he did not want to let her out of his sight.

Something in her eyes lightened, as if pleased to spend more time with him.

Lenore pushed the covers away, revealing her glorious naked body. Gavin's mouth went dry as he hardened immediately.

"First, there's something I've been wanting to do," she purred and reached out to grasp his length. When she leaned forward and flicked her tongue across the swollen length of his shaft, Gavin lost all ability to argue.

He threw his head back and groaned as her lips wrapped around his cock, sucking him deep into her mouth.

Gently, he threaded his fingers through her tousled hair, unable to stop from moving his hips in tandem with her erotic ministrations. Hungry bliss flowed through his body as she wrought magic with her lips and tongue. When he looked down at her, drinking in the sight of her sucking him, she peered up at him beneath her long lashes and he nearly climaxed right then.

"Enough," he growled and reluctantly, he drew back. "Lie down."

With a seductive smile, Lenore complied.

Remaining standing, Gavin seized her legs and pulled her closer. Positioning his shaft at her entrance, he was awed at how hot and wet she felt. Cautioning gentleness, he slowly slid inside her tight heat, listening to her moan.

In a slow, teasing rhythm, he withdrew nearly all the way before thrusting back in all the way to the hilt. Cradling one of her legs, he released the other to reach down and stroke her hard pink little bud in undulating circles.

Lenore cried out and ground her hips against him. Her free leg hooked behind his waist, pulling him deeper inside her.

Sweat beaded on his brow as he fought not to pound into her in a mad frenzy. Instead, he closed his eyes and let the pleasure of this tempo flow through him. With this slow pace, he could feel every last bit of her, savor her heat, and even experience each instant that she tightened around him.

A low moan tore through Lenore as her fists bunched in the sheets and she undulated against him. "Faster," she panted.

Still trying to be careful, he quickened his thrusts only slightly.

"Faster!" she cried out, meeting his thrusts.

With a growl, Gavin threw away caution and once more seized her hips, pounding into her with the fervor of one possessed. He felt her spasm around him just as her moans turned into cries of ecstasy. Lightning seemed to jolt through him with his own release and he continued his thrusts, riding the climax until he collapsed atop her, panting with exhaustion.

"I do not want to leave this bed," he grumbled.

"Then don't," she whispered and licked his ear.

His dejected sigh reverberated through their bedchamber. "We have to, if there's to be time to hunt and do our investigating before I have to meet with Benson."

And just like that, the reality of their danger returned like a plague.

Quickly, they dressed and rang for the carriage.

The ride was quiet, as if Lenore knew the depth of his turmoil at the prospect of the inevitable confrontation. As they arrived at the Medway, a large cobblestone structure that somehow gave the impression of a homey cottage, his wife squeezed his hand in support. He may have lost his best friend, but at least he had gained another.

When they entered the bright, smoky common room, several shouts echoed around them.

"Lord Darkwood!" A young pup barely old enough to shave darted forward to clap him on the shoulder. "I haven't seen you hereabouts in months."

"Yes. Lady Darkwood wishes to sample the famous trout." Belatedly, he recognized the lad as Lord Lumley's son and heir, but couldn't recall the boy's name.

"I adore trout," Lenore said breathlessly, plying a lace fan.

"I would be honored if you'll share my table. Alfred, Squire Nilson's son, and I were having a pint." The boy stilled, his gaze suddenly distant. "There was something I'd wanted to tell you, but I cannot recall." He shook his head and grinned. "No matter, I'm sure I'll remember it soon."

"We would be delighted," Gavin told the cheerful, albeit dim-witted boy.

After they joined the young lordlings, who fawned upon Lenore in a comical fashion, Gavin affected a bland tone of minor interest. "I'd heard the most curious rumor. Do you recall my old friend, Justus de Wynter? He was infamous for his games of hazard."

Both lads shook their heads, which wasn't surprising. Both would have been too young to have frequented Justus's haunts eight years ago. But Sampson, the innkeeper, nodded when he delivered their wine and trout. "Aye, the Red Fox, we called him. Haven't seen him in nearly ten years. Heard he took off to India to become a nabob."

Gavin nodded. That was the lie he'd spread across the countryside. "I'd heard that he'd returned."

"Wouldn't that be something?" Sampson drummed his fingers on the table. "Wouldn't surprise me if that scoundrel made a fortune. Clever as a fox, he was, hence his nickname. I'll keep my eyes and ears open for you, my lord."

"Thank you, Sampson." Gavin said. "Perhaps someone mistook him for another stranger in the village."

"Haven't had any strangers here neither. I don't mind though. I like familiar faces." A clatter echoed from the kitchen and Sampson cursed under his breath. "Blast it, I must go."

Gavin rested his elbows on the table. They should go as well. There was nothing to be learned here. Perhaps Justus was now frequenting more lowly pubs. It would make sense for him to avoid places where people could recognize him. But he'd be damned before taking Lenore to such crude places.

He leaned back in his chair and watched her delicately nibble the butter and herb crusted trout, her eyes closed in pure bliss.

"Careful, my dear," he whispered. "You don't want another upset stomach."

She blushed and nodded. He would never tire of her blushes.

Suddenly, Lord Lumley's son clapped him on the shoulder. "I remember what I wanted to tell you!" He hiccupped. "Actually, I wanted to tell Her Ladyship. It's rather unpleasant news, I'm afraid."

"What is it?" Lenore looked at him like she wanted to stab him with her fork if he didn't spit it out.

The boy took off his cap and held it to his chest. "Your friend, Doctor Elliotson was struck down by a carriage."

Lenore's face went chalk white. She dropped her fork. "When did it happen?"

"Just after sunset," the Lumley boy said, looking more interested in exciting gossip than actual concern. "Doctor Hodgkin is with him now."

"Was he…" she swallowed, "killed?"

"I'm not certain. Dudley said he heard his ribs were crushed." He pointed at a pair of dandies playing cards. "Squire Guilford's son heard he just had his leg snapped. Neither of them actually witnessed the incident, however."

Lenore made another small, grieved sound and shifted to rise from her seat, but Gavin clamped a hand on her arm. "Did anyone have a description of the carriage? Or know who exactly did witness it?"

"I heard it was black," the lad said.

Alfred looked up from his pint. "Like yours." He narrowed his eyes at Gavin. "Where were you two hours ago?"

Behind them the patrons whispered and muttered.

"He never did like his wife's friendship with the doctor," someone said.

Gavin's chest tightened. He'd had a quick meeting with Benson then. But would Lenore think he'd do such a terrible thing? Cautiously, he glanced down at her.

His wife glared at Alfred. "My lord husband was with me. He is teaching me how to ride. I never learned when I lived in London." Her chin lifted as she looked down her nose at the squire's son. "And if you would care to look at our carriage, you will see that it is unmarred. The conveyance was polished only three days ago."

The invisible fist squeezing his heart relaxed its painful grip. He looked down at his wife in wonder at her impassioned defense. "Though I do confess, I *was* jealous of her friendship with the doctor while I was pressing my suit. All of that nonsense vanished when she accepted my proposal. Besides, I would never resort to such monstrous actions. Now I must take my lady wife home. This news has upset her."

He slammed a guinea on the bar and Lenore gave him a grateful look as he escorted her from the Inn.

"We have to go see him," Lenore said as he helped her into the carriage.

Gavin shook his head. Dread pooled in his belly. "I'm sorry, but that would be too dangerous. Someone is targeting him, which means you are being targeted as well."

"I must! He was my friend!" She almost shouted, a hysterical note in her voice. "Surely people would talk if I do not visit my friend when he is hurt."

"There will be talk from my people if you disobey me," he struggled to remain firm.

Her brown eyes blazed with fury and defiance. "Well, they can all hang! And so can you."

Before he could protest, she was up from her seat in a blinding flash, the carriage door flew open, and Lenore vanished into the night.

***

Lenore ran in a circuitous route. If she went straight to Elliotson's home, Gavin would likely intercept her on the way. She needed to hide, then pay her visit discreetly before dawn.

After darting through an orchard, a crumbled arch came visible over the crest of the hill.

Triumph welled in her belly. The cathedral. She would hide there. Perhaps she could even climb the bell tower and keep a look out for Gavin and the other vampires he'd send to pursue her.

Guilt knotted her belly for her fleeing him. Guilt and anger. Gavin had so much compassion for his friend, why couldn't he muster a scrap for hers?

She was about to leap up to climb the castle walls when a sharp crack rent the air and something hard and unyielding wrapped around her throat, jerking her backward. The world rushed before her eyes before she slammed down hard on the ground.

A man laughed, low and mirthless, as he stood before her, pulling the whip even tighter around her throat. She tried to wrap her fingers around the thick coil to snap it, but it was too wide and thick.

"I had thought to find my prey inside this old ruin," he said in a cold, flat voice that made her shiver. "But not for *you* to leap into my trap, Lady Darkwood." He reached in his pocket, never breaking eye contact. "Everyone thought your mad doctor friend was a vampire. He still may be a witch, so I ran him down with my carriage just in case. But the true demon was you all along, the saintly baroness, tending to the common folk only to feast on their blood. Well, you've drank your last, demon wench."

The Hunter withdrew a bottle, uncapped it, and splashed its contents all over her dress. The acrid odor of kerosene choked her nearly as much as the whip strangling her.

Lenore frantically struggled to break the thing. Her fingers found purchase and she tugged, loosening the punishing coil enough to suck in a tainted breath.

The Hunter lit a match and dropped it on her skirts. The velvet ignited in a flash of brilliant heat, licking the fabric with orange tongues that would soon consume her. Lenore screamed as her attacker reached behind his back and withdrew a gleaming axe.

He raised it above his head and she thrashed wildly as the heat of the flames reached her legs. *Oh God, why did I have to be so foolish?* She cried inwardly. *He's going to go after Gavin next!*

Refusing to close her eyes like a coward, she stared death in its face and thanked the fates that she had at least had some happiness before the end. She entreated the lord or whatever powers that be to protect her husband.

The axe began its slicing downward stroke.

In a blur of crimson motion, a vampire appeared behind the Hunter. Their eyes met for a split second before the vampire raised his hands in two joined fists, and struck the Hunter atop the head. The human collapsed like a felled deer.

Then the vampire seized her shoulder and rolled her on the ground until the flames were extinguished. She couldn't help but whimper as rocks and grass came in contact with her burned flesh.

"Hold her." His voice rang with command as he looked past her.

Another pair of hands clamped on her arms, as a second vampire crouched behind her. He lifted her to a sitting position, pinning her further with his knees.

Her rescuer turned back to the fallen Hunter and plunged his fangs into the human's throat, draining him with famished gulps. His long red hair gleamed in the moonlight. Lifting his head, he returned to Lenore and held out his arms. The other vampire thrust her at him.

"Your turn," he told the other rogue. "But save some for Will. You'll take the vermin's body, I'll take our prize."

Wrapping his arms around her wrists, he dragged her to the cathedral.

"Justus," she breathed in shock.

He glanced back over his shoulder and raised a brow. "So, you *have* heard of me." His arched lips curved in a sinister smirk. "That should make things more interesting."

Thirty-one

By the time Justus hauled Lenore through a winding tunnel beneath the cloisters, she couldn't stop shaking and gasping for air. The pain in her legs reminded her of how the shackles had rubbed her skin raw in Clayton's cellar.

Rogues had taken her again! Panic consumed her, filled her lungs, boiled in her blood. Visions from the past flashed before her vision until she couldn't tell whether she was in the present, or in the past.

When they reached a dark, dry chamber with only a meager lantern, all she could do was shake and gasp incoherent mewls of terror.

"What's the matter with her?" the other rogue asked as he dragged the vampire hunter's body to a dark corner.

"I do not know," Justus said. "I've never seen anyone shake so much. Perhaps it's some sort of fit."

Their voices echoed dully around her, like she was under water.

"Who is she?" a third rogue asked. "And why is her dress burned?" He glanced over at the corpse. "And who is *he*?"

"That," Justus pointed, "was the Hunter. I killed him when he was trying to burn Lady Darkwood and slay her. We saved you a pint or two."

"Lady Darkwood?" The vampire gaped at her like she was a rare species of bird. "The Lord of Rochester's wife?"

"And the key to us getting full pardons and Rochester renouncing his lordship." Justus cast her a triumphant smirk.

The second rogue who'd pinned Lenore while Justus killed the vampire crept closer, ogling her limbs exposed from the charred tatters of her gown. "Pretty thing. It's been a long time since I've had me a woman. And she has lovely legs. Perhaps we could help her out of that burned dress and have a bit of sport." He reached for her, and all Lenore could see was the last rogue who'd raped her.

Lenore cringed back with a scream, thrashing against Justus's grip.

Justus thrust her behind him and backhanded the other vampire so hard his head snapped back and he collapsed to the ground.

"Enough!" he roared. "Lady Darkwood is our guest and will be treated fairly. And I do *not* tolerate rape in my band. You told me you were exiled for thievery, Rolfe. Now I wonder if it was for something else."

"No, my lord," Rolfe protested, though there was a crack in his voice and a glint to his beady eyes that hinted of dishonesty.

"Stay away from her and go through the Hunter's satchel. Look for something useful." He looked at the other vampire. "Will, have yourself a bite. The blood is still warm."

As the rogue gave him a grateful look and scrambled off to feed, Justus turned Lenore around to face him. Such close contact with a man who was not Gavin, even if he had saved her, made her body break out in renewed tremors.

"Hush," Justus spoke softly, like he was trying to coax a cat down from a tree. "We won't hurt you."

Lenore wished she could believe him. "But you'll kill me if my husband doesn't do what you want."

"I don't want to kill you." His voice hardened. "Though if Gavin doesn't listen to reason…" He shrugged.

"He doesn't want to kill *you*, either," she hissed, at last finding a semblance of courage. "Unfortunately, after you arranged for Cecil to be killed, he has no choice."

Justus paled. "Cecil?" he choked, gripping her upper arms until she whimpered in pain. "Are you saying he's dead?"

Lenore nodded, brows drawn in confusion. Shouldn't he know, if he were the one responsible for orchestrating the murder?

"Rolfe!" Justus roared. "Why?"

"He killed Charlie," Rolfe snarled. "I had to avenge him."

Lenore blinked in astonishment that this other rogue had done such a dangerous, abominable thing as to recruit a vampire hunter… and that it had happened without Justus's knowledge. Though she also couldn't help a wisp of relief that Justus was not responsible for this atrocity. Would Gavin be relieved to hear that his former friend was innocent? Would it prod him to mercy?

"Bloody hell!" Justus's eyes glowed with deadly green light. "Charlie's death was the fault of his own stupidity. Our quarrel was never with Cecil. He did not deserve to die." In a flash, Justus was on the vampire, knocking him over the head and wrapping him in a length of chain that was pilfered from the hunter's pack.

Lenore turned to run, but Justus seized her before she reached the mouth of the tunnel. "It is incredibly rude for a guest to depart so quickly. Especially when you have so much news to impart." He glanced at the third vampire, who rose from the Hunter's body, wiping his mouth. "Will, guard the tunnel while I finish securing Rolfe."

Lenore watched, dumbfounded as one rogue imprisoned the other, even using the Hunter's whip to silence the vampire's protests, by wrapping it around his head and gagging him.

"Rolfe of no surname," Justus boomed with the authority of a Lord Vampire, "as leader of our group, I place you under arrest for the murder of Cecil Brenton. You will remain in your restraints until I decide whether to try you myself or turn you over to the Lord of Rochester. Will, watch him."

"Why would you do that?" Will gaped at his leader in shock. "Rochester's your *enemy*. And why would he believe you?"

"Just because I am a rogue does not mean I lack honor," Justus said firmly. "And I have his lady wife's testimony to verify that Rolfe orchestrated Cecil's death. Now search the Hunter for anything useful." He turned back to Lenore with a raised brow. "Did he truly believe that I was responsible for luring the Hunter here? And having him kill Cecil?"

Lenore nodded, still gasping for air. Twice this vampire had saved her, first from the Hunter, then from one of his own. He seemed to truly mean his assertion that he would not hurt her. "He thinks you want revenge for what happened with that mortal girl you fell in love with."

"I *do* want revenge," Justus said through gritted teeth. "But I do not want him dead. I want him to suffer." He cocked his head to the side, his eyes softening to wistful longing. "He told you about my Bethany?"

She nodded, touched by the reverence in which he spoke his love's name, despite herself. "He found your locket with her miniature beneath the castle ruins."

"Did he tell you what he'd done with her?" The naked pleading in his eyes invoked reluctant pity.

She shook her head, squirming in his punishing grip on her wrists. "He thought you took her away and Changed her after you were exiled."

"I'll believe that only from his own lips and a blood oath." He growled, eyes skeptical. "I find it hard to believe that not only would he be so negligent as to leave her be when my actions had rendered her a threat, but that he also had nothing to do with her vanishing without a trace." His gaze lingered on her a moment before darting back to Will. "What have you found in the Hunter's belongings?"

"Stakes, crosses, holy water, salt, kerosene, another axe, and two pairs of steel shackles."

"Bring me the shackles," Justus commanded. "I can't fight Rochester with his Lady in my arms. Though I hope we can resolve this without bloodshed."

Lenore bucked and kicked as her ankles and wrists were shackled together.

"Be calm," Justus scolded, running a gentle hand along her forehead. "You'll hurt yourself." He sank his fangs into the thick flesh of his palm and lowered his bleeding hand to her blistered knee. "And hold still while I heal those burns."

Even as his healing blood cooled and mended the stinging burns on her legs, Lenore couldn't stop flinching at another man's touch. A man who was not Gavin.

Once finished, he removed his cloak and covered her exposed legs, his eyes narrowed with scorn as she trembled. "I cannot fathom why Gavin fell in love with such a cowardly weakling."

A sudden burst of fury surged through her. "I am *not* a coward, nor a weakling. I survived abduction, imprisonment and torture. I escaped my captors, swam the river Medway in the cold of late October, and with Gavin's aid, I took a ship to the Elder's motherhouse in Amsterdam to bring a traitor to justice. I only have a reasonable distaste for being shackled and touched by strangers. You would too if you'd endured half of what I had." Her mouth snapped shut and her eyes widened in shock at her own outburst. "Ah, thank you for healing my burns," she added softly.

But her astonishment paled in comparison to that of her new captor. Justus's gaze roved over her with awe and a touch of respect. "Now I understand why he loves you."

"What makes you think he loves me?" Her pulse skipped a beat as something that suspiciously felt like hope bloomed in her heart. "Our marriage was an arrangement for his convenience."

"All of his marriages are." He chuckled before his expression sobered. "But he's never before wed a bride in this cathedral, nor courted one so fervently, much less paid one such devout attention once the vows were uttered." His fingers grasped her chin, forcing her to meet his gaze. "And for your sake, you had best pray that he has enough affection for you to track you here and agree to my terms. Either way, tonight will be the last time you'll see him."

Dread pooled in her stomach. "What do you mean?"

"Gavin deprived me of my love," Justus said coldly. "It is past time I return the favor."

Thirty-two

Gavin stood outside of the cloisters of the cathedral, where Father Dunaway used to take him to his chambers to subject him to nightly sessions of violation and pain.

Bile rose up in his throat and he couldn't suppress a shudder. Justus had chosen his latest hideaway well. He was the only vampire aside from Lenore who knew what had transpired in this accursed building.

He held the note that the young urchin had delivered to him at Dr. Elliotson's house, where he'd been waiting for Lenore to make an appearance.

If you want your young wife to live, come to the cathedral alone.

The handwriting was definitely Justus's, however, the messenger insisted that a blond man had paid him to deliver the missive.

Gavin wondered how many rogues Justus led. It didn't matter, he thought as he glared at the cloisters. Even though Justus hadn't said where in the cathedral he would be waiting, he didn't have to. There was only one area that Gavin had always avoided. Thus a perfect place for Justus to take refuge.

If he or any of his rogues hurt Lenore, Gavin would tear them all limb from limb. He held up his hand for Elena and Benson to remain behind with Chandler and the carriage. He would enter alone as Justus dictated, but hell if he was going completely without reinforcements. After all, there would be prisoners to haul when this business was concluded.

His gaze traveled across every stone of the cloisters. Only this time, instead of being haunted by memories of the priest who'd violated him, his focus remained solely on finding the woman he loved.

Was Justus holding Lenore inside the actual structure, or below it?

They had to be below. Justus wouldn't risk the vulnerability of such an open position, where he could be surrounded by Gavin's vampires. No, they would be underground, holding a tunnel where Gavin would have no choice but to fight one at a time.

Searching his memory, Gavin crossed the grounds, seeking the hidden tunnel where the monks and priests had fled from King Henry VIII's forces during the dissolution of the churches. He paused as he came upon a blackened patch of grass. The acrid scent of burnt vegetation and kerosene wrinkled his nose.

What had happened here? Only sunlight, fire, and— his heart stopped as he spotted a gleaming axe a few feet away— decapitation could kill a vampire. Did this mean one had been slain? Had the Hunter come here first? Or had Justus lied and killed Lenore already?

Throat tight with fear, he picked up the axe. There was no sign of blood, but perhaps it had been burned away. Gripping the handle, he quickened his pace, his pulse pounding the same refrain with every step. Lenore... Lenore...

At last, he found the tunnel, concealed by tangling wild rose bushes. The scent of rogue vampires, along with Lenore's sweet scent, emanated thickly from the area. It took every vestige of his will not to charge through the dark passage, swinging the axe like a Viking Berserker. Instead, he made his way carefully through, trying to move quietly, even though he was under no illusion that they weren't expecting him.

As Gavin descended further down the tunnel, Justus called out, "Darkwood, my old friend! I was starting to worry that your little bride didn't mean anything to you." There was a pause as if the vampire was thinking. "Are you alone?"

"Aye," Gavin replied, though with one shout, the others would join him. "Is Lenore alive and unharmed?"

Mocking laughter echoed through the tunnel. "Yes, no thanks to you."

"Let her speak then." He issued the words in irrefutable command.

"Gavin," Lenore's beloved voice calmed a measure of his fear. "They didn't hurt me. And it is all right, Justus only wants to talk."

Gavin let out a bitter chuckle. "I'm certain he wants more than that."

Unbelievably, she laughed. "Yes, he does. What I mean is, you're not walking into an ambush."

He listened to his wife's voice for any sign of coercion or a lie. "How many are down there?"

"Three rogues, including Justus, but he's arrested one of them." Awe tinged her breathless voice.

Before Gavin could digest *that* unexpected piece of information, he heard Justus whisper something before Lenore spoke again. "The body of the Hunter is down here as well. Justus killed him."

At Gavin's startled intake of breath, Justus laughed. "Oh yes, it seems you owe me a debt of gratitude, Darkwood. Come along, so we may discuss our terms. The lovely Lenore was correct. You will not be harmed. Be aware, though, that I have a knife to her heart, so if you think to ambush me…"

"I won't," Gavin said quickly and walked faster.

Justus wouldn't really kill a woman, would he?

He emerged into a meager chamber with a bare dusty floor and a dim lantern casting shadows over the occupants. Just as Lenore had said, there was a vampire chained to the wall, glaring at him with enraged defiance. The brutish brown-haired one who had fought with Cecil, Gavin surmised. Another rogue stood in the corner, gaping at him with wide-eyed fear. Gavin noted his shaggy blonde hair and deduced that he was the one who'd sent Justus's missive.

The body of a human male lay prone in the opposite corner, face and hands pallid as if drained of every drop of blood. The open bag beside him, with stakes, a bible, and various vials scattered on the floor, verified him as the Hunter.

But Gavin's sole concern was Lenore. Sure enough, Justus stood behind her, a dagger poised over her breast. Her wrists and ankles were shackled together. The sight of the restraints made him ache for her as he recalled how raw her limbs had been when he'd first found her on his lands. After what she'd been through, being chained again had to be traumatizing.

To his surprise, though she shook like a leaf, very little fear shone in her large, dark eyes. And the love and longing in their depths took his breath away. Something was amiss, though. Gavin looked back down at her chained ankles and realized that her skirts had been burned away all the way to her upper thighs.

"What happened to your dress?" Fresh worry gnawed his skin as he remembered the patch of burnt grass above.

Justus smiled as if sharing a private joke. "Tell him, Baroness."

"The Hunter set my gown alight and nearly cut off my head." She exhaled in palpable relief. "But Justus killed him. He then put out the flames and healed my burns."

"I told you that you'd be grateful to me." Justus said with a grin. "I also have the vampire who lured the Hunter to your lands and set him on Cecil." Genuine sorrow darkened his normally sly countenance. "I didn't know about Cecil until your wife told me. I am sincerely sorry and deeply aggrieved at his loss."

Gavin blinked in surprise. Justus hadn't been responsible for the Hunter after all. More than that, he'd detained one of his own for doing so.

"Thank you for saving my wife." He would have been grateful to the devil himself. "But why?"

Justus raised a brow. "Why did I save her?"

Gavin nodded. "I thought you were here to destroy me."

"I *am*." Justus growled. "I want you to suffer as I have." He shifted the tip of the dagger slightly away from Lenore's heart. "But I don't want you dead. Or your bride. And Hunters are not permitted to live. Just because I am a rogue does not mean I lack honor."

"Why do you want me to suffer?" Gavin demanded. "I know you were unhappy to be exiled, but surely you understand that I should have killed you for what you did. I showed you mercy at risk to myself."

"It's not that," Justus glared at him. "It's what you did to Bethany after."

Gavin gaped at him. "I didn't do anything with her." Could Justus have truly gone mad?

"Liar!" the vampire roared. "I tracked down her family in Derbyshire and she is not with them. No one in their town even knows they have a daughter. You must have done something to get rid of her."

Gavin shook his head. "I'd thought that *you'd* tracked her down and Changed her. It would have been just as unlawful for me to abduct or kill that girl as it would have been for you to Change her. I would swear a blood oath that I've done nothing to her."

As Justus digested his words, Gavin had a sudden thought. Justus said Bethany's parents were in Derbyshire. But that wasn't where they went first. Perhaps he could make use of that information.

He watched his former friend's shoulders slump and defeat shadow his face. Justus believed him.

Gavin sighed. "What do you want, Justus?"

"I want a pardon. One for Will too. As for Rolfe," He inclined his head at the bound and gagged vampire in the corner, "You can arrest him and try him, or let me kill him, whichever you choose."

"And?" Gavin prodded, knowing things could not be that easy.

Justus's green eyes went cold. "And I want you to step down, leave Rochester, and live in exile as I have. Let you always be watching over your shoulder when you hunt. Let you scramble to find a new safe place to hide from the sun. Let you be alone."

Alone. The word was uttered with such malice that Gavin felt a tremor of foreboding. "And what makes you presume that I will agree to this?"

"Because I'll kill the woman you love if I don't." Justus brought the tip of his dagger to Lenore's bodice and sliced off one of the tiny silk roses.

Lenore gasped and her eyes held Gavin's, large and pleading.

Gavin crossed his arms over his chest, resting the haft of the axe on his hip. "What would become of her after I left?"

Justus smiled. "She shall come with me and Will. She'll live the life of a rogue. We'll keep her safe, and preserve her honor, don't worry. She's a brave, yet tender youngling. I understand why this one claimed your heart, and how it will hurt you to be apart from her."

Oh, how he'd thought this through, his old, clever friend. Gavin couldn't help but be impressed. However, there was no way in hell he'd agree to such terms.

"What about me?" Lenore looked up at Justus. "*I* didn't part you from your love. I've done nothing to you at all. Why should I be punished? How could you take my love away from me, when you know how much that hurts?"

A thousand myriad emotions flickered in Justus's eyes before his jaw tightened. "Quiet, or I'll silence you forever."

Thinking carefully, Gavin measured his words. "Which matters most to you? Punishing me, or being reunited with Bethany?" Keeping a tight grip on the axe, he reached in his pocket and withdrew the locket.

Justus's eyes widened in mixed outrage and longing at the sight of the trinket. "Give that back!"

"Give me my bride," Gavin countered.

"Trade her for a painting and a lock of hair?" Justus scoffed, though his eyes were lined with pain. "I think not."

"No, you *will* trade her for the locket, your pardon, *and* some information I have on Bethany's whereabouts." Gavin faced him with a level stare. "I never reported your exile to the Elders. You could come home with a clean slate, if I decree it. If Bethany's family has truly hidden her to the point where people are unaware of her existence, that changes the restrictions on making her one of us. She's also reached the age of majority by now, so there's no impediment there either."

Justus stared at him, a spark of hope igniting in his gaze. "You have information on Bethany?"

"I know that her family spent time somewhere else other than Derbyshire right after you left," Gavin said, praying it was enough. "From there, perhaps a trail could be sniffed out."

"Where?" His former second's voice cracked with desperation.

Gavin shook his head, jaw clenched with determination. "Drop the knife and give me Lenore."

Justus's eyes narrowed with suspicion. "How do I know you don't have a group of your people waiting above to ambush me?"

Gavin kept his features composed, not giving anything away. "Because I have no reason to. I'm looking to kill the vampire who brought the Hunter here. You have him, and my wife has given testimony that you had nothing to do with his crime. My people would let you go unharmed." Gavin silently thanked the heavens that this was the case. Elena and Benson were reasonable vampires. "That is, *if* Lenore is safe and here to vouch for you."

For what seemed like an eternity, Justus silently struggled. Finally, the knife slipped from his fingers and clattered on the ground.

Then Lenore was in his arms, and Gavin could finally breathe. He dropped the axe and pulled her tighter against him with one arm, while holding out the locket with the other. Justus quickly snatched the locket away, but Gavin was oblivious to all but his bride.

His lips claimed hers and blissful heat that he'd never realized he'd missed spread through his being, warming his soul.

"I love you," he whispered when he broke the kiss.

"I love you too." She rested her head against his chest, still trembling from her ordeal.

Her chains rattled between them, bringing him back to reality. A wave of agony washed over him as he imagined the tormented memories those shackles had to have invoked.

"Unchain her," he commanded his former second.

Gavin turned and looked over his shoulder in time to see Justus pick up the axe.

Thirty-three

Lenore gasped as Gavin swiftly whipped her around and forced her down. As she fell to the dusty ground, Gavin covered her with his body. Peering over her husband's shoulder, she saw Justus lift the axe in the air...

Her heart stopped. A blur passed before her vision.

The axe sliced down in a flashing arc. Firelight glinted from the blade.

And Justus brought the axe down on Rolfe's outstretched arm, severing his hand, which held a stake.

The rogue's shriek of pain rent the air as the stake fell from nerveless fingers and clattered on the stone floor.

Lenore breathed out and clung to Gavin in helpless relief. Dear God, what if she'd lost him?

"Damn it, Will!" Justus roared. "I told you to watch Rolfe!"

"Sorry, Justus." Will scrambled from his place on the floor and secured Rolfe's legs with what was left of the broken chain, ducking the vampire's thrashing arm.

Blood splattered across the stone wall.

Justus wiped a splash of blood from his cheek and approached Gavin and Lenore with the key to her shackles and a smirk on his face that belied the relief in his eyes. "Blimey, Darkwood, love makes you even more blind than it did with me."

"Thank you," Gavin whispered, face white as linen.

"Your debts to me continue to amass," Justus replied with a chuckle and then shackled Rolfe's ankles and wrists together, keeping the cuff tight on the vampire's bloody stump. Then, he wrapped the previous length of chain around Rolfe's head, making sure the rogue's fangs were tangled in the iron links to keep him from talking until his interrogation.

Not that he'd be doing much talking anytime soon. With his hand severed and still bleeding profusely, all Rolfe could do was make incoherent, high-pitched pain sounds. Despite Rolfe's abominable crimes, Lenore couldn't help but pity him and hope he received a quick death.

"Do not think I'm not aware of how much I owe you," Gavin told Justus as he grasped Lenore's hand. "You will have your pardon and be welcomed back here after you serve a requisite sentence. I'll give you a comfortable cell."

Justus frowned and opened his mouth to respond, but Will interrupted. "What about me?"

Gavin clapped him on the shoulder. "You'll be put under guard and questioned. If you do not seem to be a troublemaker, you will be allowed to become a Rochester vampire as well."

The rogue drew back. "You mean you'll arrest me?"

"Not exactly. You will be taken into custody, yes. But you won't be treated like a prisoner, so much as supervised guest. And if you do not wish to do this my way, you are free go, so long as you never come back." Gavin fixed him with a penetrating stare. "What were you exiled for?"

Will's face twisted into an exasperated frown. "The woman I was tupping was also the Lord of Grimsby's lover, but I didn't know."

Gavin made a snort of disgust. "Grimsby is a tawdry ass. If that was the sole reason for your position, you will be welcome here... as long as you do not presume to touch my wife." He cast Lenore a sideways smile before turning back to Will and Justus. "Shall we take our prisoner and go?"

Will nodded and seized Rolfe, who'd fallen unconscious from blood loss. Justus remained still, arms crossed over his chest.

"Where did Bethany last go?" he asked, making it clear he wouldn't budge without an answer.

"Manchester," Gavin said after a long pause. "I found it odd that you said her parents were in Derbyshire and behaving as if she never existed. Perhaps they packed her off to live with a relative."

"Or worse." Justus shivered, eyes haunted. Fear and anguish tore through him before his shoulders straightened in resignation. "I *must* find her… whether she's alive or…" he broke off with a choked sound.

"After your probationary period, I'll draft up a writ of passage for you," Gavin told him coolly.

"No," Justus said with a firm shake of his head. "I must go now."

Gavin sighed, eyes clearly anguished at the prospect of losing his friend once more. "If you do, you'll have to remain a rogue. I will have a difficult time pardoning you as it is. If I allow you to roam off, free reign with a writ of passage right away, I may as well give my Lordship to Benson."

Justus held his gaze, fists clenched at his sides. "So be it."

Gavin extended his hand. "I wish you luck. Do write to me, and perhaps after you've located Bethany, you can petition for reentry into my lands." He paused a moment as if measuring his words. "Or, if you still bear me ill will, the Lord of Cornwall has told me that he'd welcome you."

The crimson-haired vampire nodded curtly and vanished in a blink.

Lenore led the way out of the tunnel as Gavin and Will followed behind with the prisoner. The dead Hunter was left behind to be recovered later. When they emerged in the cathedral courtyard, she was astonished to see the carriage awaiting along with Benson, Elena, and Chandler, the vampire who sometimes served as Gavin's driver.

Gavin chuckled at her wide eyes. "I told them to meet me here with the carriage, since I was expecting to haul prisoners." He grinned at Will. "Of course, I'd meant to collect more than one, but ah well." His attention shifted to Rolfe's unconscious form. "We'll secure him in the dickey box in back. I do not want blood on my upholstery."

Benson and Elena did as bade, and then turned back to Gavin.

Elena enfolded Lenore in a warm embrace. "I am so happy to see you alive. How terrible this ordeal must have been."

"I've endured worse," Lenore replied, though she was still grateful this rigorous trial was over.

"What about this one?" Benson pointed at Will.

Gavin sighed. "Guard him while we return to Darkwood Manor. I will explain everything then."

Elena and Benson both shot him impatient looks before they reluctantly bowed and escorted Will into the carriage. Gavin helped Lenore into the conveyance and held her hand for the entire ride. She rested her head on his shoulder, thanking the saints that they were together once more.

Two other vampires waited in front of Darkwood Manor. Lenore recalled their names. Elliot and Carolyn. They watched as Gavin handed Lenore down and followed her out, Benson and Elena emerged next with Will between them.

Before they could erupt with a thousand questions, Gavin gestured to the rear of the carriage. "This is the vampire who lured the Hunter here. Take him to the low cells."

Benson gasped. "You mean, it wasn't Justus?"

"Yes," Lenore asserted, still digesting a plethora of emotions when it came to the crimson-haired rogue. "Justus killed the Hunter and arrested the rogue who was guilty."

Elena raised a brow. "And where is he now?"

Gavin answered. "He chose to remain a rogue for the time being. The Hunter's corpse lies below the cathedral cloisters. I'll send someone to fetch it tomorrow so we can search the body and make certain he didn't have any accomplices before I make my report to the Elders."

"I see." She regarded Gavin with a knowing smirk before pointing at Will. "And what of this one?"

"As of now, he seems to be innocent of anything to do with the Hunter. He also wishes to become a citizen. I would like him taken to a secure, but comfortable chamber, placed under guard, and brought a meal before I question him tomorrow." Gavin turned to Elliot and Carolyn, who stared at Will with wariness and curiosity. "If you would like to fetch at least two other vampires and work in shifts, it would be greatly appreciated."

The two bowed and walked off with lifted chins, proud of the responsibility of guarding a prisoner. They didn't have to know that Gavin selected them for their kindness... or that he was auditioning them for new responsibilities. He'd confessed as much when assuring Will that he would be treated fairly during his confinement and evaluation.

He bade Benson and Elena to select older, more vigilant vampires to guard Rolfe... in pairs. And there would be no meal for this one, Lenore thought grimly. No waste of blood for one who would not live to see the end of the next night.

While Gavin was capable of compassion, the rumors had not lied about his ruthlessness. And for that, Lenore was grateful as she watched Benson and Elena seize the vampire who'd been responsible for Cecil's death and endangering them all.

"What happened to his hand?" Elena asked, frowning at the stump, which had begun to scab over and heal.

"He raised it to me and Justus cut it off." Gavin grinned, neglecting to mention that Justus had saved their lives with that quick action.

"And Lenore's gown?" Her eyes worriedly roved over the charred fabric.

Gavin sighed. "It is quite a long tale. Let's save it for tomorrow night, shall we?"

Elena and Benson nodded, though both looked like they'd rather argue. After Will and Rolfe were hauled away, Gavin lifted Lenore in his arms and carried her into the house.

He ordered a hot bath drawn and insisted on bathing her himself. Only when he began to scrub her back with a blissfully hot cloth did Lenore realize that her shaking still hadn't subsided. But now that she was home and safe, with the stench of burnt fabric and rogues washed from her hair and body, her tension at last began to ease.

"You don't have to pamper me so," she argued when he lifted her from the bath and carried her to bed.

"Oh, but I do," he said firmly. "You were put through hell because of my past. And yet you still said you love me."

Her drowsy eyes opened at the awe in his tone. Had he not known how she felt? She smiled. Then again... "It was strange to first learn from your enemy that you loved me."

Gavin chuckled. "I thought everyone knew how I felt about you before I did. Some nights I've been tempted to shout it from the rooftops." He held her tighter and gazed at her like she held the secrets of the universe. "In light of our mutual declarations, would you make me the happiest of men and—"

"Are you proposing to me *again*?" she giggled.

"Yes, but for real this time." His knuckles brushed her cheek, his gaze more solemn than she'd ever seen. "I am done with pretend marriages to evade scrutiny from the mortals. I want real ones… and all of them with you." He tilted her chin up, his mouth hovering over hers. "Lenore, will you be my wife and live and hunt by side for the rest of our long lives?"

Breathless joy encompassed her. "I will," she whispered against his lips.

Epilogue

May Day, 1824
One month later

Gavin smiled down at his wife as she tapped her foot and watched the chimney sweeps dance around the Jack in the Green, a man costumed as a leafy, flowering tree to herald the spring. Gavin had previously viewed the annual Sweep's Festival as an annoyance at best, and a dismal reminder of the shortened nights at worst.

Now, seeing Lenore's delight in the revelry renewed his enthusiasm for the ancient custom... especially since he now had reason to enjoy spending the longer daylight hours in bed.

Lord and Lady Villar stood beside them, watching the dancers with reserved amusement. Lenore had insisted on inviting them, so they could be reassured of her happiness. To Gavin's relief, she'd told them nothing of last month's debacle with the rogues and the Hunter.

Gavin shuddered to imagine Rafael's reaction if he learned that Lenore had been abducted a second time, no matter how brief and, thankfully, bloodless it had been.

Lenore looked up at him with shining eyes. "My father had always dreamed of visiting Rochester to dance with the other chimney sweeps and awaken the Jack in the Green."

Cassandra gave her that same indulgent, yet uncomprehending smile that the nobility frequently bestowed on the lower classes when hearing of their customs, but Gavin regarded Lenore with a broad grin. Though many of her tales about her past were dismal and heartbreaking, she also had a plethora of cheerful stories, and he never tired of hearing of them.

"Perhaps he is watching them with you from above," he told her. "I do hope he would have approved of me."

"He would have, I know it," she said so fiercely that he couldn't help pulling her into his arms for a kiss. That was another thing he liked about festivals. Wantonness was encouraged, and he intended on taking full advantage of the customs later, in a secluded grove under the stars.

"It is good to see you so happy," Cassandra said when they broke apart.

Rafael nodded stiffly, still scowling as if he didn't believe Lenore was truly happy. Gavin couldn't fault him as he also found it hard to fathom that a curmudgeon like Villar could be so in love with *his* wife.

Still, that didn't stop him from extrapolating on how well Lenore had settled into life in Rochester. "Lady Darkwood has become a sort of physician for emotions to the vampires here... and sometimes others from neighboring lands." He beamed with unrepressed pride. "They tell her of their troubles and she offers comfort and counsel. She really seems to cheer them." He met Rafael's gaze and smirked. "Perhaps you could benefit from a session."

Lord Villar's scowl deepened. "Better her than her former colleague. I don't want his fingers probing my head."

Lenore and Gavin nodded. Dr. Elliotson had left for London before his leg was even fully healed, grumbling at the ignorance and superstition of village life. Gavin had taken Lenore to visit him and all the man could do was rant about how his practice of phrenology would revolutionize medicine forever. At first Gavin had been concerned that the carriage accident had addled the man's mind, but Lenore assured him that he'd already been fanatical.

Cassandra changed the subject. "Thank you again for inviting us to this wonderful festival."

"You are welcome any time," Gavin said. "Another benefit of these events is the easy hunting. The bushes are a veritable orchard of hidden lovers to feast upon… that is, unless you have the same idea and wish to find a secluded bower."

Lady Villar gave her husband a sultry smile. "I do so love the country air. Will you walk with me to enjoy the night?"

Rafael's amber gaze burned with love and desire. "Of course, *Cara.*"

As the couple wandered off in search of pleasure, Gavin led Lenore in the opposite direction. "I thought I'd never have you all to myself. I know of a private glade not far from here…" he trailed off and frowned as he saw Benson approaching with Will at his heels.

"I'm sorry to disturb you, my lord, but I have a letter for you." Benson handed him an envelope.

Gavin's chest tightened as he recognized Justus's scrawl on the front. Quickly, he broke the seal and read:

My old friend,

I have found my Bethany. She is imprisoned in the Manchester Lunatic Asylum. I will stop at nothing to free her.

As I know that if I brought her to Rochester, people would recognize her, it will be some time before I return. Tell Will that he is in my thoughts and that I hope he is adjusting well.

Regards,

J.

Gavin folded the letter with a sigh. "It seems Justus will be away for a few more years. He's planning a jail break, and doesn't wish to burden us for harboring a fugitive."

Benson snorted. "How very considerate of him, after all he's brought upon us already."

"He slayed the Hunter who killed Cecil and delivered the rogue who'd lured him here," Gavin reminded him. They'd executed Rolfe the next night, after a very brief trial. "And he provided us with a competent and useful vampire."

After Will's testimony, Gavin had approved the former rogue to join his ranks, though he would remain under supervision for the next three months. Will had proved to be extremely sharp and had an endless fount of information about the Lord of Grimsby, who was so despised that his neighboring Lord Vampires longed to find a way to oust him.

Benson continued to frown, despite his fondness for Will. "We wouldn't have had to contend with any of that if Justus hadn't brought them here in his madcap quest for revenge."

"People make mistakes," Gavin said firmly. "Remember that when it is your turn to rule in my place in about twenty years or so."

Benson's eyes widened with the realization that he would take on the duty that had been previously reserved for Justus. "Yes, my lord."

Gavin met Lenore's gaze with his next words. "Also remember that people can be prone to a bit of madness when they are in love."

Author's Note

John Elliotson (1791-1868) was an English physician who specialized in mesmerism (the precursor to modern day hypnotherapy) and phrenology. He was also one of the first doctors who regularly used a stethoscope.

He was at first a colleague of Thomas Wakley, surgeon and founder of the medical journal, *The Lancet* (who appears in Bite at First Sight), but later on, Wakley denounced him as a fraud when Elliotson's medical practices became too eccentric.

Elliotson first practiced mesmerism on poor working class women before eventually opening his own clinic and founding *The Zoist*, a medical journal focusing on his practices.

He was known to be a short, ugly man, but well admired as a lecturer because he could combine structure and theater.

Although Elliotson's practice in mesmerism didn't begin until 1829, and his visits to Rochester, where he befriended Charles Dickens happened much later, I used my author's license to have him practice in 1824, so he could befriend Lenore.

I also had his mysterious 1828 carriage accident occur sooner.

Elliotson could also be considered a forefather of modern psychology, a primary theme in this story.

Acknowledgements

Thank you so much to everyone who helped make this story possible. Thanks to Bonnie R. Paulson for telling me to write this book, when to release it, and for giving priceless feedback. Thank you to Shona Husk, Layna Pimental, and Merrilee Remmick, for helping me whip the book into shape.

Thank you to my proofreaders, Alicia Braby, and Bonnie Maestas.

Thank you to my friends and family for your encouragement and support.

Thank you to my newsletter readers for helping me choose the title and cover image.

Thank you to Bad Movie Club for giving me a much needed escape from this stressful process.

Thank you to my son, Micah Turner, for being the best son a mom could ever wish for, cheering me on while I was riding deadlines, and accompanying me to Red Lobster when it was finally done.

And thank you to Kent Butler for being my real life romance hero.

About The Author

Formerly an auto-mechanic, Brooklyn Ann thrives on writing romance featuring unconventional heroines and heroes who adore them. She's delved into historical paranormal romance in her critically acclaimed "Scandals with Bite" series, urban fantasy in her "Brides of Prophecy" novels and heavy metal romance in her "Hearts of Metal" novellas.

She lives in Coeur d'Alene, Idaho with her son, her cat, and a 1980 Datsun 210.

She can be found online at http://brooklynann.blogspot.com as well as on twitter and Facebook.

Keep in touch for the latest news, exclusive excerpts, and giveaways! Sign up for Brooklyn Ann's newsletter!

Works:

SCANDALS WITH BITE

BOOK 1: BITE ME, YOUR GRACE (April 2013)

Dr. John Polidori's tale, "The Vampyre," burst upon the Regency scene along with Mary Shelley's Frankenstein after that notorious weekend spent writing ghost stories with Lord Byron. A vampire craze broke out instantly in the haut ton.

Now Ian Ashton, the Lord Vampire of London, has to attend tedious balls, linger in front of mirrors, and eat lots of garlic in an attempt to quell the gossip. If that weren't annoying enough, his neighbor, Angelica Winthrop, has literary aspirations of her own and is sneaking into his house at night just to see what she can find.

Hungry, tired, and fed up, Ian is in no mood to humor his beautiful intruder...

BOOK 2: ONE BITE PER NIGHT (August 2014)

He wanted her off his hands... Now he'll do anything to hold on to her ...Forever.

Vincent Tremayne, the reclusive "Devil Earl," has been manipulated into taking rambunctious Lydia Price as his ward. As Lord Vampire of Cornwall, Vincent has better things to do than bring out an unruly debutante.

American-born Lydia Price doesn't care for the stuffy strictures of the ton, and is unimpressed with her foppish suitors. She dreams of studying with the talented but scandalous British portrait painter, Sir Thomas Lawrence. But just when it seems her dreams will come true, Lydia is plunged into Vincent's dark world and finds herself caught between the life she's known and a future she never could have imagined.

BOOK 3: BITE AT FIRST SIGHT (April 2015)

When Rafael Villar, Lord Vampire of London, stumbles upon a woman in the cemetery, he believes he's found a vampire hunter—not the beautiful, intelligent stranger she proves to be.

Cassandra Burton is enthralled by the scarred, disfigured vampire who took her prisoner. The aspiring physician was robbing graves to pursue her studies—and he might turn out to be her greatest subject yet. So they form a bargain: one kiss for every experiment. As their passion grows and Rafe begins to heal, only one question remains: can Cassandra see the man beyond the monster?

BOOK 4: HIS RUTHLESS BITE April 2016

The Lord Vampire of Rochester doesn't do a favor without a price. And now it's time to collect

Gavin Drake, Baron of Darkwood is being pestered by nosy neighbors and matchmaking mothers of the mortal nobility. To escape their scrutiny, he concludes that it's time to take a wife. After witnessing the young vampire Lenore's loyalty to the Lord of London, he decides she is sufficient for the role.

After surviving abuse from rogue vampires, Lenore Graves wants to help other women recover from their inner wounds. She befriends mesmerist John Elliotson and uses her vampire powers to aid him with his patients. When the Lord of London declares that Lenore is the price the Lord of Rochester demands for aiding him in battle, she is terrified. Will all of her hard work be destroyed by Ruthless Rochester? Yet she can't suppress stirrings of desire at the memory of their potent encounter.

After Gavin assures her that the marriage will be in name only, Lenore reluctantly accepts Gavin's proposal. Determined to continue her work, she invites John Elliotson to Rochester. As they help women recover from traumas, Lenore explores her own inner turmoil and examines her attraction to her husband.

Gavin realizes his marriage is a mistake. His new baroness's involvement with the mesmerist is dangerous. He knows he should put a stop to Lenore's antics— yet her tender heart is warming his own and tempting him to make her his bride in truth.

As Lenore and Gavin's relationship blossoms, the leader of a gang of rogue vampires embarks on a quest for vengeance against Gavin... using Lenore as his key.

BRIDES OF PROPHECY
BOOK 1: <u>WRENCHING FATE</u> (February 2014)

She's haunted by her past.

Akash Hope trusts no one. Her parents were shot down by uniformed men, which forced Akash to spend most of her life on the run.

She's so close to getting out on her own, making her own dreams come true when he shows up and disrupts everything.

Her new legal guardian.

His kindness makes suspicious, while his heart-stopping good looks arouse desires she'd kept suppressed.

He promises her a future.

Silas McNaught, Lord Vampire of Coeur d'Alene, has been searching for Akasha for centuries.

He's perplexed to discover that the woman who has haunted his visions is anything but sweet and fragile. Her foul mouth and superhuman strength covers a tenderness he's determined to reach.

While government agents pursue Akasha and vindictive vampires seek to destroy Silas, they discover the strength in their love.

Can they survive the double threat?

BOOK 2: IRONIC SACRIFICE (October 2014)

Jayden Leigh wants to commit suicide.

Her clairvoyant powers have become so intense that she lost her job and home. Death is the only way to make them stop. Opportunity presents itself when she comes across a sinfully handsome vampire ready to make a kill. Jayden begs him to take her instead. A blissful death in his arms, or the visions ravaging her mind? She'd gladly take the vampire.

Razvan Nicolae is captivated with the beautiful seeress who sacrifices herself for a stranger. Killing such a pleasing asset doesn't interest him. If he could get her powers under control, she could be the key to finding his missing twin.

Controlling her visions and working for a seductive vampire? Razvan's offer is like a dream come true. But her dream turns into a nightmare when a mad vampire cult leader seeks to exploit Jayden's powers to stop an ancient prophecy.

As Jayden finds herself at the center of a vampire war, she realizes that the biggest threat isn't losing her life, it's losing her heart.

BOOK 3: CONJURING DESTINY (October 2015)

Famous rock star, Xochitl Leonine, has dreamt of a world with two moons where a black cloaked man beckons her. One Halloween night, she meets the mysterious stranger of her dreams… literally… and their shared dance becomes a rendezvous in a place of endless night.

Zareth Amotken has no idea how important Xochitl's heavy metal band is to her. As an immortal sorcerer, he doesn't care. He has one goal: to find the prophesied savior of his world. Her voice holds the power to bring back his world's vanished sun.

Xochitl's compassion urges her to help in any way she can. Yet learning the mysteries of her past causes conflict with her future in music. Her destiny in his world and her obligations to her band pull her in opposite directions. How can she long for one while the other is so dire?

As Zareth introduces her to his people and teaches her to control her powers, she aches for his enchanting kiss. Zareth tries to resist, for their passion will unleash serious consequences, both political and magical.

As the time to fulfill her destiny draws closer, she must choose between her heart, her duty, and her friends. The wrong choice could ruin everything.

But if Zareth's evil half brother succeeds in taking control of her for his own ends, he will take away her choices… and destroy the world.

BOOK 4: <u>UNLEASHING DESIRE</u> 2016

HEARTS OF METAL (Heavy Metal Romance)

Book 1: KISSING VICIOUS (August 2015)

Aspiring guitarist Kinley Black is about to get her first big break—as a roadie for Viciöus, her favorite heavy metal band, and for the rock god she always dreamt might make her a woman.

The Roadie

At 15, aspiring guitarist Kinley Black wished she were a boy. At 16, after hearing Quinn Mayne sing, she wanted him to make her a woman. Now, at 22, her dreams have come true. Quinn's band Viciöus needs someone to lug their amps around the country, to strive and sweat with the guys. She just has to act like one of them.

And the rock god

Quinn had to admit the new chick could pull her weight, but that didn't mean his road manager made the right choice. Taking a hottie on a heavy metal music tour was like dangling meat in front of a pack of feral hounds—and Quinn could be part dog himself. But more surprising than her beautiful body are Kinley's sweet licks, so that no man could help but demand a jam session. Quinn will soon do anything to possess her, and to put Kinley in the spotlight where she belongs. And to keep her safe and sound from the wolves.

Book 2: WITH VENGEANCE (2016)

Book 3: ROCK GOD (2016)

Made in the USA
Middletown, DE
02 April 2017